KU-687-140

SPECIAL MESSAGE TO READERS

THE ULVERSCROFT FOUNDATION
(registered UK charity number 264873)
was established in 1972 to provide funds for
research, diagnosis and treatment of eye diseases.
Examples of major projects funded by
the Ulverscroft Foundation are:-

- The Children's Eye Unit at Moorfields Eye Hospital, London
- The Ulverscroft Children's Eye Unit at Great Ormond Street Hospital for Sick Children
- Funding research into eye diseases and treatment at the Department of Ophthalmology, University of Leicester
- The Ulverscroft Vision Research Group, Institute of Child Health
- Twin operating theatres at the Western Ophthalmic Hospital, London
- The Chair of Ophthalmology at the Royal Australian College of Ophthalmologists

You can help further the work of the Foundation
by making a donation or leaving a legacy.
Every contribution is gratefully received. If you
would like to help support the Foundation or
require further information, please contact:

THE ULVERSCROFT FOUNDATION
The Green, Bradgate Road, Anstey
Leicester LE7 7FU, England
Tel: (0116) 236 4325

website: www.foundation.ulverscroft.com

The winner of eight BAFTA awards, Graham Norton is one of the best-known faces on British television. His long-running and ever-popular Friday night chat show, *The Graham Norton Show*, continually features some of the world's biggest stars. Since 2009 he has presented the *Eurovision Song Contest*. He also charms Radio 2 listeners each week on his Saturday morning show. Born in Dublin and raised in West Cork, Graham now lives in London. His debut novel *Holding* was a commercial and critical success, winning him the Irish Independent Popular Fiction award at the Bord Gáis Irish Book Awards in 2016.

A KEEPER

The mystery of Elizabeth Keane's father is one that has never been solved by the people of Buncarragh, though not for lack of speculation. Her mother Patricia had been assumed a spinster until she began dating a mysterious man from out of town, and within months had left Buncarragh and had married. Less than two years later, Patricia was back, with a new baby but no husband by her side, and unbendingly silent about her recent past — a secret she would take with her to her grave. When Elizabeth returns to Ireland after her mother's death, she finds the house of her childhood stuffed full of useless things, her mother's presence already fading. And perhaps, had she not found the small stash of letters, the truth would never have come to light . . .

Books by Graham Norton
Published by Ulverscroft:

THE LIFE AND LOVES OF A HE DEVIL
HOLDING

GRAHAM NORTON

A KEEPER

Complete and Unabridged

CHARNWOOD
Leicester

First published in Great Britain in 2018 by
Hodder & Stoughton
London

First Charnwood Edition
published 2019
by arrangement with
Hodder & Stoughton
An Hachette UK company
London

The moral right of the author has been asserted

All characters in this publication are fictitious and
any resemblance to real persons, living or dead, is
purely coincidental.

Copyright © 2018 by Graham Norton
All rights reserved

A catalogue record for this book is available
from the British Library.

ISBN 978–1–4448–4154–1

TOWER HAMLETS LIBRARIES	
C001674209	
ULVERSCROFT	
F	£20.99
THBET	

ᴇd by
(Publishing)
cestershire

Graphics Ltd.
:estershire
n Great Britain by
, Padstow, Cornwall

on acid-free paper

For Jono

BEFORE

He longed for silence. The roar of the wind churned with the rasping rhythm of the waves and filled his head. Every morning Edward woke to these sounds and when his aching arms pulled the blankets up at night the same wall of noise filled his dreams. When would he find peace?

Edward Foley was hunched on the small promontory of rocks that marked the border between the front paddock and the sea. Clouds had robbed the night sky of stars or a moon, which made the dark hood of sounds feel even thicker. His tears had dried but now his face was wet once more with the salty mist of spray from the pounding surf. Behind him he heard occasional voices and the thin slam of a car door.

If only he could think. He had to consider the future. What to do next? He wasn't what anyone would have called young, but still, at forty-one you couldn't declare your life was over. He thought of his brother James, claimed long ago by the waves. He didn't have the luxury of giving up, but that was precisely what Edward wanted to do. To sit and hug his knees till the tide came to take him.

Through the wet crackle of the wind and waves he heard an engine start and the damp grass around him glowed red, then blue. He turned his head and watched the ambulance making its way slowly down the lane, past the orchard towards the road. He felt so foolish. What right had he to expect happiness? This suddenly seemed like the ending of the story that had been written for him all along.

He stood and looked back towards the house. Every light was burning, or so it seemed. A boat out at sea might have thought they were having a party. Behind the bright grid of windows, he could just make out the looming shadow of the castle ruins that gave the house its name. The countless decades of Foleys that had lived on this land. All that history, now hanging on to the future by a thread.

He knew he should go back, but he couldn't bear the thought of seeing his mother. He pictured her sitting at the kitchen table. A cup and saucer in front of her. His mug of tea on the opposite side. Her endless stream of words would fill the silence, but it would be her face that told him what she really thought. Somehow this was all his fault. It would be the same look she had given him when James had died. An expression that told him that she still loved him but that she could never forgive him.

His mother was not the sort of woman to bounce you on her knee or pull you into the comfort of her breast when everything seemed too much, but she was strong, resourceful and determined. He knew that if he was to get through this he would need her. He lifted his collar against the howl of the night and started across the field towards the lights of the house. Of one thing, he was certain.

His mother would have a plan.

NOW

1

Two strands of Christmas lights sagged across the main street. Some red, some green, mostly spent, they swayed forlornly in the driving rain.

Elizabeth Keane sighed as she drove her small rental car over the bridge into the town. Partly because she was weary from her overnight flight from New York to Dublin, but mostly due to the memories conjured up by the sight of Buncarragh on a wet afternoon in the first week of January. The shiny gifts long forgotten, the last few unwanted Quality Street sweets being poked listlessly around the bottom of the tin, the novelty of films being on the television in the afternoon well and truly over, each house was just a waiting room for school to reopen. She wondered if anything had changed in the twenty years since she'd lived here. Probably not. The kids were no doubt stabbing at their phones, and though they had hundreds of television stations she could almost feel the overheated boredom oozing from the terraced houses leading down from Bridge Street.

She was surprised by how fast her journey had been. Growing up here, Dublin had seemed like some distant metropolis, but now with the gleaming new motorway, Buncarragh was just a couple of exits north of Kilkenny. Had the country shrunk or had America changed her sense of distance? The crisp blue road signs, with their bright reflective lettering and kilometres, seemed at odds somehow with the places they led to. Sleepy grey market towns that remained rooted in the past.

Would this be the last time she ever made this trip? Now her mother was gone she had no real ties to the place. Of course, there were a few cousins and her uncle and aunt but they had never been close, and once the house was sold what reason would she have to return? Ahead of her on the left just past the railings of the small Methodist church, she could see the family shop: 'Keane and Sons'. The name was picked out in ornate plaster on the façade that had been painted, for as long as Elizabeth could remember, in an insipid colour that reminded her of uncooked chicken. She slowed down to look in the windows. To the left of the doors was a copse of artificial Christmas trees, while the display on the right consisted of some flat-screen televisions and a trio of gleaming black and chrome baby buggies.

Her car was just passing the doors when they opened and an incongruously glamorous woman stepped out. Shit. It was Noelle, her cousin Paul's wife. They ran the shop now. Had she seen her? Elizabeth glanced in her rear-view mirror and saw a long thin arm waving. Christ, she must have the eyes of a hawk. Elizabeth groaned. She had hoped to make it all the way to Convent Hill unobserved, but knew she would have to stop now. That whole side of the family

4

already thought she was a stuck-up bitch. She put the car into reverse and pulled up alongside Noelle who was holding a plastic Keane and Sons bag aloft to protect her bright blonde hair from the rain. Elizabeth took in Noelle's skin-tight jeans and short padded jacket that allowed people to fully appreciate her trim figure. How was it possible that this woman had produced three babies? Elizabeth considered her own forgivingly loose hooded sweatshirt and her cropped dark hair with streaks of grey which her son Zach delighted in telling her was less of a hairstyle and more of a haircut. She prodded ineffectually at some buttons till the passenger window went down. Bravely trying to banish her concerns about just how bad her make-up-free, sleep-deprived face might look, she leaned across and called out.

'Hi, Noelle! Terrible day, isn't it?'

'It is. It is. I thought it was you! It was the hair I noticed first.' Noelle emitted a small shriek, to indicate how pleased she was by her perceptiveness. 'You must have had a fierce drive. We didn't know you were coming back.' There was a slight accusatory tone in her voice.

'I didn't know myself,' Elizabeth lied. 'Zach has gone to see friends so I thought I'd come back and sort out the house before term time starts up.' This was also a lie. Her son had gone to visit his father on the west coast. She wondered why she hadn't just told the truth. Was she saving herself from embarrassment, or Noelle?

'You should have let us know. We'd have put

5

the heating on for you. You'll come down for dinner now, won't you?'

'You're very kind but I won't. I grabbed a few bits and pieces on the way out of Dublin and all I really want to do is sleep. I'll call down tomorrow. You should get in, Noelle, you're getting soaked.'

'Well, if you're sure, and if you get up there and change your mind just come down. We're still eating Christmas! We missed having your mother this year of course.' Noelle pushed the corners of her bright red lips down to indicate the sort of regret you might show a toddler that had banged their knee. 'Anyway, welcome home!'

Elizabeth forced a smile and waved. Judgemental bitch. Did Noelle not understand that she could never make Elizabeth feel any guiltier than she already did? The horrible tug of war between being both the single child of a dying woman and a single parent living thousands of miles away was finally over and she had to admit she was glad. Elizabeth put the car into gear and drove on.

The road opened out into what was known as The Green, even though it was just a narrow wedge of paving in the middle of the road with a park bench and two litter bins. Just beyond that the town's only set of traffic lights turned red. Elizabeth stared out at the wet, deserted street, the windscreen wipers wearily slicing away, and a strange fury bubbled up in her. She slammed her hand hard against the steering wheel. Not five minutes back in Buncarragh and all the feelings that had made her flee the place had come flooding back. It didn't matter how hard she had studied or who she had invited to her birthday parties, she was always made to feel less in this town. Poor Liz Keane. Growing up with no daddy. It was surprising how often the word 'Father' came up in a convent education and every time it did she had felt all eyes on her.

Now she was a single mother herself — worse, Zach's father refused to do anything as useful as disappear — she understood how strong her mother must have been to endure all the sideways glances and wagging tongues that stopped abruptly as she pushed her pram along the streets in the 1970s. She sometimes wondered if the humiliation of her own married life was a form of punishment for being so judgemental of her mother when she was a girl. Oh, how she had hated her mother for not having a husband! What sort of woman couldn't manage to get a man? She examined her friends' parents. These women weren't as pretty as her mother, with their unkempt hair and sometimes not even a smear of lipstick, and yet they had all managed to find someone to say 'I do', someone to hold their daughters' hands as they walked in large broods after mass. The memory of her and her mother clicking along the pavement from the chapel to their house while car windows stuffed with sweaty small faces gawped at them still brought back a deep pang of loneliness. That feeling of being somehow incomplete. No daddy, no siblings, no sense of being a real family.

Christmas. No wonder Elizabeth hated it so

much. Knowing that everyone else was surrounded by boisterous clans squashed around tables on mismatched chairs while she and her mother sat in Sunday silence scraping at plates. Of course, her aunt and uncle had issued invitations to join them and her three cousins but her mother always refused. 'We'll just have a nice quiet family Christmas. The two of us. Let them get on with it.' As an adult Elizabeth understood her mother's pride and all the guilt she must have endured, but as a child she felt she was being punished. She always thought her mother had put appearances — the house, her hair, new school shoes — above her actual happiness.

Nobody, certainly not her own mother, had ever sat her down and told her the story of her father in detail, but over the years she had gleaned the main thrust of the tale.

Her mother, Patricia, had nursed her grandmother until she died, at which point most people considered her to have missed the boat when it came to men. She was the spinster sister and aunt, nothing more. But then, out of the blue came news that she was dating and almost before people had time to absorb that fact came word of a wedding. Her mother had left Buncarragh to begin her newly married life. However, within a suspiciously short space of time she had abruptly returned, carrying the baby Elizabeth in her arms. There was no sign of any husband. The rumour mill went into overdrive. The husband had beaten her, the mother-in-law had driven her out, there had never been a wedding. The fact that she had retained Keane as her surname only added to the mystery and scandal. Nobody knew the truth. When Elizabeth was older she had tried to talk to her mother about what had happened to her father but was always given the same stock answer: 'He died very young, but he was a lovely man, a kind man.' If Elizabeth persisted her mother assured her that he had been an only child and that there was no other family. She imagined her family tree as a couple of bare branches with an ancient vulture perched on one of them.

It was only three months since the funeral and yet the sight of Convent Hill still seemed strangely unfamiliar. The size of the houses increased along with the gradient until she reached number sixty-two. The street lights spluttered on as she pulled up outside the home where she had been reared. Lots of spaces. People must still be away, she thought. Getting out of the car the rain felt good on her face as she looked up at the house that still managed to appear imposing. Three storeys tall and double-fronted, it had been built for a bank manager but her grandfather had bought it when the shop had started to do well. She remembered her mother telling her how Uncle Jerry and especially his wife Auntie Gillian had tried to get it after her granny had died. But their mother's will had been very clear: Jerry got the shop and Patricia got the house.

The rain streaked down the dark glass of the windows and dripped off the windowsills.

9

Elizabeth struggled to remember ever being happy here and yet she knew she had been. Balloons had been tied to the black railings that separated the house from the street and small girls in candy-coloured dresses had been deposited by mothers in heavy winter coats. One of her earliest memories was her mother taking her by the hand across the street so that they could admire the lights of their own Christmas tree through the dining-room window. So long ago. Elizabeth felt as if these were the memories of another person, her life was so removed from this house, these people, the town of Buncarragh.

She thought of where she lived now. A cramped two-bedroomed walk-up apartment above a nail salon on Third Avenue. Her own and Zach's lives stuffed into a space not much bigger than her childhood bedroom. She was glad her mother had never come to visit. Seeing it through her eyes would have ruined it for her because, despite its many limitations, Elizabeth loved her little nest. The warm glow of lamps in the evening, the morning sun that squeezed through the gaps of the surrounding buildings to fill the tiny kitchen, Zach sitting proudly at the rickety desk he had found on the street and inexpertly painted himself, but most of all the sense of achievement it gave her. Life after Elliot hadn't been easy and there had been sleepless nights when she thought her only option might have been to return home to Buncarragh, so every time she turned the key in her own Manhattan front door, it felt like a victory.

Now she was searching for the keys to Convent Hill in her overstuffed handbag. Around the worn stone steps outside she noticed the green trim of weeds. She hoped the lock wouldn't be too stiff but the key turned easily. Probably Auntie Gillian sniffing around for what she wanted to take. Elizabeth was considering what her aunt might have coveted when she noticed the absence of the two rose bushes in pots that had stood sentry on either side of the shallow porch. That bloody woman. She pushed the door open with a small grunt of irritation and felt for the hall light switch. An untidy mound of post lay on the ground in front of her and more had been placed by someone on the thin hall table. Everything looked the same: the gold and green patterned carpet runner going up the stairs; Cinderella herself had fled from the ball on those steps, pop stars had greeted adoring fans as they made their way from jumbo jets down to the tarmac. The framed Chinese prints still hung on either side of the living-room door; the narrow passage still led past the stairs to the kitchen, which had been her first port of call every day returning from school. So familiar that it was like looking at her own face in a mirror and yet something had changed. Mixed in with the comforting smells of furniture polish and coal fires were the unfamiliar scents of damp and neglect. Nobody lived here and that realisation struck Elizabeth with a greater force than she had expected. She felt as if something had been stolen from her.

The car unpacked, Elizabeth sat at the kitchen table with a bowl of tomato soup in front of her. She felt oddly self-conscious as she raised the spoon to her mouth but of course there was no one here to watch her. Nobody would walk in. It occurred to her that she had probably never been alone in this house before. Babysitters, neighbours, school friends and of course her mother meant that there had always been another heartbeat. She put down the spoon and looked around the kitchen. Every surface was piled with ancient crockery now coated in dust and grease. Behind each pine-door-fronted cabinet she knew there were more plates and pots and pans. Jars of chutney and cans of marrowfat peas that were probably older than she was. So much stuff and this was just one room. A heavy wave of fatigue swept over her and she felt defeated by the enormity of the task ahead of her. She checked her watch. Only eight o'clock. She didn't care. She was going to bed with the hope of waking up fully motivated. She grabbed her small carry-on case and headed up the stairs.

On the landing she hesitated. Where should she sleep: her childhood bedroom or her mother's room? The thought of sleeping in her small single bed didn't appeal and somehow she felt it would make her mother's room seem even emptier. Back in New York she had felt guilty for not missing her mother more, but in this house she felt her absence like a physical ache. She opened the door to her mother's room. The overhead light was far too bright so she quickly switched on one of the bedside lamps instead.

12

Apart from the abandoned walking frame and the ugly utilitarian commode that her mother had needed before she died, the room was as she remembered. She sat on the shiny dark green comforter that covered the bed. The springs creaked beneath her weight and suddenly she was a little girl alone in her room hearing that sound, knowing that her mother was in bed and all was safe. She would never have that feeling again. Unexpectedly she found that she was crying. She braced her hands on her knees and with her head bowed, let the tears fall. Her mother was gone and she could never come home again. Some of her tears were for her own child. She hoped she made Zach feel as safe and loved as she had been but she doubted it. The world was terrifying and nobody could be stupid enough to think that a lecturer in Romantic poetry living in a tiny rented apartment could ever protect a sensitive, easily distracted young man from all its dangers. She lay down and fell into the emotional void that the time difference, jet lag and the welcome escape of sleep provided.

2

The warm light of the lamp was still glowing through the peach silk shade when she woke. Glancing over at the window she could see no hint of daylight. She looked at her watch. Six, but what six? Had she changed her watch? She couldn't remember. Shoving her hand into her jeans pocket she retrieved her phone. Six in the morning. Knowing that she probably wouldn't fall back to sleep she padded across the landing to brush her teeth and go to the toilet. Everywhere she looked there were 'things'. Pointless stuff lined every surface. Turning her head as she scrubbed at her teeth she could see bottles of No More Tears shampoo and Matey the Sailor bubble bath that must have been there since she was a girl. She opened the mirrored door of the cabinet above the sink. Packed. Every prescription from the last forty years appeared to be crammed onto its shelves.

Back in the bedroom there was less obvious clutter, but Elizabeth knew what lurked inside the large rosewood wardrobe and the matching chest of drawers. Why had she decided to do this herself? Was there a single thing in this house she actually wanted or had missed in the last twenty years? She should have just let a house clearance company loose on the place or allowed Noelle and Aunt Gillian free rein to scavenge whatever they wanted.

Tentatively, she opened the door of the wardrobe. The first thing that confronted her was a full-length reflection of herself. God, she looked awful. She examined her face, which certain girlfriends said gave her boyish good looks. Odd that those women were usually button-nosed, plump-lipped beauties. She wondered how they would have coped with her square jaw and long straightish nose? Even in this light her normally ruddy complexion looked pale and drawn. Her bright hazel eyes peered at her from puffy eyelids and heavy bags. Oh God — had that stain been on her top the whole journey or was it just the soup from last night? Her hair had a strange ridge across the left side of her head. She smoothed it down but to no effect. Turning her attention to the inside of the wardrobe, she managed a small grin. Yes, it was stuffed to bursting, but running her hand along the rail of coats and dresses was like visiting a museum of her memories. The blue tweed of that coat her mother had worn standing stiffly at the school gates, the slim fitting dresses bought for a lifetime of christenings and weddings, including the knitted navy blue two-piece that she had worn when Elizabeth had married Elliot in Ann Arbor. Her poor mother. The warmest March anyone could remember Michigan having. The red sweaty face peered out from every wedding photograph. Elliot's mother standing beside her looking like she'd been carved from marble. Elizabeth shuddered at the memory of the day. The way both mothers had come up to her with an expression of concern and suspicion. 'No champagne for you?'

She glanced up at the shelf above the hanging rail. One side was full of folded jumpers and cardigans. The other half seemed to contain nothing but a rolled-up yellowing duvet. Elizabeth thought it might be useful if the heating didn't come on, so she pulled it forward. It spilled out into a large soft pile at her feet. With the duvet gone she could see a dark wooden box shoved right to the back of the wardrobe. She couldn't remember ever having seen it before and reached in to retrieve it. Disappointingly, it didn't feel very heavy. She placed the box on the floor and knelt in front of it. Wiping the dust from the lid, the dark sheen of the wood was revealed. Walnut? The corners were protected by small inlays of brass. She hoped it wasn't locked. No, the lid lifted easily. Peering in, the contents were a bit of an anti-climax: a tiny yellow knitted baby booty and beneath that a thin pile of letters held together by an ancient cream ribbon. Elizabeth slipped the first letter from the pile and began to read.

★   ★   ★

Castle House,
Muirinish,
West Cork
30 November 1973

Dear Lonely Leinster Lady,
I'm not really sure how to begin. I have never replied to one of these ads before. I suppose I should just tell you a bit about myself and you can see if you like the sound of me!
I'm forty-one, so well below your cut-off age of fifty! I'm six feet tall and I still have most of my hair. I enclose a photograph so you can decide if I am decent-looking or not! I'm a farmer, which you specified you were looking for. The farm is near Muirinish in West Cork. It is one hundred and twenty acres but if I'm being honest only

eighty are any good, the rest being a sea marsh. It's a dairy farm, which I enjoy even though it's a bit of a tie.

So why is this great catch on the shelf? Well, things haven't been easy at home. My brother was running the farm after my father died but then when I was seventeen he was killed in an accident so I had to take it over and help my mother as much as I could. It meant I have found it very hard to get out to meet anyone and to be honest it has also made me a bit shy. Time has a way of slipping by and I felt I had to do something about finding a wife before it was too late.

Because of milking it would be difficult for me to get up to see you but I would be happy to meet you in Cork city for lunch or even a cup of tea. If you wanted me to send you the train fare I'm sure that could be arranged. I don't want to sound rude but it would be good if you could also send me a photograph so I can see if you are as lovely as you sound!

I hope to get a letter back but if I don't then I wish you happiness in your life.

With every good wish,
Edward Foley

★   ★   ★

17

Castle House,
Muirinish,
West Cork
15 December 1973

Dear Patricia,

Thank you very much for your letter. I was very happy when I got it. Thank you also for your photograph. You are as lovely as I had imagined. Well guessed about my photo — yes, it was taken at a steam rally in Upton!

My sympathies for the loss of your mother. It must be very hard for you especially with Christmas coming. It is a shame your brother has not been more help to you. I didn't mention in my last letter but I live with my mother. Don't worry! If I find a wife we have planning permission for a bungalow so you would be the lady of the house! Not that I'm counting my chickens of course!

I am very happy that you want to meet up in the new year. My mother says the Metropole Hotel do a nice carvery and it is almost beside the station. Does that sound suitable? To tell you the truth I am very nervous about it and I hope I'm not too quiet for you.

I hope you have a good Christmas and you aren't too sad.

With every good wish,
Edward

Castle House,
Muirinish,
West Cork
3 January 1974

Dear Patricia,
Thank you for your card. Was the town on the front Buncarragh? My mother says thank you as well.

I am very excited about next week. I'll meet you off the train. Hopefully we will recognise each other from our photographs but just in case I'll be standing by the Cork Examiner *kiosk* just by the entrance. I'll be wearing a tweed jacket, because to be honest I only have the one decent jacket!

It'll be a bit early for the lunch but maybe if the weather isn't too brutal we could go for a walk along the river first. If I am a bit quiet please don't think it is because I don't like you. I'm just not sure how I will be with the nerves.

See you on the 10th — oh and if your train is delayed don't worry, I will wait.

With every good wish,
Edward

PS If you change your mind please let me know.

Castle House,
Muirinish,
West Cork
11 January 1974

Dear Patricia,

Words can't describe how wonderful it was to meet you yesterday. You are even lovelier in person and funny and kind.

Afterwards, on the drive home, I thought of all the things I wanted to ask you and what I wanted to say. Next time! I hope you want there to be a next time.

Sorry about your arrival. I was just so overcome by nerves. I wasn't going to let you walk past without saying hello — just tongue-tied! I enjoyed it all — even the windy walk! I thought the lunch was good, though your chicken did look a bit dry, even if you said it wasn't. You are too nice.

I hope you don't think I'm being too forward if I say that my favourite part of the day was the goodbye kiss. I loved the feel of your lips. I wish I had held you for longer. I have been thinking about it ever since. When will I get to give you a hello kiss? I hope it is soon.

My mother says you are very welcome to come and visit us at Castle House. She will be there to supervise so there will be no chance of any scandal! She wonders would you like her to write to your brother to put his mind at rest?

20

I cannot lie. I haven't felt this happy for a very long time.

Hoping to see you again soon,
Edward

★   ★   ★

Elizabeth put the pile of letters on the floor and leaned against the wall. Her father! Edward Foley. That name had been all she had ever known about her father. She picked the pages up again and her hand was trembling. The man her mother had never let her know had touched these bits of paper. She knew it was ridiculous but seeing the neat handwriting, the black ink soaked into the blue Basildon Bond, she felt connected to him. Had her mother put them here knowing that she would find them? Were they her gift to her from beyond the grave?

Elizabeth read on. Another visit to Cork. A weekend spent at Castle House. They became full-blown love letters. There was more kissing and even a blush-inducing reference to feeling her mother's breasts. Maybe she hadn't been meant to find them. Then at the bottom of the pile there was a page of the same fine writing paper but this one was marked with blue biro. Just five large letters spread across the sheet. They were scrawled in a thin spidery hand but Elizabeth was certain that the word they spelled out was SORRY.

THEN

1

The extra bowl mocked her. The neon strip of the kitchen light was reflected as a shiny toothless smile in the bottom of the dish and Patricia Keane resolved to leave her single life behind.

It had been almost five months since her elderly mother had died and still she found herself routinely setting the table for two or putting a pair of cups beside the kettle. Her mother had been ill for so long, barely there really, and yet her death had seemed so sudden when it finally came. The rasping breath of the old woman had become like the ticking of a clock or the rustle of leaves outside the window. You didn't notice it till it stopped, and then the silence was as vast as it was shocking. Of course, the void had been quickly filled with the sound of people calling by with plates of sandwiches and strange women she hardly knew indulging in competitive cleaning in her kitchen. It was only after the funeral that the silence returned. But it was more than that. The rooms weren't empty, they were filled with the absence of someone. The dead don't vanish, they leave a negative of themselves stamped on the world. Patricia had read an article in the *Reader's Digest* about how people who had an amputation still felt an itch in the severed limb. She imagined it must feel the same as when she shouted, 'Tea, Mam?' up the stairs, before remembering.

The idea of a Lonely Hearts advertisement hadn't been hers. That brainwave belonged to her friend Rosemary O'Shea, the only other girl from her class in the convent to still be single. At the age of thirty-two Patricia and Rosemary were most definitely on the shelf. Everyone seemed to have found a man. Even greasy Annie and the unfortunate-looking Niamh Rourke, otherwise known as Beaky, had managed to march down the aisle. Rosemary was different. She seemed perfectly happy in her own company. She worked as a hairdresser in Buncarragh Beauty, though not even the kindest would have described her as the greatest ambassador for the salon. She had left her parents and four brothers out on the family farm and rented a small flat above Deasy's the chemists. Last year she had even bought herself her very own second-hand Fiat. What use did she have for a man? Patricia didn't really know why, but she trusted Rosemary's judgement. She hadn't seen that much more of the world but her certainty about things was infectious. It was Rosemary who had convinced her to cut her hair. The straight brown locks that she had worn at shoulder length for as long as she could remember had been turned into a short bob, with a side parting replacing her fringe. 'You aren't in the convent any more, you need hair for life,' Rosemary had argued and somehow Patricia had known what her friend had meant. It was also Rosemary who had talked her out of shapeless pinafores. 'You're so lucky — you have a waist,' she had said, indicating her own fuller figure. 'Show it off!' A pile of Simplicity patterns had been borrowed and Patricia had dusted off her mother's sewing machine to make herself a few skirts that she had to admit did suit her. Rosemary made her feel as if life was possible, that you didn't have to simply accept your fate. It was a lesson that Patricia badly needed.

At eighteen her life had been completely rewritten. After a car crash that killed her father and left her mother unable to manage by herself, she had found that instead of going to university or having a nice steady job in the bank, she was a full-time carer. As the unwed daughter, there was never any question that it would be otherwise, so she had turned her back on the idea of having a life of her own and wrapped herself in an apron. The last fourteen years had been spent waiting for her mother to get better or die. Now she had nothing. Well, that wasn't technically true. She had inherited the large family home in the town and until they could find a way to wriggle out of it, a small allowance from the family business run by her older brother Jerry and his wife Gillian. She was already under pressure to sell up or do the decent thing and give the house to her brother and his young family. 'What do you need with all those rooms?' But she was holding firm. 'That house is your reward,' Rosemary reminded her.

They were sitting in the Coffee Pot, which was the nearest thing to urban sophistication that

Buncarragh had to offer. It was owned and run by Eileen Moore, who was married to Cathal the printer. After a much-heralded trip to Paris, Eileen had decided to open her very own café. A vast gleaming coffee machine had been imported from Italy along with a huge marble bar top. Sadly, the counter had been broken in two in transit but Eileen put her sausage roll display case over the join and now you'd only notice the repair job if you were looking for it. There were even tables and chairs placed out in the street. Patricia's mother had never approved. She couldn't understand why anyone would want the world and his wife driving by looking at what you were eating. She would have felt like a cow in a field.

Rosemary carefully divided their chocolate éclair in two. 'Well, there are no fellas around here. None you'd want, anyway. Anyone decent is gone.'

'Cormac Phelan was about the only one I sort of fancied and slutty Carol got him.'

'She's a fierce whore,' Rosemary observed while licking some cream from the side of her mouth.

'Fierce,' agreed Patricia and the two of them sat silent in mutual contemplation. How could a man be found?

'Kilkenny!'

'I couldn't.'

'You could. I could drive us in one Sunday. There are those big dances at the Mayfair. That's where all my brothers went to shift girls.'

'Rosemary, look at me. I'm thirty-two. They'll

25

think I'm a mother come to collect my kids. I could no more go to a dance . . . '

'You could. You look great.' But her reply lacked conviction.

'I just want a nice farmer. He doesn't need to be too young. I don't even care if he doesn't live around here. A farmer's wife. Doesn't that sound lovely?'

'Yes.' Rosemary sounded unconvinced.

'I just think you'd feel useful. You'd be a team.'

'I suppose.'

'How do I find a farmer?'

This conundrum rendered them silent once more but then Rosemary sat up straight and fanned both of her hands in front of her. She had the answer!

'The *Journal!*'

'What?'

'The *Farmers' Journal!* They have ads in there. I read it in the salon.'

'You get the *Farmers' Journal* in the salon?'

'People leave it behind. The point is they have ads in there, the 'Getting in Touch' section. It's farmers and women who want to meet a farmer.'

Patricia's face indicated she still didn't fully understand.

'Looking for love, like. Lonely Hearts. That is your best bet, I'm telling you.'

'Oh God, Rosemary. I'm not sure.'

'Well, it's worth a try anyway,' Rosemary said and crammed the last of the éclair into her mouth.

★ ★ ★

Two weeks later an over-excited Rosemary was doing her best to run up Convent Hill, her purple coat flapping behind her, a newspaper gripped in one hand while the other tried to control her black patent shoulder bag. She looked like a bishop fleeing the scene of some nocturnal indiscretion. Outside number sixty-two she rang the bell and leaned panting against the pillar of the porch. When Patricia opened the door, she was confronted by the face of her friend, even redder than normal and framed by her coarse dark curls glistening with sweat. Rosemary didn't speak — she simply thrust the rolled-up newspaper into Patricia's hand. They both looked at the paper and then simultaneously began to shriek. It had arrived!

At the kitchen table they smoothed out the paper and then Rosemary quickly flicked to the section at the back. Her chewed nail ran down the various ads, Bantry Bachelor . . . Fermanagh Medium Sized Farmer . . . Romantic T/T . . . here it was . . . Lonely Leinster Lady! The wording had been Rosemary's handiwork. Patricia had favoured something a little more discreet but she was told in no uncertain terms that discretion was not going to help find her a husband. Rosemary had also advised lowering her age or not mentioning it at all but Patricia had insisted, arguing that she didn't want any potential relationship to start with a lie. Early thirties had been settled upon though if Rosemary had been totally honest she thought that made her friend sound forty if she was a day.

After the initial excitement of actually seeing the ad in print and reassuring each other about how well it looked and the quality of it compared to the other advertisements, the women felt oddly deflated. There was now nothing to do but wait.

Days, then a week, then a fortnight and still no response. Every morning Patricia found herself waiting for the postman. Some days nothing, on other days the familiar clank of the letter box as an envelope hit the mat with the most gentle of thuds, but every day disappointment. She cursed herself for ever listening to Rosemary. This was worse than before. At least in the pre-advertisement age of her life she had just been lonely, but now she was rejected as well. She had taken to walking the long way round just to avoid Buncarragh Beauty and Rosemary's face peering expectantly at her through the window. She imagined people smirking at the sight of her because they had worked out that she was the lonely Leinster lady. She berated herself for daring to think that she might have had a chance at a second beginning. Why hadn't she simply accepted what everyone else knew — she was a spinster. She tried the word out as she combed her hair in the mirror. 'Spinster.' Her skin was still free of wrinkles and yet, as she repeated the word to her unsmiling face, she imagined her hair starting to take on a greyish hue.

It was the day before the three-week anniversary of sending away her ad and postal order when the thud on the mat sounded just a little more substantial. Patricia stood frozen in the kitchen. She wanted to run and check, but hated herself for being so easy to humiliate. Forcing herself to take another sip of her tea, she put the mug down on the table and walked at a steady pace to the door. She leaned against the frame and slowly craned her neck around the corner into the hall. A large brown envelope. Too big for a bill. Could it . . . She inched forward and bent to turn it over. A gasp. There, clear as day, in the top left-hand corner was the legend 'The Irish Farmers' Journal'. She picked it up and scampered back into the kitchen.

Inside there were four further envelopes. Inside the first was a postcard depicting the ruins of Ennis Friary beneath a chemical blue sky. An odd choice, Patricia thought. She turned it over and read, 'You sound like a ride.' She dropped the card on the table with a start. Why on earth would anyone write that? Why would the Journal send it on to her? Pushing the postcard to one side she cautiously opened the next envelope. This at least was a letter. It was written on lined paper in what appeared to be a very unsteady hand. With difficulty Patricia deciphered that this was from a man who lived in Tullamore. Not too far away, she thought. He had been married twice before. She didn't like the sound of that. As if reading her thoughts, he continued by reassuring her that his past relationships ensured he knew what he was doing. Patricia doubted this was the man for her. He had been a farmer but was now living in a care home. Oh, for God's

29

sake. Did she have her own house? She crumpled the thin paper into a ball. The third envelope contained a card with a drawing of a blue tit perched on a branch on the front. It was from a man in Carlow who thought it perfectly acceptable to ask her for a photograph of herself in her bra and panties. She was torn between being furious with Rosemary and impatient to share these shocking replies with her just to hear her friend's big throaty laugh. What a waste of time and money!

The fourth letter looked different. It was written in black ink on the same Basildon Bond blue notepaper her mother had favoured. The handwriting was neat and, more importantly, didn't look insane. A small black and white photograph fell on the table. A middle-aged man, forty? was standing beside an old-fashioned steam engine. His hand rested on the large metal rim of the wheel by the driver's seat. He was staring straight into the camera and oddly wasn't smiling, but nor did he look too serious or sad. Patricia decided that 'benign' was how she would describe him. His dark hair receded on either side of his forehead leaving a widow's peak and his large dark eyes seemed kind. She peered closer. Yes, definitely kind. He was dressed simply in a white shirt open at the collar, with the sleeves rolled to the elbow, and the belt of his dark trousers showed off his slim waist. He didn't set Patricia's heart racing but she wasn't repulsed either and at this point that seemed like winning. She started to read his letter.

2

Could people tell?

Patricia scanned the other passengers in the train carriage. A bald, rubber-faced businessman engrossed in his newspaper, a young woman playing I spy with her two bored children, an older lady absent-mindedly sucking her teeth as she knitted something small and pink. Not one of them seemed aware of her existence. They appeared to be oblivious to the fact that at the age of thirty-two, she was embarking on the most exciting and scandalous, yes, that was the very word, scandalous adventure of her whole life.

Rosemary had given her a lift to the train station in Kilkenny. They had hugged each other on the platform and then as the train pulled in she had tied a bright red and yellow scarf around Patricia's neck.

'To brighten you up a bit.'

Patricia looked crestfallen and cast a glance down at her navy coat and black shoes. 'Do I not look all right?' she asked with an edge of panic creeping into her voice.

'No, no! You look beautiful.' Rosemary held her arms and looked into her friend's eyes. 'You really do.'

The train had come to a standstill. Whistles were being blown. Doors slammed.

'Good luck! I can't wait to hear all about it. I'll be waiting for you here tonight.'

'Thanks so much, Rosemary. You're great.'

Patricia stepped onto the train and looked back. 'Bye!' Then she let out a loud nervous laugh that was almost a cry for help.

'You'll be grand!'

Whatever confidence she might have had slowly evaporated during the long journey, which involved having to change trains twice. By the time they went through a series of long tunnels approaching Cork station Patricia felt very unsure indeed. One of the children had begun to cry because they didn't want to put their red wool hat on and the businessman was heaving himself into his overcoat. The end of the line.

Patricia stood on the platform for a moment to get her bearings. The large sign showing the way out was down the platform to her right. She retied the belt on her coat and twisted Rosemary's scarf so that the knot was to one side in what she hoped was a jaunty fashion. She put one foot in front of the other and gripped her handbag tightly in an effort to stop her hands from shaking. Her heart felt as if it was vibrating, it was beating so quickly. In her mind, she repeated her mantra, 'You'll be grand. You'll be grand.'

Outside seemed very bright and loud. Cars were streaming along the road beyond the car park in front of the station. Looking around she quickly saw the kiosk with the large 'Cork Examiner' sign above it and there . . . just behind it, she recognised Edward waiting for her. In truth, the way he had positioned himself it seemed closer to hiding than waiting. She wondered if he had seen her. He was staring studiously in the opposite direction. God, this had all been an awful mistake. She wanted to walk straight back into the station and get on the next train home, the next one anywhere. No. She had come all this way and his letters had been lovely. Edward Foley was going to meet her whether he wanted to or not.

'Edward?'

No response. The man's head remained facing the other way. Could she see him quivering?

'Edward?' she repeated a little louder. This time the old man selling papers tapped him on the shoulder and he was forced to turn around. The dark eyes that had seemed so kind in the photograph were wide with fear. His mouth hung open. Patricia wasn't sure what to do next. She offered her hand and said, 'Hello. I'm Patricia.'

Edward looked at her hand as if he had never seen one before and certainly didn't know what to do with it. Patricia felt the hot flush of embarrassment. The old paper seller was smirking as he observed their slow, stiff puppet show. She worried that she might cry but then as if someone had flicked a switch, Edward took her hand and shook it. His skin was warm and rough. The simple handshake seemed strangely intimate. Their eyes met for a moment before he quickly turned his gaze to the ground. 'Hello.' His voice was deep and hoarse. Even from one word she could hear his thick Cork accent. As if worn out from his efforts to be social Edward let his arm fall to his side and uttered no more. Patricia sighed deeply. This was going to be a very long day.

'Will we take a walk?' she suggested. He risked

a quick peek at her face and then began to walk away. Patricia took this as a sign of agreement, so she followed him. They walked in silence till they reached a set of traffic lights. Edward indicated to the left and informed Patricia, 'The river is down there.'

'The banks of the Lee,' Patricia said, referring to the old song.

Edward stared at her as if she had just made a statement in ancient Hebrew. 'Yes. Just down here.' He began to walk again. Patricia wondered what he would do if she didn't follow him, but she did.

They walked down to a metal bridge. On the other bank of the river buses were shuddering their way in and out of the station. The people on the pavement brushed past them, all seeming in a great hurry. Lives being lived all around her while she was lumbered with this strange man who didn't seem to have the slightest interest in her.

Halfway across the bridge Edward stopped and looked over the balustrade down into the murky water. Patricia did the same. There was a strong wind off the river and her hair blew around her face. She knew she must look a right state but she didn't care. She heard something and looking at Edward realised he was speaking quietly. She leaned in to hear him.

'I loved her dearly both true and sincerely. There is no one in this wide world I loved so much as she.'

What in God's name was he talking about?

'Every bush, every bower, every wild Irish

flower, it reminds me of my Mary on the banks of the Lee.'

Of course. Now she understood. Her head bowed, she began to speak and their two voices found each other on the wind.

So I will pluck my love some roses, some wild Irish roses
I will pluck my love some roses, the fairest that ever grew
And I will place them on the mound of my own darling true love
In that cold and silent valley where she lies beneath the dew.

The lyric ended, their voices silent, he turned to look at her and smiled. His face *was* kind. Patricia smiled back. She tried to think of something to say, a way to keep the momentum going, but she couldn't. When he turned and began to walk again, she followed.

The lunch was torture. He slurped down his vegetable soup without comment while she sipped at her small glass of grapefruit juice. When the young waitress was clearing their starters away she gave Patricia a small smile of encouragement and sympathy. A series of questions about his journey, the farm, his mother, all failed to ignite anything that resembled conversation. The solitary question he asked her during the whole day was when he enquired if her chicken was dry.

'No. No, it's fine, thanks.'

'Looks dry,' he commented as he sawed a thick slice of lamb.

Somehow the fact that he was right, and her meal had the texture of chalkboard, only made things worse. It was as if it was his fault.

Finally, they were back at the station, half an hour too early for her train but Patricia really didn't care. She just wanted the day to end. They stood facing each other at the entrance and she was just about to shake his hand and thank him for the lunch when he thrust his head forward like a cuckoo exiting a clock to announce the hour. Before she knew what was happening he had pecked at her lips. She let out an involuntary yelp of surprise.

'Oh sorry, I . . . ' He searched for one of his few words.

'No. It's . . . ' Patricia too was struggling.

'Well.'

'Yes.'

'I'll leave you, so.'

'Right. Thanks for the lunch.'

Now he was staring at her, his shoulders hunched, his hands knotting and twisting his fingers. Patricia longed for him to go but still he stood there. 'Go!' she silently screamed at him in her head. Surely he wasn't enjoying this either? His face looked as if he was thinking about something else, remembering a great sadness. 'Sorry,' he whispered and turned quickly to walk away.

Patricia suddenly wanted to call after him, to somehow reassure him, make him feel better about how the day had gone. She thought about the man who knew all the words of 'The Banks of the Lee'. Why hadn't she been able to spend the afternoon with that man? How had the man who had written her such sweet letters been turned to stone in her presence?

Patricia walked beneath the large station clock, confident there wouldn't be a next time.

NOW

Carefully, as if her mother might discover she had read them, Elizabeth folded the letters and returned them to the dusty oblivion of the box. Who had her mother been back then? She couldn't imagine the strict, dispassionate woman who had raised her replying to these sweet, coy notes. The mother she had known had almost sneered at any hint of romance. A little knot of sadness and regret tugged at her heart. She would never know the young woman who had hoped for a different life. She thought of the old photographs downstairs that she had pored over as a child. Uncle Jerry in short trousers holding her mother's hand before she went off for her first communion. Two teenage girls standing outside the front door of Convent Hill, their arms Irish-dancing stiff by their sides while a summer breeze whisked their hair around their laughing faces. A smooth, unblemished forehead framed by a pale blue satin hairband that matched her bridesmaid's dress as she stood beside Aunt Gillian on her big day. The smile on her face, her eyes that glinted with a mixture of hope and excitement. Not a hint of concern or care. Elizabeth had never known that woman.

She thought back to how she had felt when she first met Elliot in New York all those years ago when she was studying for her doctorate. He wasn't her first boyfriend but what she had felt for him was nothing compared to the callow boys at UCD. Elliot was dangerous. He both thrilled and frightened her. That tanned skin and the tiny ridged ladder of bone that climbed up his chest from his open-necked shirts. The confident way he touched her body, his hands mysteriously finding themselves in just the right place. Rushing essays, skipping shifts at the coffee shop, all because she had to be with him. She hadn't felt as if she had a choice. She had been hooked. High on love. Surely her mother had never felt like that? But then again, if she hadn't, then she had also managed to avoid the excruciating ten-year comedown that Elizabeth had endured. The years of suspicion, never knowing what was wrong but always aware that things weren't right. Then, seven, almost eight, years ago, leaving the college after lectures, noticing the dark-haired young man in his oversized coat staring at her. She had thought he was a student.

'Elizabeth?'

He was standing in front of her. She noticed the little rim of dirt around his nose ring. 'You don't know me but . . . ' and soon she knew everything and could never unknow it. The physical revulsion she had felt thinking about the things that Elliot had been doing at the same time as sharing her bed, kissing their child — it was still all too easy to recall. She hated how the revelations had made her feel, the way Elliot twisted her reactions to accuse her of being homophobic. The frustration and fury could still make her vibrate when she thought of him standing at the foot of their bed full of smug outrage, as if somehow her disgust made him the injured party in this mess of his making. So many of her friends had tried telling her that this was better. It would have been worse if he'd left her for a woman. Stony-faced she had listened but inside she was screaming. There was no better! From now on there would only be layers of worse. Her marriage was over, washed away by a tidal wave of lies. Now Zach was the only worthwhile souvenir from her journey into the deepest, darkest depths of romance. His good-natured way of approaching the world seemed so remarkably unmarred by his parents' failings. He was her defence that it had all been worth it.

She stood up abruptly to avoid sinking into a now-familiar swamp of regret. The box was returned to the wardrobe and with a sigh Elizabeth accepted that she would have to share this secret. Breaking her dead mother's confidence made her feel disloyal, but she had to tell someone about what she had found. Who would know more about Edward? She imagined her mother turning in her grave but she was going to have to speak to her Uncle Jerry and Aunt Gillian. She looked at her phone. It was still only seven thirty, too early to talk to anyone. She would make herself some toast.

Opening the kitchen door she didn't notice it right away. It was the rustle of paper that drew her attention, and then she saw it. Sitting up in her canvas tote bag, holding an energy bar between its small dusty pink paws, was a rat.

Elizabeth screamed and slammed the door. Panting with fear she leaned against the wall and scanned the hall for any other rodents. Her body shuddered as she considered how many of them might be in the house. Had they been in the bedroom with her last night? Of course she was used to seeing rats weaving around the black plastic hills of rubbish on the streets of New York late at night, but this was different. Seeing one at such close quarters seemed almost pornographic in its horror. She considered all the things that were in the kitchen. Her car keys, the house keys, her handbag with her passport and purse. She needed a trap or poison or whatever new methods had been developed since she was a girl. The obvious place to go was Keane and Sons, which for as long as she could remember had been an Aladdin's cave full of anything you might want that wasn't food or clothing, though of course her cousin Noelle had added a baby boutique, despite the protests from Uncle Jerry.

The shop wouldn't open till nine. After having a very brief, heart-stopping cold shower, she got dressed and came back downstairs. The kitchen remained off limits and it was still only eight o'clock. The large pile of post was spread across the console table. She sighed and sat in the high-backed mahogany chair that had always been used when anyone was speaking on the phone. It creaked as it always had and the back hit the wall as she knew it would. Ripping open the various envelopes, she found appeals from donkey sanctuaries, cancer charities, guide dogs for the blind, several electricity and phone bills, a

41

letter from the refuse collection company acknowledging the end of service from that address and then a letter from her mother's solicitor, Ernest O'Sullivan.

She assumed it was going to be a bill, but the letter was addressed to her. He wanted to speak to her about her mother's will and a codicil that had come to light. Elizabeth checked the date on the letter. A week after her mother's funeral. She folded the paper and slipped it into the back pocket of her jeans. Hopefully it could be dealt with over the phone. She didn't fancy having to drive all the way over to Kilkenny. As long as it didn't involve her Uncle Jerry or complicate her plans, she didn't care. Her goal was just to sell up and head back to New York with enough money to help Zach through college. He claimed he didn't want to go but she knew that Elliot would read him the riot act when he got wind of their son's plan. It was one of the reasons she had agreed to let Zach head west by himself to San Francisco for a visit with his father. She pulled her phone from her pocket. It would be after midnight in California, too late to call. She would ring in the evening. Looking at the screen she saw that she had a missed call and a voicemail. Zach! Even as she wondered how she hadn't heard the phone ringing, she remembered she had left the phone on silent from the night before.

'Hi, Mom. It's me. Just to let you know I've arrived. Dad picked me up from the airport and everything is great. Really warm compared to home. Hope Ireland isn't too depressing. I'm

42

shattered so I'm going to crash. Love you.'

It was so lovely to hear his voice. His New York swagger trying to mask his adolescent excitement about his trip. She thought about calling him back but decided against it. He'd done what she had asked and called her, so she would let him enjoy his little taste of independence. She would wait to return the call. She wasn't going to be that sort of mother, or more precisely she didn't want to be her own mother.

One of the most enduring memories she had of her mother was the day Elizabeth was leaving Buncarragh to begin her studies at university in Dublin. She had expected her mother to perhaps be a little upset but what she was not prepared for was the emotional outburst that her departure had provoked. Her mother hadn't just shed a tear as she waved her off from the door, she had collapsed into full-scale sobbing. Elizabeth remembered being embarrassed and impatient. It wasn't as if she was heading off to war or a hospital for major surgery. She was just doing what dozens of other teenagers from Buncarragh were doing and their parents weren't holding on to porch pillars, wailing as if they were watching their family trapped on a sinking ship. Afterwards, on the bus to Dublin, she had recalled all the excuses her mother had made over the years for not allowing her to go on any school trips. She had assumed it was to do with money, but in retrospect it seemed far more likely that her mother had an unhealthy attachment to her. Some might have said she was just being overly protective but to Elizabeth it had felt more like possessiveness. When the idea of her doing her postgraduate work in America had been broached, her mother had come up with a thousand reasons why Elizabeth shouldn't. When the day finally came for her to fly to JFK, there was no sign of her mother at the airport to wave her off. She'd claimed she was ill, but Elizabeth knew the clingy truth.

In need of a caffeine fix, and with the twenty-euro note she had found in the pocket of her hoodie, she left the front door on the latch and headed out. The burglars of Buncarragh could help themselves. The only thing she cared about was her passport and that was being guarded by a rat.

★ ★ ★

Walking into Boost she fought the desire to roll her eyes. It was like stepping into one of the self-consciously hipster haunts in Williamsburg that Zach and his friends thought so much of. The exposed brick behind the counter, the chalkboards hanging from chains, the metal stools placed around old butcher's blocks. It was a source of amazement to Elizabeth that such a place could exist in Buncarragh. She remembered the old café that Mrs Moore used to run, what had it been called? Coffee something . . . Pot? The odd thing was that the two women standing in front of her waiting at the counter could have been customers in Mrs Moore's but here they were ordering skinny lattes and dry cappuccinos. She herself had always felt she was holding on to her Irish roots by stubbornly refusing to order anything other than an adjective-free coffee or tea, but now she found that the whole nation had moved on without her.

Sitting on a high stool, she perched her laptop on a wooden shelf that ran the width of the window. The Wi-Fi password was fullofbeanz. She scrolled through her emails, deleting the junk as she went. She was left with only two that she felt she should actually read.

The first was from Linda Jetter, their downstairs neighbour who had volunteered to look after Shelly the cat. In fact, she had been so keen that Elizabeth was considering offering her the creature full time. Zach had lost interest in Shelly shortly after his persistent pleas to get a cat were answered. Elizabeth had been dealing with her single mother guilt after Elliot's departure, and she'd agreed to the pet against her better judgement. It didn't help that she felt obliged to explain to everyone who encountered the cat that he hadn't been named after the poet. Shelly was simply young Zach's way of describing the cat's tortoiseshell markings. The email consisted of four photographs of Shelly in Linda Jetter's apartment. At best he looked bored, at worst contemptuous. Linda had just written 'Shelly — feeling right at home!' Elizabeth quickly typed a brief response, thanking Linda again for her kindness. She wasn't sure why, but she couldn't help feeling sorry for Linda Jetter. All she knew about her was that she was in her late fifties, had never been married and worked as a paralegal secretary in midtown somewhere. It was just that she never seemed to have any sort of social life, and came and went with clockwork precision in one of her sensible suits, carrying her work shoes in an old Lord & Taylor bag. She was probably perfectly happy. In fact, it was likely that she felt just as sorry for the divorced single mother living upstairs.

The other was from Jocelyn, one of her friends at work. They were both in the English Department and shared the Romantics between them. Elizabeth scanned the content. Christ, this was not good news. Jocelyn was wondering if she knew already that Brian Babst and Nicole Togler had dropped out. They had both been taking her 'Romantics and the Celtic Tradition'. With them gone she had only five students left. Her course felt doomed which was, she thought, strangely Celtic and Romantic. She marked the email unread — she would reply later. The shop must be open by now. She'd grab another coffee to go and head over.

Homemade muffins that looked the same on 34th street as they did in Buncarragh were sitting in a basket by the till and Elizabeth was just about to pick one up when she heard her name being whispered in her ear. She turned to find her cousin Paul with a wide grin spread across his face.

'I heard you were back!'

'Yes.' She wasn't sure what else to add. She was clearly back.

'Noelle said she saw you.'

'Yes. She did.' Elizabeth searched for a phrase

46

to add so that she seemed less curt. 'She looked well.'

Happily, the barista interrupted them by asking what she wanted. After she'd ordered she turned back to her cousin. He really hadn't changed at all. Arms slightly too long for his body, dark hair still falling into his eyes, and that gormless grin. Elizabeth didn't mind her cousin. As her mother used to say, he had no harm in him.

'I was coming into the shop to see you, actually.'

'Always welcome. What do you need?'

'I saw a rat in Convent Hill.'

'In the yard?'

'No. In the house. It was sat up on the kitchen table. I nearly died of the fright.' Elizabeth liked the feel of the words in her mouth. It was an expression her mother might have used and certainly something Elizabeth herself would never have said on campus or at home.

'Jesus, that's fierce. I'll send young Dermot up later on with a few traps and lay a bit of poison at the back there.'

'Thanks. That would be great.' The barista leaned forward and asked for nearly six euros. Elizabeth refused to consider how many dollars that might be. She turned to Paul. 'Can I get you something?'

'Are you sure?'

'Of course.' She remembered these strange little dances.

'I'll have a latte, so. Thanks very much.'

Having placed the order, the two of them were sentenced to wait.

47

'This place is new. O'Keefe's opened it here last year. It's nice, isn't it?'

'Lovely,' she replied, wondering whether she was lying or not.

'Will you come over? Mam and Dad would love to see you.'

'Are they there? Yes, I'd love to. There is something I'd like to talk to them about.'

'Right.' Paul looked confused and Elizabeth immediately regretted saying anything. Doubtless he would assume it was to do with the will or what was going to happen to Convent Hill.

Walking through the town back to Keane and Sons several people said hello, or shouted 'welcome home' from car windows. Each time she turned to her cousin Paul and mouthed, 'Who the fuck?' and when he enlightened her she nodded as if he had solved the mystery but in reality, she was none the wiser. Had she forgotten these people, or had she in fact never known them? It reminded her of climbing the steps at 68th Street on her way to lecture at Hunter and the way unfamiliar faces of students occasionally broke into wide smiles as they greeted her like an old friend.

In contrast, walking through the doors of Keane and Sons shocked her precisely because of how familiar everything seemed. The smell! Nowhere else on earth had the same aroma. Chemical fertiliser mixed with plastic and cardboard all layered over the decades of long-gone scents that lingered in the wooden floors. The look of the shop was more or less the same as well. The central staircase that led up to electrical goods and small pieces of pointless furniture was covered in the same worn grey linoleum, the Christmas display remained twinkling and unwanted at the left-hand side of the shop while garden supplies and tools took over to the left of the stairs. At the back, dog beds jostled with paints and cleaning products, while the light of the new baby boutique glowed from the small alcove that used to sell paraffin and loose seeds.

'They're up in the flat. Head away up and see them.' Paul encouraged his cousin towards the stairs.

'Elizabeth!' It was Noelle descending the stairway, putting one foot in front of the other with great care like a beauty pageant contestant exiting a private jet.

'How are you today?' she enquired, peering over the cellophane-wrapped Babygros piled high in her arms.

'Great. Yourself?'

'No rest for the wicked!' Noelle almost shrieked, punctuating the end of the sentence with a strange nasal honk.

'I'll let you get on.'

'Talk later,' she called over her shoulder and headed past the long-life bulbs.

A wide smile full of teeth and lipstick fixed on her face, Noelle hid her disappointment well. This was so very far from any life she had imagined for herself. Folding Babygros, dusting unsold birdfeeders, sticking prices on colanders. She sighed and headed towards the rear of the shop. When she had met Paul he had been studying at the College of Commerce out in Rathmines and somehow she had assumed that meant he had a certain amount of ambition. He had confidence, money in his pocket, people liked him, he was what she imagined a young empire builder might be like. When she realised that she was pregnant, she hadn't even panicked. It could be part of the plan. Paul and Noelle were a team and together they could achieve great things. It was only after the wedding that he had mentioned something about returning to Buncarragh. She remembered the way he said it seemed to imply that they had discussed it or that it was an idea she had always known about. Noelle made it very clear to her new husband that she had no intention of rotting away running some Mickey Mouse family shop in Buncarragh. He had pleaded. Promises had been made. They would save up for a couple of years and start their own business back in Dublin. She hadn't been thrilled but at least it was a plan, but then two more babies had come along and by the time her in-laws had decided to retire, the whole country was in the toilet. Keane and Sons was worthless, and their savings were hardly enough to buy new bikes for the kids, never mind start a new life. It was obvious that Paul didn't mind a bit. This was what he had always wanted; for Noelle it was just what she had. Buncarragh. She could see that her kids were happy and even she acknowledged that leaving wasn't an option, so every morning she got up, looked at herself in the bathroom mirror and put on a brave face.

Up in the flat Elizabeth was wrapped by her Aunt Gillian in a hug that was both too long and too tight.

'Elizabeth!' the older woman hissed in her ear, turning the name into a mournful incantation. Finally releasing her niece, she then grabbed both her hands and peered into Elizabeth's eyes. 'How are you? It must be hard. Hard. Is it? Hard being back?'

A heavy gold bangle on her aunt's wrist caught her attention. Surely that had been . . .

'Oh, you noticed it! Your mother insisted I have it. Insisted. So, so precious.' Gillian stroked the bangle before wrapping it in a firm grip that suggested she would not be parting with it before her own deathbed.

Elizabeth was a pinball machine of emotion. Suspicion, fury, jealousy, sadness, but mostly a strange regret because the one person who would really appreciate this story was no longer at the end of the phone. Laughing at her aunt and uncle or listening to her mother relating her sister-in-law's latest transgression had been a staple part of their family bond for so many years. Elizabeth realised that moments like this would continue to catch her unawares, a thread of memory being snagged on a nail from the past.

'Sorry. Seeing it just took me by surprise. Everything seems so strange, you know, being in the house without her.'

'Of course, of course.' Gillian now grabbed her niece's arm and pulled her down beside her on the green brocade sofa.

'Will you have a cup of tea?'

'No thanks. I'm just after a cup of coffee.'

'Ah, you will.' Gillian heaved herself back out of the sofa. 'I'm making one anyway. Jerry will be gasping.' She made her way towards the kitchen and Elizabeth noticed the way her aunt leaned on the backs of chairs and rolled slightly from side to side as she walked. How many more years had Aunt Gillian got? A whole generation slipping away like a crumbling cliff face into the sea.

Left alone, she looked around the room. A new flat-screen TV was really the only noticeable change from when she had spent time here as a girl. The white horses were still galloping out of the surf in the large print hung above the brown and beige-tiled fireplace, electric bars now glowing orange where coals had once burned. A faded tapestry map of Ireland, which she was fairly sure her mother had made, was in a thin brown frame next to the corner cabinet where Aunt Gillian kept her Waterford crystal, so special that it wasn't used even for special occasions.

A shadow fell across the room and turning she saw her Uncle Jerry in the doorway. Another hug, but this one not trying to compensate for the months and years of silence between them. He seemed smaller than he had been but the manly scent of hair oil and cigarettes was as strong as ever.

'Jerry? Is that you?' came Gillian's voice from the kitchen. 'Can you give me a hand with the tray?'

Like a well-trained dog, Jerry turned and walked away. His trousers hung loose around his legs and seemed too long. Elizabeth wondered if she should volunteer for tray duties, but then reminded herself that this elderly high-wire act probably happened on a daily basis.

The tea poured, the three of them sat and talked of the mundane. How retirement was going, what a great job Paul and Noelle were doing with the shop, the grandchildren growing so fast and there were even a few questions about Elizabeth's life in New York and how her son — 'Zach,' she reminded them — was doing. Any mention of her marriage or Elliot was delicately avoided.

When the small talk had talked itself out, Elizabeth put down her cup and cleared her throat.

'I wondered what either of you could tell me about Edward Foley?'

Gillian pursed her lips in thought and Jerry simply stared at his wife and rubbed his slick head of thinning hair because this was the sort of question that was more suited to her.

'Foley? I don't think I know a single Foley. Jerry?' Her husband shrugged his shoulders and gave her a look that suggested she might as well have asked him to perform open heart surgery.

'Why do you ask?'

'My father? Edward Foley,' Elizabeth prompted.

Cups were put down. 'Oh, that Edward Foley,' said Gillian slowly and deliberately. She threw a glance at her husband.

'Your father,' Jerry repeated unhelpfully.

'What, well, I'm not sure, what sort of thing, what did you want to know?' Her aunt seemed uncharacteristically flustered.

'Well, it's just that up in Convent Hill last night I found some letters, quite a few letters, from Edward Foley.'

'Letters?'

'Yes, from when they were courting. It's just that I know so very little. Mammy never spoke about him.'

'I don't know if we should . . . ' Jerry began and turned to his wife for assistance.

'Sure, Jerry, Patricia is gone, God rest her, what harm is there in talking about it now?'

'Well, we know so little.'

'What?' Elizabeth just wanted answers.

'Tell her, Jerry.' Her aunt had granted permission.

'Well, to be honest I don't know a lot. Your mother was doing a line with this farmer down in Cork somewhere, we didn't even know his name at the time, did we?'

'No clue,' his wife confirmed.

'Anyway, she visited him down there a couple of times and then out of the blue, no word of warning, the next thing we hear she's married. That's right, isn't it?' He turned to his superior for confirmation.

'Just a notice in the paper, wasn't it, Jerry? No letter, nothing, not a note, not a phone call. It was all very peculiar.' Gillian had taken over the story and her husband sat back, relieved of his duties.

'We wrote to her of course, but nothing.

Eventually, we did get a letter, didn't we, Jerry? From the mother-in-law explaining that your mother wasn't well but she would be sure to write when she felt better. I probably have it somewhere.' She looked around as if she might notice it framed on the wall. 'Anyway, about a year later, not even that — '

'A few months,' Jerry chimed in.

'Well, again no warning, no phone call, your mother was back here and she had you wrapped in a shawl. We never asked any questions and you know your mother, she never apologised or explained. We were never any the wiser. Isn't that right, Jerry?' Vigorous nodding. Gillian picked up her cup to indicate the story was over.

'You never asked her anything?' Elizabeth was incredulous.

'Well, you asked her if she was back for good, didn't you, Jerry? Would she be staying? She said she would. And that was that. Now a few other people did ask her about the husband and apparently, he had died. I assume he must have left her some money though, because she never worked.'

'I always thought she had got money from the shop.'

'No, no,' Gillian said, sounding slightly sheepish. 'That stopped after your granny died.'

Jerry coughed and without looking at Elizabeth or his wife said quietly, 'To be honest we had a bit of a falling out around that time. It was little wonder she didn't confide in us.'

'She just swanned off and left that house sitting there.'

'It was her house.'

Gillian ran her tongue around the inside of her mouth. This was clearly a conversation that had been repeated many times. Elizabeth wondered if the parts of this story that were clearly missing involved her mother at all. Perhaps they were just part of an ongoing battle between her aunt and uncle.

'There is a woman who might know more than us,' Jerry volunteered. Gillian gave him a quizzical look.

'Your mother was great pals with a Rosemary O'Shea.'

'Rosemary O'Shea?' Aunt Gillian raised her eyes to heaven. 'Sure that one is half-cracked.'

'Is she still in Buncarragh?' Elizabeth asked, attempting to keep her uncle on track.

'Oh, she is. You'd know her house. The small ivy-covered one on Connolly's Quay. It's just beside what used to be the bike shop. It's the St Vincent's charity shop now.'

'Do you think I could just call in to her?'

'I don't see why not. She's retired. Used to have that little barber shop where the new coffee place is.'

'I was in it only this morning,' she said, seemingly delighted at the coincidence.

'Half-cracked,' repeated Aunt Gillian, crossing her arms. Elizabeth had been warned.

THEN

This time he was on the platform. When he saw her, a smile flashed across his face and he half-raised his arm, less of a wave, more like flagging down a bus, but still, Patricia saw it as progress.

She really didn't know how or why she was back at Kent station in Cork. She wanted to blame it on the enthusiasm of Rosemary, but she knew it was more than that. In the few weeks since their first date she had begun to grow fond of him. The man who could barely look her in the eye in person, on paper became sincere, direct and self-deprecating. She looked forward to his letters during the dark days that offered little else. Somehow, she found herself remembering her visit to Cork the way he did. Viewed through his eyes it seemed sweeter than stiff, romantic rather than awkward. She felt she needed to give him a second chance and the sight of his broad grin, however brief, gave her confidence that she had made the right choice.

When she reached him at the end of the platform by the exit, Edward stretched out his hand to her. A gentleman, she thought and offered him the small cream suitcase she had retrieved from under her mother's deathbed. The bag smacked into Edward's unsuspecting palm and she realised that he had been going to shake her hand, not carry her case.

'Sorry.' She pulled the suitcase back.

'Sorry. No, let me.' He fumbled for the handle.

'No, it's fine.'

'No. No, I should,' and he managed to squeeze his hand under the handle with hers. The touch of his flesh against hers made her immediately release her grip.

'Thank you.'

He led them wordlessly out to the car park, the noise of the city amplifying their silence. She wondered what sort of car he would drive.

Leading her to a dark green estate car, some sort of Ford perhaps, that didn't look too ancient, she was pleasantly surprised. As she slipped into the passenger seat however her first impressions were overwhelmed by the smell of the interior. A combination of stale milk and what her father used to call 'A grand country smell' — in other words, shit — hung thick around her. Her hand fumbled to roll down the window as soon as Edward had shut her door. She tried not breathing through her nose but she could still taste the stench. She prayed she wouldn't be sick. Her hands tightened their hold on the leather handle of her handbag. Time was not going to fly.

Edward drove hunched over the wheel, emitting grunts and sighs as he made his way through the city traffic, peering over the dashboard to see if he was in the right lane. Patricia felt it was unwise, unsafe even, to distract him with any of her prepared small talk. Once past Bishopstown, however, as the houses gave way to fields he seemed to relax and sat back in his seat. Patricia tried out some of her questions.

'Are you busy on the farm at the moment?'

'So-so.'

'Are you near a village?'

'Not really. Muirinish, but there's nothing there.'

Patricia closed her eyes and breathed as deeply as she dared. She ran through the rest of her questions in her head and accepted that every answer would be a variation on 'no'.

'Are you not cold?'

Edward had spoken. The shock of it meant that she hadn't actually heard what he had said.

'Sorry?'

'Your window. Are you not a bit cold?'

'Oh. Well, I might close it a little. I like the fresh air.' She wound the window up two thirds, almost excited that he had actually engaged in some sort of conversation. 'Are you cold?' she asked.

'No.'

They drove on with nothing but the steady growl of the engine filling the emptiness.

The jolt of a pothole woke her. How long had she been asleep? The bright winter light of earlier had gone and now the hedges blurring past were being swallowed by a grey gloom. She sat up and discovered a long string of saliva connecting her mouth to a dark stain on the front of her coat. She quickly wiped it away. Edward glanced at her and smiled. It was nothing, but to the starving, crumbs can feel like a feast. Patricia smiled back. 'Sorry. I had an early start. Was I asleep for long?'

'A while all right. You missed Bandon and Timoleague. It's not far now.'

'Oh, right.' Patricia wondered how she could surreptitiously reapply her lipstick before she met his mother.

'That was my primary school there.' He indicated a slate-roofed box with long windows. Patricia peered out as if her guide had announced the Arc de Triomphe or the Spanish Steps. She struggled to come up with an appropriate response, even a 'nice' seemed disingenuous, so instead asked where he had gone to secondary school.

'Clonteer, but I only did a few years before my brother James died and I went onto the farm full time.'

Death. How had her small talk taken her to death so fast?

'Oh. That's a shame.' It was unclear even to herself if she meant the untimely passing of his brother or his truncated education.

'Ah, it was all right. I wasn't much of a one for school.'

The car came down a hill through some trees and then rounded a corner onto a narrow causeway. On either side of the road misshapen mounds of grass and reeds sat like giant mushrooms in a network of muddy channels.

'It's low tide,' Edward observed.

Having got used to the smell inside the car, Patricia was now accosted by a salty sulphuric fog from outside.

'You might want to close your window,' he said as she quickly rolled it all the way up. 'It's not always this bad,' he added apologetically.

The road rose up slightly over a small bridge where the channel through the marsh was wider.

'This is where old Pat Whelan went in. Drunk as a lord, riding his bike back from the pub.' Edward gave a low chuckle and Patricia was very happy to join in.

'Was he all right?'

'No. Never found. They did find the bike at low tide but no sign of Pat. The mud just swallows things up. We've lost a couple of cows over the years.'

'I see.' Patricia wasn't sure how to respond so just stared out the window at the wide flatness of the marsh, imagining the horrors that lay beneath the smooth dark sheen of the mud.

Ahead of them was the reassuring solidity of hedges and trees. As they reached them Edward spoke again.

'This is where the good land starts. That's all grazing in there.' He pointed to his right and Patricia's eyes followed dutifully though in fact she had no idea what she was looking at. The car slowed down.

'Here we are.'

They went through a pair of unpainted stone pillars and up a lane with a long thick Mohawk of green down the centre. At the top of the hill, Patricia gasped. It was the sea! Just a field away was a long sandy beach. At either end the land reared up into tall dark cliffs. Backing onto the rocks furthest away from them was a large white and blue farmhouse and behind that the jagged silhouette of a ruined castle.

'It's beautiful,' she said and she meant it. The

whole landscape that stretched before her looked like something she might have seen in a gallery in Dublin on a school trip.

'It's home,' Edward replied matter-of-factly.

As the lane came down to the shore and towards the house Patricia could hear the waves and the rushing of the wind. She felt strangely invigorated, as if maybe she had made the right decision. The whole trip wasn't the worst idea she had ever had.

Edward brought the car to a stop just before the house. Patricia could see that the lane continued on to a farmyard where a line of outbuildings joined up with the old castle and the back of the house to form a U shape. A sheepdog roused himself by the door to one of the outbuildings. His tail wagged but he didn't approach them. When Patricia tried to open her door, it was yanked from her hand by the wind. Edward hurried around the car to help her out.

'Are you OK?' His voice was raised against the gritty din of the surf and storm.

'Yes,' she called back and stood up, the wind catching her hair and coat, tossing them without mercy. Edward was holding her case. 'Let's get you in.' He led her through a small gate painted the same shade of Virgin Mary blue as the windows of the house. A narrow gravel path led them up the side and around to the front, where a neat grey-haired woman was waiting at the door for them. Her dark eyes quickly surveyed the new arrival and for a moment Patricia felt like a rabbit that had just been spotted by a fox. Her hostess bared her teeth into a smile and then waved Edward forward with one bony hand while the other held her lemon cardigan closed against the weather.

The door shut behind them, and it was as if heavy machinery had stopped. The silence was abrupt. Patricia tried to smooth down her hair and readjust her coat simultaneously.

'You are very, very welcome. You must be Patricia. I'm Edward's mother. Please call me Catherine.'

Patricia noticed a look flicker across Edward's face. She guessed that not many people got to call Mrs Foley by her Christian name. The women shook hands and the lady of the house led them down the dark hall and to the left into a living room that seemed too small for the house.

'I've just lit the fire. I wasn't expecting you for a while. You made great time.'

Edward stood in the doorway holding the case and still wearing his coat. He looked as much of a visitor as Patricia did.

'There was very little on the road.'

'You weren't speeding, I hope. Was he speeding?'

Patricia opened her mouth to reassure her that he hadn't but it turned out the question was rhetorical. 'Sit down there,' Mrs Foley continued, patting the back of the small over-stuffed sofa. 'Will you take the poor girl's coat, Teddy? I have the kettle on.' The last few words were called over her shoulder as she left the room.

Edward and Patricia stood and looked at each other. He reached out his hand and Patricia

63

unbuttoned her coat and gave it to him.

'Teddy?'

'My mother calls me that.' He paused and something unsaid passed between them. The sense that they were on one team and Mrs Foley was on another. 'You can call me Teddy if you want,' he offered.

'I think I prefer Edward.'

He held up her coat and case to indicate he was going to deal with them. 'Sit, so.'

'Thanks.'

Alone, she looked around the small room. Everything seemed to be shades of brown and orange. The wallpaper was a dense mesh of autumn leaves and the fire burned in a small beige-tiled fireplace that looked much newer than the house. A rug in swirls of gold and hazel covered most of the floor, with a border of wood-effect lino covering the gap between it and the wall. Patricia was struck by how unlived-in the room seemed. Apart from an underwhelming oval mirror on the chimney breast, the walls were bare. Small wooden tables were pushed against the walls but there were no ornaments, books or magazines. The only light came from the shadeless single bulb hanging from the ceiling. It looked like the people who lived here had moved out.

The door burst open and Mrs Foley appeared with a tray of cups and saucers and a fat brown teapot. She hesitated, unsure of where to place it, and then opted for the low table to the right of the fireplace.

'Where's Teddy? Is he hanging your coat? You

must be parched after that drive. I'm boiling a ham for the dinner. I hope that will do you. It's Teddy's favourite. Do you take sugar?' A pause for breath. Patricia shook her head and took the cup of milky tea that she was being offered.

'Thank you,' she said quietly, not wanting to interrupt Mrs Foley's flow.

'Aren't you a great girl to make that journey all by yourself? Outside Kilkenny you're from, is it? Teddy told me. I've never been there myself. The ICA did a trip there once to see the castle and they had a tour of the brewery but sure, why would I want to see that, so I didn't go. The girls loved it though. Said it was a very nice city. Narrow streets. Sure, I suppose you go there rarely enough yourself. You were looking after your mother, weren't you? Teddy mentioned it. Very sorry for your loss. It must be hard for you being all alone. You have a brother, I think Teddy said. Are you two close?'

The room suddenly fell silent and Patricia realised that she was being asked to speak. It was becoming clear to her why Edward was a man of so few words.

'Not especially, no.'

Edward stepped sheepishly back into the room and was handed a cup of tea and encouraged by a cushion-patting hand to sit next to Patricia on the sofa. All of this occurred while his mother continued her monologue.

'Of course boys and girls are very different. I would have loved a little girl but it wasn't to be. I just have Teddy now, and it's a long time since anyone called him a boy. He works hard, don't

65

you, Teddy? Dairy isn't an easy life but it's the life we know and we get by, don't we, Teddy?' Edward didn't even look up. He evidently understood that the tsunami of chat would just wash over him and it did. Patricia sipped her tea and occasionally nodded or smiled when she felt it was appropriate. Somehow, like a ventriloquist drinking a glass of water, Mrs Foley had managed to consume her tea without pausing for breath. Putting her cup back on the tray she concluded. 'Look at the time. You should be getting on with the milking. I have the dinner on. Would Mary like to go with you?'

Edward froze and stared at his mother, who at first didn't seem to have noticed her mistake, but then a ripple of horror crossed her face.

'Patricia! Patricia! My mind is away!'

'Don't worry about it.' Patricia wasn't sure what had just happened but she knew it hadn't offended her. Edward had his back to her and his mother.

'Where did you put Patricia's coat?' Mrs Foley was back in full flow. The two young people were herded into the hall and towards the back of the house. Patricia's coat was retrieved from a heaving row of pegs and Edward slipped on a pair of waiting wellington boots. He opened the back door and the rush of wind came as a welcome relief from the incessant chatter of the last few minutes.

Head bowed, Edward looked sideways at Patricia.

'She likes to talk.'

'She does.'

They exchanged a look and again she felt that they were somehow on the same side.

Edward pointed back towards where the car was parked. 'That's the orchard.' Patricia looked at the couple of dozen stunted trees permanently cowering at right angles against the tireless wind. She followed him as he walked towards the ruins of the castle. Mounting what she assumed had been the steps to the main entrance, she took his arm for balance. Under the rough material of his jacket, he felt solid, manly.

Once inside, the rough stone walls provided some protection from the storm.

'Is it always this windy here?'

'Not all the time, but there's nearly always a bit of a breeze off the sea.'

Through what might have once been a window or a door Patricia could see the waves crashing against the bottom of the cliff. Edward leaned close, closer than was necessary. He smelled of soap, not the sweet perfume of Camay or Imperial Leather, but the fresh tang of that hard butter-yellow block her mother had used for hand-washing her smalls. She liked it. 'That's the beach down there but if you follow it around behind this, it turns into the start of the marsh.' Patricia craned her neck to see where he was pointing. 'We drove across it,' he added by way of explanation. 'They say the Foleys built the castle because they were protected by the marsh behind them and any boats coming from the sea would be frightened of running aground.' She nodded to show she understood. His voice soothed her. Not as deep as his monosyllabic grunts had led her to believe, the lazy lilt of his West Cork accent made her feel oddly calm. Their eyes met and neither of them looked away. She could feel the heat of his body in the cold damp cave of the ruined walls. She wondered if he might try to kiss her again, but then without warning he simply reached out his right hand and gently squeezed her breast. It was so unexpected, she didn't flinch. Her eyes looked down at the mottled pink of his hand and then back up to his expressionless face. He removed his hand and said, 'I'd better get on with the milking.' Edward turned and walked away leaving Patricia to ponder if it had been her modest bosom that had prompted him to seek out the heaving udders in the milking parlour.

NOW

The sun changed everything. The bare branches of the horse chestnut trees looked jubilant against the blue sky, and the shimmering water of the weir took on an air of celebration. Elizabeth found she was swinging her arms as she walked down Connolly's Quay. It had always been one of her favourite streets in the town. The long row of trees and the strip of grass separating the road from the steep drop down to the river. The houses were much as she remembered them and Busteed's lounge bar still had its hanging baskets bursting with brightness even in January. Wedged between the former bike shop and a large grey house that used to be the home of Dr Wilson was, just as described by her uncle, a small ivy-clad cottage.

Standing in front of the door with its frosted glass panels, Elizabeth hesitated. Why was she here? What good would answers do her now, especially when she didn't really know what the questions were? Before she could ring the bell, an aggressive burst of yapping broke out behind the door. She could just make out the blurred silhouettes of two small dogs jumping and clawing at the glass. Before she could decide to change her mind about this visit, a much larger form loomed towards the panels and the door was pulled ajar.

A ruddy-faced woman stuck her head out,

younger-looking than Elizabeth had been expecting, but with a strong ridge of grey roots topping the rest of her hair that had been dyed a glossy aubergine colour.

'Maxi! Dick! Shut up!' The woman kicked at the small dogs trying to make good their noisy escape from behind the door.

'Hello. Are you Rosemary O'Shea?'

'I am. Will you stop it?' she said, still addressing her pets.

'Sorry to bother you. I'm Elizabeth, Patricia Keane's daughter.'

Rosemary's face changed. She looked her visitor up and down, as if searching for some hint of her old friend. 'Oh, I'm so sorry for your loss.' Both women paused for a moment before Rosemary continued, 'Will you come in? Then these pests might calm down.'

A plain hall with bare pine floorboards led back towards a bright cluttered kitchen. The dogs, now revealed to be black and tan Yorkshire Terriers, ran rings around their ankles, quickly deciding that they were delighted that the woman they had been zealously keeping out had been invited in.

'Maxi, Dick, go to your bed.' Rosemary pointed at a pile of old towels and chewed-up dolls below the large window that looked out onto a small courtyard garden.

'Wasn't there a group, Maxi, Dick and Twink?'

'I did have three but Twink got hit by a car.'

Elizabeth looked confused. 'I hadn't heard.'

'Twink the dog. Actual Twink is still with us as far as I know. Tea?' She brandished a kettle.

'Yes please. That would be nice.'

'Sit down there.' Elizabeth assumed she was referring to the one kitchen chair that wasn't piled high with newspapers and magazines. 'I have herbal if you'd prefer.'

'No. No thanks, regular is fine.'

'Builder's it is!' she said, turning to the sink and stove.

From behind, Elizabeth was able to get a better look at her. The hunch of her shoulders was the only thing that betrayed her true age. Her thick wool cardigan was long and appeared to be weighed down by the over-stuffed pockets. Underneath it she wore a strange shapeless green and yellow shift that came almost to her ankles and on her feet she had a pair of burgundy velvet slippers, the rubber heels worn away like ancient steps.

Rosemary O'Shea had never been a woman with a plan. As a young girl she had preferred to wait and see what came along. Now that she was in her mid-seventies she wondered if that had been a mistake. Financially things had turned out all right. The sale of a site carved from the family farm as part of her inheritance had been enough to start up her little barber shop. Over the years, it hadn't always been easy, but she had managed to keep going. Fashions changed but she had always stuck to what she called 'a boy's cut'. They either liked it or lumped it. That's why she had got out of ladies' hairdressing with the fanciful pictures ripped from magazines and the tears and tantrums when a mirror revealed that they would never look like one of Charlie's

71

Angels. Men weren't like that and the odd few she had encountered that wanted some trendy style or look never came back. She could operate on autopilot, which suited her, and there was enough chat from the men or mothers bringing in their kids to make the days pass in a pleasant blur. Oddly it was age that had forced her to confront the future. Painful varicose veins and knees that were aching by lunchtime made her realise that she couldn't work forever. The problem she had was that she couldn't see how she would ever be able to afford to retire, but then along came the offer from the coffee company and now she was sitting prettier than she ever had.

Committees and night classes in painting up at the Tech kept her busy enough. Her nephews and nieces still brought their children in to her to have their hair cut. Most of the time she felt content. Things have a way of working out for the best, she often reminded herself.

The question that bothered her, or if not exactly that, then at least pecked away softly at the back of her brain, was about being alone. Had she *really* not wanted to meet anyone? She remembered laughing at the girls who spent every waking moment trying to catch a man. The very idea of falling in love had seemed so stupid to her, but now she worried that perhaps she had been too clever for her own good. She had to admit there were some nights when she wished her bed wasn't quite so wide and cold. The dogs were good company, but lately she wanted to slap the girls from school, now stooped and grey, who presumed to tell her that the dogs must be like her children. There had been a few boyfriends, well, men who called, over the years but none had seemed worth changing her life for. She had attempted to shut down that side of things. Of course, she still had physical urges now and then but when she closed her eyes late at night she never saw her gentlemen visitors from the past, or handsome detectives from the TV. No matter how hard she tried to banish it, the face that loomed into the heated haze of her imagination belonged to her eldest brother's first girlfriend. Her name had been Anne, Anne Lyons. One night before Rosemary had moved out of the home place, they had shared her bedroom. Anne was a few years older and had a small case full of make-up and creams. Rosemary had just said how nice the body lotion smelled. That was all. She hadn't said anything else. Then Anne offered her some and before Rosemary had a chance to reply, Anne had started rubbing it into Rosemary's arms, then her shoulders and then without any hesitation, as if it was the most natural thing in the world, she slid her hands down under her nightie and began to caress her breasts. Rosemary's whole body had quivered from that touch. Warm lips on her neck and then she turned and their mouths met. Sometimes, as a grown woman, when she pleasured herself, she found that tears were rolling down her cheeks. These episodes left her feeling confused and anxious. Her desires frightened her and besides, what was the point of them? Anne had broken up with her brother soon after their night together and was last heard of living in Galway with a marine biologist.

Now Rosemary read articles and interviews or saw characters on television shows and wondered if that might have been her life. She thought not. She hoped not. That wasn't a choice she could have ever made, was it? She knew people talked about her and called her strange or eccentric and she had to admit she enjoyed the attention. She had a certain notoriety in the town that gave her pride, but that was very different from having a label. She didn't want strangers to think they knew her, to assume things about her. No. Her life had happened and it was the one she had lived. No regrets.

'I was sorry not to be able to get to your mother's funeral, but my brother's was the same day over in Durrow.'

'Oh dear, I'm sorry to hear that.'

'Ah, he was old. We're all old. It'll be me soon.'

'I'd say you have a fair few years left in you yet.'

'The funny thing is, that is how I feel, and yet I know it's not true. My time can't be far off. Still, no one but Maxi and Dick to give a flying fuck.'

This was a friend of her mother's? Elizabeth couldn't imagine the Patricia Keane she knew being close to this vibrant, seemingly fearless creature.

'Have you no family yourself?'

'No. That never happened for me. Not that I minded. I like an easy life. My little shop filled my days. A barber shop. I gave up on women's hair years ago. Men are much simpler. Ten minutes, you're done. No complaints. No fuss. The rest was friends, books and red wine!'

The two women laughed. 'Sounds all right to me.'

'What about yourself? Any family?'

'A son, nearly all grown up. I was married but that finished a few years ago.'

'Oh yes! I remember hearing about that. That must have been a bit of a shock?'

Elizabeth hated to think of the people of Buncarragh gossiping about her but at least she didn't feel like Rosemary was judging her or, even worse, implying it was somehow her fault.

'It wasn't the best.'

Sensing her guest's discomfort, Rosemary broke the silence by placing two steaming mugs on the table. Elizabeth didn't want to be a germ-phobic American, but her mug was filthy.

'Thank you,' she said, trying to summon up some enthusiasm.

The old lady moved some papers to an already large pile and sat down. Without any sign of self-consciousness, she dipped her hand into her bra and began to rearrange her still impressive breasts. Elizabeth studied a dream catcher in the window that thus far had ensnared only cobwebs and a few dead flies.

'I was very fond of your mother but we weren't close. Well, not for many years.'

'It was my uncle who told me you were friends. I'm afraid I don't remember you from growing up.'

'You wouldn't. We were friends before you came along.'

Elizabeth picked up the mug but glancing at it again thought better of the idea and replaced it on the table.

'That's sort of what I want to talk to you about.'

'Oh, yes.' The old lady leaned in.

'I'm here to clear out the house and I found some letters.'

'Letters?'

'Yes. They are from an Edward Foley. I think he was my father.'

Rosemary let out a short sharp yelp, which made Maxi and Dick come running to see if their mistress required some assistance.

'Edward Foley! I haven't thought about him in years. And you found the letters? That's gas.'

'So, you remember him?'

'Well, not really. I mean, I never met him, but I knew all about the letters.'

'So, you weren't at the wedding?'

'No. Sure, no one was. It was all very odd. She had gone to stay with Edward and the mother and then she just didn't come back. Not a word. Nothing. Your mother had given me the number for down there but I had no joy. I wanted to call the guards but I remember old Mrs Beamish, she ran the salon I worked in at the time, she told me I'd get in trouble for wasting their time. So, and I don't know what possessed me, I got in my car — a little Fiat it was — and drove all the way down to Cork and out past Timoleague. It took a bit of asking but eventually I found the Foley

76

farm.' Elizabeth imagined a much younger version of this woman wedged behind the wheel, setting out to rescue her friend. It pleased her to think someone had ever cared about her mother that much.

'And?'

Rosemary paused and took a sip of tea.

'Nothing. I never saw her, or him for that matter. The old mother came out to me and told me that Patricia was too ill to receive visitors. She was nice enough, apologised for my wasted journey, but at the same time I knew there was no way I was getting into that house. There was a steeliness to her.'

'So, what did you do?'

'I sat back into the car and came back to Buncarragh. The next thing I hear, about a week or two later, they were married. I can't remember who told me. There was an announcement in the paper. Of course, it was only later that it all made sense.'

'What did?'

'Well, when she appeared with you in her arms. You were hardly a newborn. Anyone could have seen that.' The old woman paused and examined Elizabeth's face, trying to gauge how much of the story she already knew or had guessed. Rosemary took a breath and continued. 'She was obviously pregnant when she left Buncarragh. That's why I couldn't see her. That's why no one was at the wedding.'

'Really? Are you certain?' Elizabeth found it hard to imagine that her mother had ever been a sexual being, and certainly not someone who couldn't control her desires.

'Put it this way, when is your birthday?'

'The twenty-first of March,' Elizabeth replied automatically.

'When you were a baby, there were no birthdays. It was only when you went to school, I saw balloons tied to your railings. That date was plucked from the air, I'd say.'

Elizabeth remembered all the fuss about her birth certificate when she had been applying for her passport. Her mother claiming to have lost it and getting it re-issued. At the time she had thought it had been delay tactics by her mother because she didn't want her to travel abroad, but maybe this woman's theory was correct.

'She never told me any of this, mind, but it is the only thing that makes sense. It was all very . . . ' She searched for the right word. 'Well, sad, I suppose. Your mother was never the same when she came back. We used to share a joke, talk about everything, but the woman who returned to Buncarragh, well, I never saw her laughing. Her whole life was raising you and looking after that house. I suppose that gave her a certain kind of joy. Maybe it was just me that never grew up. You never really know what is going on in someone else's head, do you?'

'No. You don't.' Elizabeth wondered what gave this dishevelled old woman in front of her joy. What was in her badly dyed head?

'And Edward? What happened to him?'

'I managed to get out of her that he was dead but that was all, and she made it very clear that she didn't want to talk about him. She didn't want to talk about any of it.'

Elizabeth leaned back in her chair and tried to absorb what Rosemary was telling her. The woman she was describing was a stranger.

'Sorry not to have been of more help.' Rosemary drained her mug and got up to bring it to the sink. Elizabeth's tea sat untouched. 'If I think of anything else, I'll let you know.' The interview, such as it had been, was over. Elizabeth got up and allowed herself to be ushered back to the front door.

'Thank you. So strange to think that my mother could ever have done anything so scandalous!'

'And she wasn't a girl. She was a grown woman. Still, it was a different time. We were all a bunch of innocents.'

'I suppose.' Elizabeth turned to step back out into the street but then, remembering, added, 'Oh, and thanks for the tea.'

Rosemary just raised an eyebrow and shut the door.

The blue skies were gone and pencil-grey clouds now lurked overhead with the promise of rain. With nothing else to do Elizabeth headed back towards Convent Hill. She was nearly at number sixty-two when her cousin Paul emerged from the house and greeted her.

'Perfect timing!'

'Is it? What can I do for you?'

'I'm glad I caught you in time.' Paul sucked his teeth and pushed his hair back from his eyes. 'There's no way you can stay in there. The place is coming down with rats.'

'Oh, Christ.' She shuddered.

'Did you not see the droppings? They are all over the carpets, shelves, everywhere. I got young Dermot to take your bags down to the flat. Mam and Dad are only delighted to give you a bed for a few nights.'

The person who didn't share their delight was Elizabeth. What fresh circle of hell was this? She had hoped to slip quietly in and out of town and now she was going to be sharing a bathroom with Uncle Jerry. It was too much. She struggled to think of some excuse to avoid the unthinkable.

'That is so, so kind of them but I . . . ' Elizabeth twisted her head left and right searching for inspiration. Nothing. 'The thing is I'm actually . . . ' And then suddenly it came to her. The letter in her back pocket. 'Kilkenny!' she cried as if it was Gaelic for eureka. 'I have to head into Kilkenny to see the solicitor and I'll stay there tonight.' She was almost panting with relief.

'But sure, just come back tonight. There is no need to be spending money on hotels,' Paul argued, knowing that he was sure to get the blame if his cousin slipped through the family net.

'I'd be afraid to drive back tonight. You know, jet lag. I don't want to fall asleep at the wheel.' She was on a roll now and Paul's face seemed to accept defeat.

★ ★ ★

80

Half an hour later, having retrieved her overnight bag from the flat above the shop — 'Why Patricia had to use a solicitor over in Kilkenny I'll never know.' 'Never wanted anyone to know her business, your mother.' — Elizabeth was parked in a lay-by just outside Buncarragh on her phone. Having called Ernest O'Sullivan to explain that she happened to be in Kilkenny, an appointment had been made for later that afternoon. Then she left a message on her son Zach's phone and was now leaving one on Elliot's unanswered phone. 'Just wanted to check in. Zach let me know that he made it there safely. Hope you two are having fun. Talk later. Bye.' Hanging up, she immediately regretted her message. She always hated it on the rare occasions when Elliot actually took up his role as parent. Much as she complained, in truth, she had found that the last eight years as a single parent had suited her better than the endless discussions, bickering and uneasy compromises that had made up the bulk of Zach's childhood. What sort of mobile to hang over the cot. When he should get his first pair of jeans. Some things were not meant to be decided by committee. She was her mother's daughter, she supposed.

O'Sullivan and Company, solicitors, were easy to find. Housed in a tall stone-fronted building that must have been a former home to some fat cat, it was located on the Parade just opposite the walls of the castle. Arriving early, Elizabeth sat in the Design Centre up the street and had a coffee and a small slice of a tray bake that tasted even healthier than it looked. She left most of it.

Elizabeth felt nervous, she didn't know why. Her mother was not the sort of person to leave loose ends or ambiguity. The house was hers and hers alone. She really hoped that Jerry and Gillian or even Paul and Noelle had not tried to meddle in her affairs.

Ernest O'Sullivan's offices were slightly less impressive once you entered the building. They occupied only the second floor; what must have been a beautiful room had been sub-divided by cheap partitions and the ornate cornices visible in the hallway were covered by a low ceiling of tiles interspersed with strange metallic grids protecting those below from the neon strip lighting. A bored young girl who looked as if she could be heading straight to a nightclub after work showed Elizabeth into the cubicle that housed Mr O'Sullivan himself. She had resolved to refuse any tea or coffee but then realised that she hadn't actually been offered any.

'Hello, Miss Keane, very nice to meet you.' A soft manicured hand was offered but Ernest O'Sullivan didn't stand. Elizabeth was slightly taken aback by his rudeness but when she leaned in to shake his hand she noticed a black plastic handle at his back. He was in a wheelchair. Ernest was asking her about her journey and telling her what a pleasure her mother had always been to do business with but all Elizabeth could think about was how this man had got behind his desk. There didn't seem to be room to navigate a wheelchair around it and besides, they were on the second floor. Was there a lift? She doubted it. Could it be he was just using a wheelchair to sit in? This was neither the office nor solicitor she had been expecting.

'So, I wrote to you because, and I must really apologise, we found a codicil to your mother's will. It should have been discovered along with everything else but it had slipped out of the file. I hope you understand. These things happen with old papers.' His eyes blinked behind his thick glasses. The neon light made shiny tracks across his gleaming bald head.

'Of course. Is it something I should be concerned about? Is there any dispute?'

'Oh, no. On the contrary, you have had some added good fortune. You've been left another house.'

'Another house?' Elizabeth repeated, not understanding how this was possible.

'Yes. It's all very straightforward. Your mother held it in trust for you but now it is all yours to do with as you wish.'

'A house? But where is it?'

'Mmmm, let me just check.' He riffled through a thick pile of papers on his desk and retrieved a large Manila envelope. 'Here it is. Muirinish, in West Cork. Castle House, Muirinish, County Cork. I have no idea about the state of the place but congratulations. It must be worth something!'

The Foley farm! Why had her mother said nothing? She knew this day was going to come and what if Elizabeth hadn't found the letters?

'Does it come with much land?'

'No. Looking at this, the title deed is fairly new.' He studied the papers again. 'Yes. Just six years ago, so my guess is the house was split from a farm and somebody else got the land. The map here just shows a house, with a farmyard to the rear and a strip of garden at the front.' Ernest seemed delighted for her. He held out his smooth pink hand again and Elizabeth shook it. She was dumbfounded. Her father, who had never existed, never been spoken of, was in death suddenly very present in her life. She had read his heartfelt thoughts and now she owned his house. She felt like she might cry, so quickly made good her escape with the envelope in her hand.

On the street, she hesitated. What should she do? Where should she go? She stepped beneath a tree to avoid a large group of Japanese tourists following their guide back towards the bus from whence they had come, like spawning salmon dressed in Burberry raincoats. Elizabeth reached for her phone. She had to share this news with someone. Zach? Yes, she would call Zach, but when she opened her phone she saw that she had received a text message. It was from Elliot.

Hi, Liz. Did you mean to call me? Zach isn't here. No plans to see him this holiday.

Her knees buckled and she steadied herself against the rough grey bark of the tree. A father found, and a son lost.

THEN

Castle House,
Muirinish,
West Cork
11 Feb 1974

Dear Patricia,
I just wanted to say thank you so much for coming down to visit us in Castle House. I hope you got home all right and the journey wasn't too boring. I know I get very quiet in the car. Sorry. I think it is half my nerves, and half making sure I don't have a crash with such precious cargo!

It was a real pleasure showing you around the farm and seeing everything through your eyes. Sometimes I forget how lovely it is here with the sea on our doorstep. Mam wanted me to tell you how much she enjoyed meeting you as well. She has talked of little else since your visit. Were your ears burning?

I've been thinking about you so much since you left. It sounds silly I know, but I miss you. That time we spent together sheltering in the old ruins keeps turning around in my mind. The memory of you in my arms and your softness under my hand won't leave me. I know I'm probably not the man of anybody's dreams but I

*can tell you for sure, that you are the
woman of mine.*

*When do you think you might visit
again? The thought of seeing you is all that
is getting me through these dark cold
mornings. Let's plan another trip as soon
as possible. I want to touch you and put
my lips on yours so badly it hurts.*

*I have never felt like this before. Please
write back soon.*

*Warmest regards,
Edward*

★   ★   ★

Patricia didn't know what to think when she
finished the letter. The things he talked about
had happened but it was just that he had
experienced them in such a different way from
her. For every flash of connection between them,
a shy glance or a hand touched accidentally,
there had been hours when Edward seemed
completely oblivious to her existence. Her
memory of the weekend was spending most of
her time with Edward's mother or hiding in her
room. She knew she hadn't much experience of
men, but surely they weren't all as confusing as
this one. Then she wondered if she was being
unfair or if her expectations were too high. She
had read horrific stories about men and at least
Edward was sweet and hadn't tried to stick his
fingers in her knickers the way she heard fellas
did the second you let them kiss you. Patricia

folded the letter and put it in the small pile with the others. She would write back but she wouldn't encourage him. Edward Foley, she decided, was not the man for her.

The next day, a Thursday, Patricia was taking advantage of the dry weather by hanging a few things out on the washing line that sagged between the walls of the small yard at the back of the house. Her efforts were interrupted by the doorbell. She hurried through, still with a couple of clothes pegs in her mouth. Patricia opened the door to find a slim, oily-haired man almost obscured by the largest bunch of flowers she had ever seen outside of a funeral procession.

'Patricia Keane?'

'Yes,' she replied, the pegs falling to the floor. She found herself backing away from the large collection of red and white blooms.

'These are for you,' the man said, thrusting the bouquet into her arms.

She tried to protest. 'But who are they from?'

'There's a card.' The man was already heading back towards his van emblazoned with an enormous Interflora logo.

Patricia's hands were trembling with excitement as she ripped the card from its doll's-house envelope.

'Happy Valentine's Day, Lonely Leinster Lady, from your Munster admirer!'

It was Valentine's Day! Patricia had completely forgotten. In her life she had received two Valentine cards, both of which had come from her uncle after her father had died. When her mother discovered who had been sending them she asked him to stop and he did. Now she was holding a huge bunch of flowers from a real man who had actual feelings for her. The scent of them filled the hall and their sweet fresh fragrance banished all her negative feelings. She wasn't a spinster. She was a woman who was desired by a man. He wasn't perfect, well, he was so very far from perfect, but he was kind and worked hard and he had sent her flowers!

Patricia knew she was being silly but over the next couple of days the fantasy of her wonderful boyfriend took shape. Old Mrs Curtain had seen the Interflora van and asked about her secret admirer. Rosemary had shrieked like a bird in the zoo when she saw the arrangement displayed reverentially on the unused dining-room table. Even her sister-in-law Gillian had heard about the delivery and asked about her 'love life'. After all the years of watching the other girls walking with their boyfriends, showing off engagement rings, pushing prams, Patricia felt as if she had finally joined some sort of exclusive club. She had a man! Despite repeatedly trying to remind herself of who that man was and all his failings, she found she was developing feelings, if not for him, then for the notion of being somebody's girlfriend.

When she wrote to thank him for the flowers, she found she didn't attempt to draw a line under their courtship. She told him how much she had enjoyed their weekend. The pen also seemed to form the words that told him she would in fact like to come and visit him again. As she licked the envelope she wondered if it would be different this time.

Certainly in his next few letters Edward seemed to have found a new frankness. He spoke directly about how much he yearned for her physically and Patricia found that as she read his words she shared his desires. He promised to be more talkative and told her he was planning a couple of short day trips so that they could spend some time alone together.

This time on the train Patricia refused to listen to her doubts. Edward would be different and suddenly things would be easy between them. She unwrapped the tinfoil around her cheese and ham sandwich and ate with gusto. She felt like a woman who had cracked the code.

Early signs were hard to read because he had brought his mother with him to the station.

'Our neighbour Mrs Maloney has been up in the Mercy Hospital for weeks. Tests and more tests. They still don't know what is wrong with the poor creature. The family have found it very hard to get up to see her so when Teddy was driving up I thought I'd take advantage of the lift. I think she was delighted to see someone from home. Just to get all the news . . . '

Mrs Foley's advancing army of talk laid waste any possibility of a conversation with Edward, so Patricia sat patiently with her cream case in the back seat.

'Do you mind? I hope you don't mind. I get fierce car sick in the back. I'm all right in the front, amn't I, Teddy?'

The wind welcomed them back to Muirinish. Like a washing line of coats and scarves the trio made their way from the car to the back door. Patricia was impressed by the way Edward's mother strode through the storm, unmoved by its force. Once inside Edward disappeared almost at once. 'The milking, I better . . . ' He looked at Patricia and she felt he wanted to say more, but before she could speak he was gone.

'Now I suppose you'd like to go and settle yourself. I put you in the same small front room again. Do you want a hand with your case? Sure, it's light. You'll be grand. Up you go.' Edward's mother ushered Patricia from the room and she walked up the creaking stairs. The house seemed darker than before and now that she was alone the noise of the storm outside was louder than she recalled. On the landing, through the gloom, she looked around. Five doors. One was the bathroom, even colder and damper than her own at Convent Hill. The central door in front of her led to her small room with its single bed and tall narrow window that looked out to sea. She wondered what was behind the other three. She wasn't even sure which room belonged to Edward or where his mother slept. From the outside the house seemed much larger than this. Did one of the doors lead to a corridor of further rooms? Pushing open her door she turned on the light, the fringed shade casting a shadow all around the room. The curtains hadn't been drawn and the glossy golden material shifted slightly as the window rattled against the elements. From outside came the complaining cries of seagulls being buffeted high above the house. She sat on the bed, still wearing her coat.

A sinking feeling had replaced all her optimism of earlier in the day. This was just going to be another weekend of awkward silences. She sighed and lifted her case onto the bed.

Opening it, she reached for her toilet bag. Like so much else in her life now, it had been her mother's. She remembered the day it was purchased. The two of them had been in Deasy's Chemists looking in the section to the right of the door that she normally only visited at Christmas searching for fancy soaps or bath salts. Her mother had picked the bag out because of the butterfly resting on the cornflower that adorned it. 'Won't that cheer me up when I'm in hospital?' It was an uncharacteristically positive remark for her mother to make which was probably why Patricia always recalled it. She reached for her toothpaste and toothbrush so that she could freshen up before heading downstairs, but the small bag slipped from the bed onto the floor. Patricia bent down to retrieve it and when she did, she noticed something else under the bed. What was it? The object was just beyond her grasp and she had to lie flat on her stomach to reach it. As she re-emerged from under the bed she looked down at her hand and stared for a moment. Something so familiar and yet it had been so many years since she had seen one, never mind held one in her hand. A baby's dummy. A soother. Pink plastic, the rubber of the teat not yet perished. It couldn't have lain there for forty years. She would ask Edward about it. At least it would be something to talk about.

Back downstairs a random selection of pots sat on the Aga, steam billowing up to the ceiling, but there was no sign of Edward or Mrs Foley. Patricia wasn't sure what to do. She hated the awkwardness of being a guest. Through the window she saw a light spilling from the door of one of the outhouses and a shadow moving. Perhaps she could help with something rather than just sitting around waiting to be fed. She didn't want her hostess to get the impression that she was lazy.

Outside the wind was so strong it made her laugh. Somewhere in the distance a door or a shutter had come loose and was banging in protest. Patricia weaved her way across the yard, one hand trying to control her hair, the other preventing her skirt from billowing skywards. She could see Mrs Foley's back, a few chickens pecking at the dirt floor around her. Suddenly, wings spread wide and Patricia realised that the old woman was holding one of the birds by its feet. Almost before she could understand what was happening Mrs Foley grabbed hold of the chicken's head and twisted sharply. The squawking ceased and the neck hung limp but the wings took longer to understand that all hope of flight was lost. The other chickens went about their business, seemingly unaware that one of their number had met its grisly end. Patricia was standing just outside the door now and was wondering how she should alert Mrs Foley to her presence, when the old lady slapped the dead bird on the rough bench in front of her and with one swipe took its head off with a large knife.

The violence of it made Patricia gasp.

Mrs Foley turned and held the headless corpse upside down. The red juice steamed as it trickled noisily into a waiting bucket.

'Oh, there you are!' she said by way of greeting.

'Yes.' Patricia wondered if she had been meant to witness this gruesome scene. As if to reassure her Mrs Foley raised her free hand and absent-mindedly licked the blood that was dripping from it. Something shifted in Patricia's stomach.

'That's Sunday lunch sorted,' Mrs Foley said, holding the bird aloft with a smile, but all Patricia could see was the smear of blood across her teeth.

Back in the house Mrs Foley disappeared with the dead chicken and when she re-emerged began checking pots, poking their contents with a well-worn wooden spoon. Patricia was standing by the back door, unsure if she should sit down or not.

'I was saying to Teddy, dinner's going to be a while, so maybe he'd like to take you down to Carey's for a drink. I don't keep drink in the house. Myself and Teddy would never have one. Christmas maybe. The odd sherry. I was telling him it would be nice to take you out. Show you around the place. It's a nice little pub, with a lounge bar as well. Quiet enough. You'd never get any trouble in there. Not like a city pub. I suppose you'd never go to the pub in Buncarragh, would you?' Patricia shook her head, knowing better than to try and interrupt

Catherine Foley's monologue, but her hostess persisted with her enquiries. 'Do you have a lot of friends back home?' The pause for breath suggested that an answer was in fact required.

'No. Not really. I couldn't get out much looking after my mother.'

'Of course, of course. But you have your family, don't you? How's your brother keeping? They're all well?'

'Yes, thank you. All fine.' Patricia felt like a fraud mentioning Jerry and Gillian as if they were one big happy family.

Mrs Foley had stopped mid-stir and was staring at Patricia. It seemed she required a fuller response.

'We aren't really that close. There have been some disagreements about our mother's will,' she confessed.

The old woman nodded sympathetically. 'Isn't that sad. Often the way of course. Often the way.'

⋆　⋆　⋆

When Edward returned from the milking, he was sporting a fresh shirt and jumper and his hair was slicked back off his face. Before he could speak his mother launched into an explanation of how she had told Patricia all about the trip to the pub and the two young people were ushered to the door.

Once outside they braced themselves against the wind.

'Is it a walk?' Patricia asked, sincerely hoping that it wasn't.

'A bit far, I'd say. We'll take the car.'

As they sat side by side in the darkness with the tight beams of the headlights making a glowing tunnel along the road ahead, Patricia felt better. It was just the two of them. She looked at Edward. His profile, lit by the instruments on the dashboard, looked strong and handsome. She liked the lines around his eyes from all the years of squinting through the winter storms and summer sun. The stubble of his chin meeting the soft pink of his lip made her shift in her seat, almost embarrassed.

'I'm glad I came back.'

'So am I.'

A short silence but then it was Edward who continued. 'Sorry about my mother. I think she is just so glad to have someone to talk to.'

'She's grand. It was nice of her to suggest we do this.'

'Yes.'

Patricia quickly lost all sense of direction as the car twisted its way through the narrow roads. They had turned right out of the gates of Castle House, away from the causeway that crossed the marsh, but after that they had turned inland into a maze of identical-looking hedgerows and ditches. Before long the car slowed down as it approached a crossroads and there was the unexpected sight of a small stone-clad building that housed the pub. The lights from the two large windows on either side of the door spilled out onto a gravel forecourt revealing a lone petrol pump and a couple of parked cars.

Inside, the room was split in two. On one side

a long bar with stools led down to a brick fireplace, while on the other side low tables and small padded seats were pressed against a long dark-green vinyl-covered banquette. A barman just past the point of being referred to as young was stooped over a newspaper and two old men, wearing flat caps and nursing pints of stout, were perched at the end of the bar nearest to the half-hearted fire. All three looked up to examine the newcomers.

'Teddy boy,' the barman called in greeting and stepped back from the counter, ready to serve.

'Andy. You're well?'

'I am. Bad enough old night.'

'It is. It is.'

'What can I get you?'

Patricia felt four pairs of eyes staring at her. She rarely, if ever, went into pubs, even the ones that boasted a lounge bar, and she certainly had no idea what to drink. She felt a small seed of panic beginning to grow.

'A pint of Murphy's,' Edward ordered and then looked back at Patricia. Her eyes darted around the bar. She tried to remember the names of drinks. 'I'll have a . . . ' she said, trying to give off the air of a woman deciding which of the many drinks she enjoyed she would be choosing this evening. Just then she noticed the poster behind the bar with the little deer. The advertisement was on television. 'A Babycham please!'

Edward looked at her a little uncertainly. 'And a Babycham please.'

The barman looked behind his head at the picture of the small deer dancing on stars. 'A

96

Babycham, is it? Well, I'll have a look.'

Patricia heard the old men chuckling and muttering the word 'Babycham'. She felt suddenly indignant. The poster was on the wall and they talked about it on TV. It wasn't as if she had ordered a cup of tea, which was in fact what she would have preferred.

Edward led Patricia to the low tables and pulling one of them away from the seating, invited her to sit down. As she sat her weight forced some air out of a hole somewhere in the vinyl. A long high-pitched farting sound filled the room. Edward pretended not to have heard it but the two old boys at the bar were shaking so hard it seemed likely one or both of them would fall off their stools. Patricia smoothed out her skirt.

The barman reappeared and plonked on the table a small bottle and glass that bore the Babycham logo.

'For the lady.'

'Thank you.' Her voice was barely a whisper.

'The Murphy's will be a minute.'

'Grand. Grand. Take your time.'

Left alone, the silence of the bar seemed to engulf them. Somewhere a clock was ticking.

'Don't wait,' Edward said, indicating the bottle on the table before her.

'Thanks,' she said, pouring the fizzing liquid into the glass. 'I've never actually tasted this stuff,' she confessed. 'I panicked!' She giggled and he gave her an easy smile that once more made her glad to be there with him.

'And a pint.' The barman placed the drink in front of Edward.

Bringing it up to his lips he said. 'Sláinte' to no one in particular.

Picking up her Babycham, Patricia echoed him. 'Sláinte!' She dared to hope this might turn out to be fun. They both took a sip and smiled at each other.

'Nice?' he asked.

'Sweet. It's good though,' she assured him.

Edward took another sip of his pint and looked around the bar. Patricia could feel them slipping back into silence. What did people on dates talk about? What could all those half-wit girls from school think of to say to men that she couldn't? A piece of turf shifted in the hearth.

Abandoned on the banquette next to her, Patricia spotted a copy of *Titbits* magazine. She was vaguely aware that it wasn't the sort of publication you should admit to looking at but Rosemary often brought her a copy from the salon and they enjoyed reading each other their horoscopes. Hoping that it might restart their conversation she picked up the magazine and held it out to Edward.

'Read me out my horoscope!'

'What?' He looked confused.

'My star sign. See what it says.' She felt slightly flirtatious. Maybe there would be a mention of a new romance.

'Sure, you can read it yourself there, can't you?'

'It's more fun if you read it and then I read out yours.' These were the simple rules that served herself and Rosemary well. She fanned the magazine in front of him temptingly.

Behind them, the barman had begun putting out beer mats on the other tables.

'Ah, don't be teasing Teddy.'

Patricia wasn't sure what he had said.

'Sorry? What?'

'Reading wouldn't be Teddy's thing.'

Edward's face had turned the colour of blood and he glared at the floor.

Patricia looked at him and then back at the smirking face of the barman.

'Edward, what does he mean?' Her voice was low, the question almost hissed.

'Sure, Teddy here can't read and write, can you, Teddy?' the barman laughed and slapped Edward's back. An echo of laughter came from the old men across the room.

Edward jerked his head towards the barman and snapped, 'Just leave us be. We're having a drink.'

'Sorry I spoke.' The barman gave an exaggerated look of apology and sauntered back towards the bar.

Patricia was frozen. Questions filled her head like small birds trapped in a net. Edward was holding onto the edge of the table and breathing heavily. She daren't look at him. Finally she spoke.

'Is it true?'

The question hung in the air. It was agony and made worse because they both understood that this was the final moment before they would both have to face the truth. Edward swallowed hard.

'Yes.'

Patricia felt her stomach drop. She thought of herself standing in the hall of Convent Hill, ripping open envelopes. The things he'd said. The private things. The things who had said? Of course, she knew the answer to that question, the unthinkable truth. Suddenly she couldn't bear to look at Edward for a moment longer. He just seemed like a great big man-baby sitting in front of her. She struggled to her feet and rushed out of the door. She had no idea where she was going but every footstep she took into the black night meant she was closer to home. The door slammed shut behind her. She could hear Edward's voice calling her name and then the loud unfettered roars of laughter.

NOW

It had always been Elliot's shortcut to victory when they fought. He would accuse her of being a control freak. Elizabeth had thought it unfair but now as she sat in her parked rental car she wondered if he had been right all along because this was the deepest pit of hell. She had no control whatsoever. Multiple messages had been left on various phones with no replies and she was thousands of miles away. She held on to the steering wheel and tried to remember the breathing techniques from the solitary yoga class she had ever attended. Calm. She was powerless and she must accept that fact, there was nothing to be gained from being hysterical. Bad things happened to daughters. Boys were strong. Boys were tough.

A moment later she was shaking the steering wheel and sobbing aloud, 'Where the fuck are you, Zach?' She let out a long, low howl and it felt good. Wiping away her tears Elizabeth considered her next move. Dublin Airport. She could drive straight there. Her passport and credit cards were all she really needed and she had them with her. No need to head back to Buncarragh. The keys to her New York apartment. Would she need them? No, she could just fly direct to San Francisco. The thought of Noelle and Gillian with their faux concern made her feel nauseous. She couldn't control her husband and now had failed to look after her son. Neither a wife nor a mother. Their judgement and pity would hang thick as cigar smoke in the air.

A peal of electronic bells. Her phone announced that Elliot was calling. She pounced on it and held it to her ear.

'Elliot! Thank God. Have you heard anything?'

'Calm down, Elizabeth. I'm sure he's fine.' The smooth, even tone of his voice made her want to smash something. How could any father sound like this when his son was missing?

'Have you any news? Did you contact his friends?'

'Well, I left him a voicemail, explaining that we had rumbled him, so I expect he'll be calling one of us shortly.'

She rolled her eyes and tightened her grip on the phone. The man was useless.

'I'm coming back.'

'Why? What good can you do?'

'Why? My son, our son,' she corrected herself, 'is missing. He's only seventeen. I think it is my job as his parent to do whatever I can do to find him.'

'Elizabeth, think about it. Don't rush into anything. You saw his ticket, right?'

'An e-ticket, yes. I think it was the real thing, but who knows? I got emails from you! Emails saying how pleased you were he was coming to stay!'

'Elizabeth, I never sent anything. Please believe me, I knew nothing about this plan of his.'

'I know, I know. I was a fool. You emailed to give me your 'new' email address and it never crossed my mind that Zach would do something this stupid, this dangerous!'

'Well, say the ticket is real, then he is in the Bay Area somewhere. There is no point you coming all the way out here.'

'I'm coming!'

'From Ireland? It'll cost you a fortune.'

This gave Elizabeth pause.

'When were you planning to come back to New York?' Elliot continued.

'In five days.'

'Look, by then I'll have found our runaway and I'll send him back for you to knock some sense into.'

'I don't know. I feel weird being this far away.'

'Elizabeth, we might never have found out he'd done this. He has been fairly unlucky — it's not like we speak on a daily basis!'

She grinned despite herself.

'That's true enough. He must be shitting himself, now that he knows we know.' She heard Elliot chuckling at the other end of the line.

'Do what you need to do. I'll let you know the second I hear anything. He'll be fine. Zach is a smart kid. Surviving in New York prepares you for most things.'

'He flew cross-country alone, without telling anyone!' She could feel her hysteria returning.

'Elizabeth,' Elliot said in a soothing voice, 'everything is going to be OK. I'll stay in touch. He knows we are going to be pissed at him, but he'll call. You'll see. Try not to worry.'

The sort of thing only a man could say. How could she possibly not worry?

'OK. Thanks. Call me. I'll call you.'

'We'll talk. Goodbye.'

'Bye.'

Elizabeth imagined Elliot rolling his eyes across the room at, what was the latest one called? Andrew? Barry? Maybe Will? There had been so many.

Outside the car the street lights had come on and a thin mist of rain had given the streets an oily sheen. She had to admit that Elliot was right. She might as well get on with things. Putting the car into gear she eased her way into the afternoon traffic. Buncarragh. She resolved to tell her family nothing about her maternal failings.

Back in the familiar streets of her home town she reluctantly headed for the shop. Paul was behind the counter on the phone and greeted her with a wave. From behind an elegant tower of stainless steel bowls Noelle emerged and when she saw Elizabeth her face took on an expression of such deep dismay and sympathy that Elizabeth wondered how on earth she could have heard about Zach. Arms outstretched, her cousin lunged at her.

'Rats! I was nearly sick when Paul told me, and you up there all alone the whole night. They could have eaten the face off you!'

'It was only one rat, Noelle. I don't think I was in that much danger.'

'Young Dermot is after killing four of the monsters and it's only been a few hours.'

Elizabeth felt the blood draining from her face.

'Really?'

'Four of them, the size of kittens. Come up to the flat and Gillian will make us some tea.'

The two women made their way up the stairs.

'We weren't expecting you tonight. Paul said you'd stay over in Kilkenny.'

'It didn't take as long as I was expecting.'

'Everything all right?' Noelle asked with a studied air of nonchalance.

'Oh, fine.' Elizabeth wondered briefly if she should mention the house in Cork, but decided against it. The less these people knew the better. 'Just technical stuff about tax.'

'Oh.' Noelle's face couldn't hide her disappointment.

Sitting around the kitchen table with her aunt and uncle, the main topic of conversation was rats and what a narrow escape Elizabeth had experienced. Everyone seemed to have a story of someone getting their throat ripped out or innocent calves being murdered while they slept. The overall impression was that rats were to Ireland what sharks were to Australia. While not exactly enjoying the conversation, Elizabeth had to admit that it felt nice to have something to take her mind off Zach and his whereabouts.

She liked hearing her relatives telling stories. It was something she missed with her American friends. They were all so articulate but somehow lacked the skills to simply spin a yarn. Of course, ask them about their feelings and they became conversational virtuosos. When she had first arrived in New York that had thrilled her. Naming every emotional scar, exploring the cartography of relationships. It was all so new and refreshing, but now she found a nostalgia for a tale well told. Stories swapped across a cup-filled table, like serves being returned in tennis.

'Oh, I nearly forgot!' her Aunt Gillian exclaimed apropos of nothing obvious. 'Remember we were talking about your father earlier?'

'Yes.' Elizabeth wondered where this was going. Questions about her trip to Kilkenny perhaps?

'Edward Foley was the name?'

'Yes?'

Noelle leaned forward. She clearly didn't know what was coming next.

'Well, I found the letter I was telling you about. The one from his mother.'

She bent stiffly and retrieved her handbag from the floor by her chair. 'I shoved it in here somewhere,' she said, unzipping the bag and rummaging in its contents. She glanced at various envelopes. 'No, that's not it, no.' Her face suddenly brightened. 'Here it is. I'd kept it all these years in with the old photo albums. I knew I had it somewhere.' She handed the slim envelope across the table to Elizabeth.

She looked at it.

'This is from Edward Foley's mother?'

'Yes. Catherine Foley, I think she signs it.'

Elizabeth stared down at the letter in her hand. It made no sense, but there was no mistaking what she held. Pale blue Basildon Bond and the neat handwriting in black ink. Both identical to

106

the letters she had found in Convent Hill. A cold hand reached across the decades and gripped her stomach. Her poor mother.

THEN

Something was wrong. What was it? Patricia lay
rigid as a corpse. Then, it struck her. The wind
had stopped. The stillness made her uneasy.
There was a metallic taste in her mouth and
her head felt thick and heavy on the pillow.
Downstairs she heard a door open and shut. She
squeezed her eyes closed and tried to banish the
horror of the night before. How could she ever
leave this room again?

Her memories came in and out of focus like a
half-remembered dream. She could picture
herself stumbling through the dark, her sobs
swallowed by the wind in the trees and the deep
pit of the night. She had never felt so pathetic
in her whole life. Even when her mother had
died she hadn't been so upset. Of course, she
understood that the tears weren't just for the
humiliation back in the pub, they were for her
life. A life so devoid of hope that she had allowed
herself to imagine that Edward could be her
knight in shining armour. She felt like such a
fool. How had she become so deluded? Placing
her feet carefully, she had marched slowly
forward, her hands outstretched to protect her
from branches or anything else that might
confront her in the blind blackness of the night.
All too soon of course the lights of a car had
pinned her to the hedge and then Edward was
out on the road, coat flapping in the headlights,

pleading with her to get in. She knew she had been screaming at him but couldn't remember exactly what. She ended up collapsed into a shuddering ball in front of the car. Edward had half-lifted, half-helped her into the passenger seat. She remembered the familiar smell of her coat which she kept pulled over her head on the drive back to Castle House.

'I'm so sorry. I was going to tell you. We weren't trying to trick you. We just thought it was the best way to do things. We . . . ' His litany of apologies and explanations washed over her and all she really heard was the word 'we' repeated over and over again. It made her feel sick to think of them working as a team, the two of them plotting and planning what to say to her. Even worse was the thought of Edward sitting still while his mother read Patricia's letters aloud to him. Private! It was all meant to be special and intimate and now she felt so exposed. All she wanted to do was go home and end this nightmare. Why had she come back? If only she had kept to her resolve to finish things she would have been spared all this. She pushed herself lower into her seat. 'Mammy can explain things. Mammy will tell you how it happened.'

Patricia groaned.

Mrs Foley was standing in wait in front of the house, her shadow stretched across the grass like a thin giant. Had she already heard that something had happened in the pub?

'What is it? Is everything all right?' She had taken Patricia's other arm in a firm grip and helped her indoors with Edward.

109

'She knows,' was all Edward said.

'Knows what?'

'The letters, Mammy. She knows about the letters.'

Mrs Foley said nothing more.

The three of them weaved their way like drunks into the house and through the hall to the brightly lit heat of the kitchen. Patricia sank down in a chair and stared at her clenched hands on her lap. She was aware of Edward and his mother standing apart and staring at her. The lid of a simmering pot rattled in anticipation.

Predictably it was Mrs Foley that broke the silence.

'Will you have some food?'

An indignant Patricia glared at her. How dare this woman think that a plate of dinner was going to help her overlook this betrayal? The expression on Mrs Foley's face suggested she was taken aback by the red swollen eyes and running nose of the young woman sitting at her table. She took a step forward.

'Edward meant no harm. It was my fault. I'm not going to be around forever and I just wanted to see him settled. He is very fond of you, Patricia.'

She shook her head. 'No. He can't.' Her voice was a high-pitched rasp. 'If he cared he wouldn't have lied to me.' She threw an accusatory glance towards Edward but he had his gaze firmly fixed on the far corner of the room.

'No, no, Patricia,' Mrs Foley said in a soothing voice. 'Edward meant everything in those letters. Those were his feelings.' She lowered her voice.

110

'I was just trying to help. He's not a stupid boy. It was just that, well, school wasn't for him.' Her hands made a strange calming gesture as if she was patting an imaginary dog.

'But, you read my letters! Out loud, the two of you sat there. Those letters were meant for him, just him.' She jabbed a finger in Edward's direction. 'I feel sick. I want to go home. I just want to be at home.' The thought of being in her own bed in Buncarragh hugging a pillow made her begin to sob once more. A long thin thread of snot left her top lip and slowly descended onto her lap. She could hear Mrs Foley moving around the room.

'We'll put the kettle on. A hot-water bottle. A cup of tea. A good night's sleep. You've had a bit of a shock, that's all. Teddy, will you make yourself useful and get down the cups?'

Patricia heard his thick-soled shoes moving across the lino. She couldn't bear to look at him. What a useless lump of a man he was! Patricia had never considered herself a violent woman but she wanted to do him physical harm. She wanted to hurt him, make him feel something. How could he have managed to never learn to read and write? She wondered if there was something wrong with him. She stole a glance at his broad back, his coarse hands holding the delicate china cups. How had she ever thought he was handsome or sensitive? He was Frankenstein's monster. He turned and she saw his big gormless face. Patricia buried her face in her hands, a hot knot of fury and regret.

The morning sun crept past the curtains and gave the small bedroom a golden glow. Patricia tried to remember coming upstairs or going to bed but couldn't. She wondered what more had been said. It was only when she thought of getting up that she realised that she couldn't. Her legs were almost like dead weights and she became light-headed if her head left the pillow. A quiet whimper escaped her lips. This was no time to be ill. She longed to go home but even she had to accept that the trip was very unlikely to happen today. A light tapping at the door.

'Come in.'

The door cracked open and Mrs Foley's foot pushed it further ajar so that she could come in balancing a tray with a small pot of tea and a rack of toast.

'I brought you up a little breakfast there. I didn't think you'd want to come downstairs just yet.'

What did that mean? Had something else happened last night? Rather than asking any questions, Patricia just said, 'Thank you.'

The older woman looked drawn and had applied some rouge and lipstick which gave her the appearance of an elderly ventriloquist's dummy.

'I'll just pop it down there.' The tray was wedged into the side of the mattress, pinning Patricia against the wall. 'Did you manage to get some sleep?'

'I did. I don't feel very well,' she blurted out like a child.

'Well, have a bit of toast. That might settle you.' Mrs Foley placed her chilled bony hand on her forehead. 'No temperature. That's something.' She turned and closed the door quietly behind her.

The toast tasted good. She ate two slices and then drank her tea. Sick or ill weren't the precise words for how she felt, but something wasn't right. Peculiar. Yes, she decided, that was just the word for it, peculiar.

She only realised that she had fallen asleep when the crash of the tray hitting the floor woke her up. Her body felt even heavier than before. She thought she remembered Mrs Foley coming in to clean up the mess but she might have imagined it. The rest of the day was a blur of sleeping and waking. There had been no sign of Edward all day but at some point his mother had spoon-fed her a bowl of soup. It had been dark outside. The old woman had helped her onto a commode by the window. Patricia knew she was supposed to be angry with this old lady but found that she was just grateful to her for her kindness.

The next day passed by in a similar fog of deep sleeps interrupted by visits from Mrs Foley with various offerings of sandwiches or soup. Patricia was vaguely aware that this was the day she was supposed to go back home to Buncarragh. She had meant to ask if she could use the phone to call her brother to explain what happened but she wasn't sure she had. The wind was back and the rattle of the window seemed to fill her head whether she was asleep or awake.

On the third day she woke to find she was wearing a night-dress that didn't belong to her and the chair where her clothes had been folded neatly was now empty. More tea. She remembered getting sick over the side of the bed and now a smell of Dettol hung in the air.

Was it the fourth day when Mrs Foley told her about the doctor's visit? Apparently they had called him out and she had slept right through. He could find nothing wrong, she was told, but maybe she was a little anaemic. She had sipped at a cup of beef tea, while Mrs Foley wiped the drips of liquid from her chin with a towel. Patricia wanted to cry but she found she didn't have the strength. Sleep.

Looking back she wasn't sure when she had lost track of the days. Had it been the fifth day or the sixth, or even a week? More? She didn't know. Time ceased to matter, and her world had shrunk to her narrow bed and the short shuffle across the room to use the commode. Sometimes she heard Edward and his mother talking downstairs. She recognised that they were not normal conversations. They were arguing. She could hear the anger but couldn't make out the words. The phone had rung a few times. It must be for her. It must, but it never was. When she remembered she repeated her plea to let her brother in Buncarragh know where she was. They would be worried about her. Even as she said the words she doubted them. Would anyone really care? Worse, she wondered if anyone had even noticed her absence. She had vanished and the world looked exactly the same.

Mrs Foley did her best to reassure her.

'I phoned the shop. I spoke to a very nice woman, your sister-in-law I think . . . '

'Gillian?' Patricia asked, trying to imagine her reaction to this call from a strange woman in County Cork.

'Gillian, that's the very woman. Well, she hopes you get well soon and you aren't to worry about a thing. Now you can stop your fretting, that's all sorted.'

Patricia put her head back on the pillow, relieved that people knew where she was.

That night she dreamt she was back at Convent Hill. The house looked the same as it always had but she knew she must have been away because she was very happy to be back home. Patricia was looking for her mother. In her dream she wasn't dead, Patricia just couldn't find her. She looked in the rooms on the ground floor and then raced upstairs to check the bedrooms. In the wall between the bathroom and her own room there was a door that she had never seen before. Finding it unlocked she stepped through it. Had she just forgotten this room? It was lined with dark wood panelling and in the centre was a round table covered with books. How had she never seen this room before? Had her mother been keeping it a secret from her? On the far wall she noticed another door. Opening it she found herself at the top of a wrought-iron spiral staircase that led down into a large conservatory filled with tropical plants. Brightly coloured parrots fluttered beneath the glass ceiling. She carefully descended the staircase. The smell reminded her of the botanical gardens in Dublin. When Patricia reached the bottom step she saw a long dark room behind her full of terracotta pots and gardening equipment but as she walked through it the room became a kitchen, but like the ones you might find in a hotel, with metal surfaces and oversized ovens. At the far end there was a grey wooden door. It was rattling and Patricia felt afraid for the first time, uneasy about what was behind it. She had scarcely touched the handle when the door exploded inwards and Patricia found she was standing in front of Castle House being whipped by the wind, staring out to sea. She was back! She had been in Buncarragh but now here she was again. She tried to scream but made no sound. When she woke the wind from her dream was still howling outside her window.

The next morning as the door was pushed open, she knew at once that something was different. She heard the clatter of the spoon against the saucer as the tray was manoeuvred into the room and looking up she was surprised to see, not Mrs Foley, but Edward. He stood by the bed holding her breakfast. Patricia patted the mattress and he put down the tray. Despite everything she found herself worrying about how she looked. She imagined how her unwashed hair clung to her brow, her pale, sweaty complexion devoid of make-up. She pawed ineffectually at her parting to try and improve its appearance.

'How are you feeling?'

116

She stared up at him.

'Where have you been?' Her voice sounded small and dry compared to his.

'Working. Busy. You know yourself.' He shrugged. 'This is more my mother's thing.'

'She has been very kind.'

Edward said nothing. She remembered the raised voices. Patricia reached for the waiting teacup on the tray. Edward gave a sudden cough. Glancing up she saw that he was shaking his head.

'What?' she asked. Edward thrust a finger to his mouth to indicate she should be quiet. Then he leaned forward and pulled the teacup away from her hand. Again, he shook his head. 'You'd like a glass of water?' His voice sounded slightly raised. 'OK, I'll get you one.' He picked up the cup of tea and left the room. She heard him crossing the landing and going into the bathroom. He returned with a small glass of water and put it on the tray along with the now-empty teacup. 'I'll let you have your breakfast.' He widened his eyes and pointed at the teacup a few more times while shaking his head vigorously, then he left her alone, closing the door softly.

What had just happened? Patricia looked at her tray and then at the flaking paint on the back of the closed door. Could Edward be trusted? Was his mother putting something in the tea? She found it so hard to think. Her head felt heavy and thick with sleep, and yet a small spark of reason told her that this must be what being drugged felt like. Why would Mrs Foley not want

117

her to leave? She took a couple of sips from the glass of water that Edward had brought her and then lay her head on the pillow, panting slightly from the effort of just trying to think.

For the next two days she made it her mission to avoid drinking every cup of tea she was given. Some she poured into the commode but it was too obvious-looking so she began to simply pour it down the side of the bed next to the wall. She hoped she would be long gone before Mrs Foley discovered the brown soaked corner of carpet under the bed.

At first, she felt a little stronger, more alert — but then she was plagued with bad headaches, stomach cramps and diarrhoea. Mrs Foley kept her plied with tea to aid her recovery but Patricia didn't drink a drop. By the end of the third day she felt a little better. She wondered if she was well enough to get to the bathroom because she was becoming concerned the tea lake under the bed might make its way into the room or cause a stain to appear on a ceiling downstairs. She got out of bed and for a moment felt so dizzy she was certain she would fall. Grabbing the chair by the bed for balance, she waited till the room steadied itself. Tentatively she moved one foot and then the other before letting go of the chair. Her breathing was shallow and rapid. Opening the bedroom door as gently as she could she stepped out onto the landing.

Patricia was struck by how big it seemed after the fog of days spent in her simple cell. She took a step towards the bathroom, holding her cup carefully. She didn't want to leave any tell-tale

118

stains on the carpet. Another step and she was able to steady herself on the banister. She held her breath and listened. Just the wind and the distant call of a gull. Putting one foot carefully in front of the other, she slowly made her way towards the bathroom. Her heart was beating loudly and her blood seemed to be rushing inside her ears. The inside of her mouth was dry. Once more she paused and strained to hear any sounds in the house besides the groans and rattles caused by the constant storm. Silence. Another few steps. She was nearly there. A floorboard creaked. She gripped the cup and held her breath. Nothing. Another couple of steps and she had reached her goal. She lunged towards the toilet and poured the tea into the bowl. Immediately she regretted it. She was a fool. Why hadn't she used the sink? If she flushed the toilet Mrs Foley would come running but if she didn't the tea would just sit there to incriminate her. Her breathing was coming in short bursts now as she began to panic. All at once the bathroom was flooded with light and turning her head she found Mrs Foley's face inches from her own. She screamed.

'Look at you, out of bed,' the old woman said, her voice betraying no emotion. 'Isn't that . . . ' She stopped short and Patricia realised she had seen the cloudy tea-coloured water in the bowl. Her eyes went to the empty cup in Patricia's hand. Mrs Foley's lips tightened and a hard cold stare took hold of her face. Edward had been telling the truth. Patricia felt sick. She realised that for reasons she couldn't comprehend, she was in real danger. Her whole body was gripped by a breath-stealing fear.

'Let's get you back to your room, shall we?' Without waiting for an answer Mrs Foley put her arm around Patricia's shoulder, the bones of her fingers digging into her flesh, and guided her with some force across the landing. Back in bed, the blankets were tucked tightly around her and then as she left, Mrs Foley smiled sweetly. 'If you want anything just call.'

Patricia stared at the ceiling as she heard the sound of a key turning in the lock.

NOW

She kept listening to the voicemail.

'To hear the message again press two.'

There was his voice, so calm and plausible as he lied to her. Life had taught her to doubt men but somehow she had always believed her relationship with Zach was different. Thinking back she realised that she had chosen to delude herself. She never quizzed him about his life or asked the really difficult questions, and she had to admit that was less to do with trust and more about her fear of what she might find out. Everything she knew about his teenage life came through the filter of what he had chosen to tell her. She remembered how she had sat quietly while Laura and Jocelyn at work recounted horror stories about their teenage sons and assured them that her relationship with Zach was different. 'He tells me everything,' she had told her friends. 'We are more like roommates than mother and son.' Elizabeth rolled her eyes, thinking what a gullible idiot she had been. She reminded herself to give Laura and Jocelyn permission to openly gloat and really relish hearing about the enormous slice of humble pie she had been served.

Elliot had called her twice but with nothing new to report. Further messages had been left for Zach and now it seemed there was nothing to do but wait. As if reading her mind, her ex-husband patiently explained that the cops couldn't help because Zach was no longer considered a minor, and hadn't been gone for long enough to be classified as a missing person. Again she suggested that she come and join him but once more he convinced her that there was nothing to be gained. She should get on with what she was supposed to be doing. Having a task would take her mind off things. The problem was that she no longer had any interest in the original reason for her visit. Even without the rats she had no desire to go back up to Convent Hill. In the brief amount of time she had spent there, she had already realised that there was nothing she needed in those abandoned rooms, no souvenirs of a long-ago childhood that she wanted to take back to New York. What filled her mind apart from her son was the opportunity to learn more about her father and her own origins. Her mother had done such a good job of suppressing her past that Elizabeth felt like an archaeologist finding a chink of light in the tomb or the glimpse of gold beneath the layers of soil. Everything in Convent Hill was familiar to her, but now she had a taste of the unknown.

Perhaps it was the dazzling low winter sun making the world seem simpler, or maybe it was just hearing the droning duet of Gillian and Noelle as they moved around the flat, but she found herself considering a trip. Lying fully dressed on her bed Elizabeth fondled the large key she had been given the day before. A greasy knot of string attached a crumpled brown label to it. The words 'Castle House' could just be made out in ancient biro. The thought of packing her car, planning her route, seeing where she had started her life, all seemed far more appealing than sitting in Buncarragh waiting for rats to die. An adventure would distract her and, in a way, deciding what to do with this new addition to her property portfolio was more pressing than clearing out her mother's hoard of unwanted treasure. She couldn't just ignore an entire house that belonged to her and surely, Elizabeth told herself, she should at least see it before instructing some County Cork estate agent to try and offload it for her.

Extricating herself from her relatives was not a simple job. Elizabeth felt she was caught in a dense, sticky web of objections. This was not the time of year to be exploring the wilds of West Cork looking for her roots. Where would she stay? No B&Bs would be open this early in the year. What if there was a bad frost, or even, God forbid, snow? They didn't grit the roads down the country. How would she ever find the place? Fancy phones and apps wouldn't help her down there. Why was she going? What did she hope to find? The last question she left unanswered for she had no desire to tell these people any more about her life than she needed to. She made no mention of the will or her unexpected acquisition of Castle House. In order to negotiate her release from Buncarragh, she reluctantly agreed to give them her mobile number, hoping that, given it was an American cell phone, the fear of expense would prevent them from ever using it.

Eventually she was behind the steering wheel. On the seat next to her was an unfolded map of Ireland provided by her uncle, which had the roads she was looking for highlighted in red marker pen — Noelle's handiwork. Elizabeth waved at the Keane family lining the road outside the shop as if in a bad amateur production of *The Sound of Music*, and set off, letting out a long sigh of relief. She had only gone a few hundred yards past the bridge when she saw a familiar figure on the footpath. Rosemary was coming down the road with a red string bag of groceries. Her aubergine hair was being buffeted by the breeze and she was wearing a tartan overcoat that appeared to be for a much larger woman. She looked like an elderly children's entertainer. Without really deciding to, Elizabeth pulled over.

'Rosemary!' she called through her open window. The older woman put her hand up to protect her eyes from the glare of the low sun.

'It's me. Elizabeth. Patricia's girl.'

'Of course it is. Sorry. I could hardly see you there.'

'I'm heading down to Castle House.'

Rosemary looked blank.

'The Foley place, where you went to find Mammy.'

'Well, good luck to you. All I remember is that it was a hell of a drive. It'll be a lot better these days, mind you. All those new roads and you won't be worried about the engine falling out of your car.' She laughed. 'What brings you down there?'

124

'I just thought it might be nice to see it once. My birthplace and all that.'

Rosemary wrinkled her face, seeming concerned. 'I see. But tell me, what do you think you are going to find?'

Elizabeth was slightly taken aback. 'Well, I don't really know. I just want to see it, I suppose.'

Rosemary nodded. 'Well, don't get your hopes up. I've always found there are far fewer answers than there are questions.' She smiled and then slapped the side of the car with her free hand as if urging a recalcitrant horse on its way. 'Drive safe!'

The roads might have improved but the traffic hadn't. It was mid-afternoon and the light was beginning to fade as Elizabeth approached Cork. It was going to be dark soon and she didn't feel confident about finding Muirinish at night. Even if she did, where would she spend the night? She decided to follow the signs to Cork Airport, reasoning that there must be a hotel there and it would avoid her getting embroiled in the city traffic.

Sitting on the bed in her plain room, she looked out of the window at her view of the brightly lit terminal building. Maybe she should have researched her trip a little more before setting off? It was doubtful she would ever make this journey again and somehow sitting in a hotel that could have been anywhere in the world seemed a waste. She inserted the charger into her phone and went to brush her teeth. Over the insistent growl of her electric toothbrush, she thought she could hear something. What was it? Her phone! She spat into the sink and rushed into the other room. The display was lit up. Zach!

'Hello! Hello!' Her voice pleaded with the phone for it to be her boy. A pause and then . . .

'Hi, Mom.'

'Zach . . . ' Elizabeth sat on the bed, heavy with relief. 'Zach, where have you been? I, we, were so worried about you.'

'I'm sorry. I'm fine.'

'Never ever pull a stunt like this again. Oh, Zach. Why did you lie to me? Where the hell are you?' Her relief was turning quickly to anger.

'I'm with . . . I'm with my girlfriend.'

'Girlfriend? I . . . ' She was surprised into silence. Was it awful that her first thought, beyond his safety or his whereabouts, was that her son was straight? She had mentally prepared for him being gay and told herself that she would be fine about it, but her relief on hearing the word 'girlfriend' suggested that maybe she had been lying. Once more she reproached herself for all the conversations she knew she should have had but avoided. Why had she been so scared? Was she homophobic? No, she really didn't believe she was. Her problem was Elliot and the thought of him somehow being able to claim a victory. Well, he couldn't. Zach liked girls. A silly grin spread across her face.

'She lives out here and I just wanted to visit her.'

'For God's sake why wouldn't you tell me?'

'I was afraid you'd say no.'

126

Elizabeth had to admit that the chances of that were pretty high. The thought of her son flying across the country to spend time with a family she had never met wasn't the sort of thing she would have readily agreed to.

'But Zach, you didn't just do this without telling me. The emails. The emails you wrote from your father. What about them?'

'I'm sorry. I didn't mean any harm. I just really wanted to visit.'

'And, oh my God, I just remembered. Your version of Elliot claimed he'd reimburse me for your flight! Well, I will be holding you to that, Zach. You are going to pay me back every last cent, do you understand?'

'Yes, Mom. You'll get it all back. I promise.'

'How did you think you were going to get away with it all? Zach, you aren't stupid. You must have known I'd talk to your father at some point.'

There was a silence on the other end of the line and then a simple, 'I suppose.' And it broke her heart. She could picture him so clearly in that moment. His head bowed, one shoulder jerking forward, a small shuffle of his feet. Elizabeth just wanted to hug him. Smell his hair and know that he was safe in her embrace.

'Have you told your father?'

'Yes.' A slight pang. He had called Elliot first.

'And?'

'He's going to drive down to collect me in a day or two.'

'Where the hell are you?'

'Sacramento.'

127

'And who is this girl? How did you meet?'

'I met her through school.' A brief silence. 'I really like her.'

Elizabeth smiled. 'Well, that's good, honey. I'm glad. I'm also very glad that you are all right. You are never, ever, ever to do anything remotely this stupid ever again. Do you understand?'

'Yes, Mom.'

'Call me when you get to your father's, OK?'

'Yes, Mom.'

'I love you and I'm very happy you are all right. Don't scare me!'

'Sorry, Mom, I love you too. Bye.'

'Bye.' And as she pressed the little red button to hang up she began to cry. Her baby was out of danger. It was as if only now, when she knew he was all right, that she was able to admit to herself how frightened she had been. The mother that had sat for hours in the dark just listening to the rise and fall of her baby's tiny chest, holding her own breath while she waited anxiously for each warm milky exhale — it turned out she was still that woman. Would it ever get easier? She doubted it.

An hour later she was sitting at the bar downstairs with a large glass of red wine she felt she deserved. Instrumental arrangements of Coldplay songs filled the air and an anorexic artificial tree blinked in mild alarm by the entrance to the lobby. It felt odd to be travelling alone. No Zach to check on now, no academics made amorous by afternoon drinking and distance from their wives to try and avoid. For the first time in what seemed like a long time,

128

she felt calm. Elizabeth sipped her wine and looked around. Four older women gossiping and laughing at a table, maybe a post-holiday catch-up, or were they heading off for a bit of winter sun? A couple of pairs of businessmen sat opposite each other, some nursing pints, others with cups of coffee. Elizabeth tried to guess which ones were really friends and which were colleagues thrown together by commerce. Sitting alone at the bar made her feel slightly conspicuous. She thought she might just have a sandwich in her room rather than face the dining room as 'a table for one please'. She was just draining her glass and debating whether or not she should risk ordering another one, when she felt the familiar vibration in the pocket of her sweatshirt. The high-pitched alert from her phone made a couple of drinkers glance in her direction before she was able to tug it free from her pocket. Elliot. A twinge of guilt. She had meant to ring him first.

'Elliot. Sorry. I was just about to call you.' She made her way across the bar and out into the lobby.

'Elizabeth. Hi. You've heard from him, right?' She noticed his voice contained a little more irritation than relief at discovering the whereabouts of their son.

'Yes. He called. What a little fool. All of this just for a girl.'

'A girl?' An odd question. Elizabeth had a slight sinking feeling. The calmness of a moment ago had disappeared.

'Yes. That's what he told me. He went to meet up with a girl.'

'That's all he told you?'

'Yes. Why, what is it? Tell me.'

'Try woman. As far as I can ascertain this girlfriend of his is in her mid-thirties.'

Elizabeth gasped and thrust an arm against a metal pillar to steady herself. Her son was barely seventeen years old.

'What? How do you know this?'

'He told me! He thought it would make me less worried to know that he was with an older person! What should we do?'

'I don't know. I don't know. I could strangle him. He was just on the phone as if butter wouldn't melt. Who is she?'

'No clue. I remember the family name is Giardino. I'm driving down to the family home tomorrow to pick him up.'

Giardino? Giardino. Why was that name so familiar to Elizabeth? Was it a celebrity? A store she went to? A student? The answer came to her with the sudden shock of walking into a glass door.

'Michelle. Did he mention the name Michelle?'

'That's it! You know this woman?'

'She's the maths tutor that comes to the house.' She stopped herself from adding, 'the one you insisted I got.'

'And you didn't notice anything?' His tone was accusing.

'Do not try to put this on me. She just shows up every Thursday after school. Normally she leaves right after I get home.' Elizabeth felt slightly nauseous. Michelle Giardino zipping up her padded winter jacket and then freeing her long dark hair

130

from the collar, before calling out casually, 'See you next week, Zach' as she went to the door. Zach cross-legged on the floor with his textbooks spread out on the coffee table in front of him. The floor. The couch. Her bed. Had Miss Giardino been rolling around with her teenage son? Had Elizabeth been paying her to . . . she could barely bring herself to consider it . . . to fuck Zach?

'Where did she come from?'

'The school! The school recommended her.'

'Well, you have to inform them immediately.'

'Yes. Yes, of course.' But if she was being completely honest she knew she wouldn't, or at least not at once. She hated talking to the office of her son's high school. The judgement in their voices as they listened to her excuses for late payment of fees or the patronising way they explained the importance of attendance. She knew this would somehow become her fault. Only a bad mother would allow this to happen. Once more Michelle Giardino's pretty face floated into her mind's eye. A rage bubbled up inside her and she longed to reach out and smack the smug look off her face. 'Well, at least now I know why he was keeping this whole thing a secret.'

'It's her I'm pissed at,' Elliot said. 'I don't blame him. I mean, my first girlfriend was a lot older than me.'

Elizabeth's blood ran cold. Was that supposed to reassure her in some way? She didn't know how to respond so simply chose not to. The silence between them was interrupted by a slight crackle on the line.

131

'I . . . ' He sounded as if he was going to try and comfort her or qualify what he had said, but then thinking better of the idea continued, 'I'll call again after I've collected him. The three of us can have a talk.'

Elizabeth bristled. She didn't like it when Elliot decided to resume the role of parent. Swallowing her irritation, she replied, 'Yes. Talk then. Bye.'

'OK then. Bye.'

'Good luck.'

'Thanks.' A little weary chuckle and then he was gone.

The next morning banished all memory of the blue skies and brilliant winter sunshine of the day before. Mottled grey clouds hung heavily across the damp fields while strong gusts of wind shook the bare branches of the trees. The dining room of the hotel was filled with disconsolate-looking guests sitting beside packed bags. 'Delayed.' 'We don't know.' 'Might be cancelled.' The mood of the room and the lack of tables prompted Elizabeth to get some coffee in a paper cup and head out to her car.

The road to Bandon was simple enough, but then she took a wrong turn in a village called Old Chapel and ended up on the top of a hill at a crossroads where nowhere she wanted was signposted. A group of windswept children peered at her over the wall of a school playground as she turned around and headed back to the village. This time she found the right way and was soon driving beneath the imposing stone walls of the ancient abbey in Timoleague.

The road then seemed to head inland away from the coast and Elizabeth wondered if she had gone wrong again but then she emerged through a long tunnel of trees and found herself driving along a narrow causeway across what looked like a salt marsh. At the other end there was a humpbacked bridge that seemed to be almost hewn from rock. Beyond that there was a wider grass verge where she pulled over to check her map. Noelle's red marker pen stopped at the village of Muirinish, which is where Elizabeth had told them she was going, but that was slightly inland. She knew that she needed to be by the sea. Peering through the windscreen she couldn't see anything that resembled a house or even an entrance. Maybe it had been knocked down years before and she was now the proud owner of some rubble? Grabbing her handbag, she decided to get out of the car and explore a little on foot.

The wind was strong, but after so long in the car she enjoyed it rushing across her face, tasting the salt from the sea. The road curved slightly and the trees became a little thicker, but then she came to a gap that was filled with dead grass. Pushing forward she saw the rusted remains of a gate leaning against the wall. This was the entrance to a lane or old driveway. Elizabeth hesitated for a moment, thinking how under-prepared she was for this sort of exploration. Her sneakers and thin jeans would be soaked. Maybe she should wait until she had got some wellington boots from somewhere? No. There were dry clothes to change into back in the car.

It wasn't ideal but it would have to do. Taking high steps and trying to flatten the grass, she continued. Back from the road the lane was slightly less overgrown and she found she was able to pick her way along a single track, avoiding most of the puddles and patches of mud. To her right behind a low stone wall were some geriatric apple trees. On the left was a sloping meadow that looked as if it had been used for grazing fairly recently. She could hear the sea but wasn't able to see it until the lane climbed gently and all at once there it was, stretching out in front of her. Elizabeth gasped, it was so beautiful. A couple of lines of a Keats sonnet she had been teaching that semester popped into her head.

'*Oh ye! who have your eyeballs vexed and*
    tired,
Feast them upon the wideness of the Sea.'

The sea. The sound of it, the smell, the ragged white edges as it met the distant cliffs. She scanned the horizon, wondering about her mother Patricia. Had she stood here? Was this the first time Elizabeth had looked out at this view or had her infant eyes already soaked it in just to forget it all? It was only then that she caught sight of the house wedged between the sea and the ruins of a castle. That must be it. Castle House. With a burst of enthusiasm, she made her way as quickly as she could down towards her legacy.

Elizabeth wasn't exactly sure what she had

134

been expecting but this house wasn't it. Not grand enough to be a country pile, but not small enough to be considered a cottage, it was a nondescript two-storeyed house that had clearly seen better days. Faded blue paint was cracked and peeling off the windows and doors. Behind the glass, net curtains hung grey and exhausted. The path from the small gate to the porch had disappeared under a carpet of weeds. Behind the house loomed the castle with its ghostly outline. The wind seemed to be pursuing itself around the walls and Elizabeth felt oddly ill at ease. She wouldn't have said she was frightened but nor was she sure that she wanted to let herself into this house alone. A few small clouds of spume danced on the air and the roar of the waves sounded almost threatening. She felt for the key in her bag and held it for a moment.

At first the lock seemed so stiff that Elizabeth thought the house had made her decision for her: she wouldn't be going inside. But suddenly it had a change of heart and the key lurched to one side. She twisted the handle and the door swung open with a long creak. Peering into the gloomy interior Elizabeth could see the dusty floor covered in a scattering of dead flies and bees, with a staircase leading up into darkness. She found a light switch and to her great surprise it worked. A weak bulb illuminated the hall and Elizabeth stepped fully inside and pulled the door behind her. A room on either side. She opened one door and then the other. Both rooms were more or less the same apart from the wallpaper. Newspapers were scattered on the floors. Only a single wooden chair splattered with paint remained of the furniture. Small drifts of soot lay in front of the fireplaces. She was struck by how loud her footsteps seemed. Moving past the staircase she went through an open door into the kitchen. A few of the cupboard doors were hanging open as if abandoned and small piles of dusty crockery were dotted along the counter tops. Against what must be the back door a broom was resting, as if someone had decided to do some cleaning but then thought better of the idea. Again, the light switch worked and the bare neon tube on the ceiling flickered into life. Somehow the brightness made the room seem even colder. Elizabeth shuddered and stepped back into the hall. She examined the staircase. Would it be safe? She wondered if the floors upstairs would hold her weight. Did she need to go up? What was she looking for? This was just some abandoned house with no trace of the people who had called it home. She wondered how long it had been empty.

Unwilling to admit defeat and determined to find some trace of her father in this house, she tentatively started up the stairs. The creaking floorboards joined in with the rattle of the window frames and Elizabeth realised she was walking on tiptoe, sneaking her way around the house as if she was afraid to disturb it. Upstairs it was almost dark. She felt for the switch but it clicked ineffectually. Turning to go back downstairs towards the light she thought she heard a noise. A clicking sound that stopped and

136

started with no sense of rhythm. It seemed to be coming from the bedroom door opposite the top of the stairs. Somehow her curiosity was stronger than her fear and she stepped across the landing. Silence, but then there it was again. Tap, tap, tap. Silence. She put her hand on the door knob and twisted. A pause. Two deep breaths and then she pushed open the door. She saw the long-toed feet moving across the floor and then a whole flapping pigeon hurled itself at her in an explosion of feathers. She felt the heavy warmth of its body graze across her face. Elizabeth screamed and fled down the stairs and out of the front door only to find her way blocked by a man. She screamed again.

'Sorry, sorry. I didn't mean to frighten you.' The man took a couple of steps back. Her heart pounding wildly, Elizabeth tried to examine her would-be attacker. He was a little taller than her but around the same age, she guessed. He had short dark hair and was wearing a tattered green V-neck jumper over a collarless shirt. He didn't look particularly dangerous.

'You gave me a shock,' she said, still panting slightly. 'I wasn't expecting anyone and I've just been attacked by a pigeon.'

He smiled and Elizabeth was struck by his white even teeth. In fact, now that she looked more closely, all his features were fairly uniform. She might even have described him as handsome.

'I just saw the lights on. I was working on the fences below.' He indicated the field between the house and the sea. 'My name is Brian, by the way.'

'I'm Elizabeth.' They shook hands and she was shocked by how rough his skin was. It was more like hide or leather than someone's palm.

'Nice to meet you, Elizabeth. What brings you down here on such a bad day?'

'Well.' Elizabeth realised she was still holding the key. 'This is where I was born.'

'Really? That's amazing.'

'Yes, it was my father's house. Edward Foley, I never knew him or this place. He died when I was very little.'

'Edward Foley? Sure, he's not dead.'

From inside the house came a crashing sound as the pigeon tried to make good its escape.

THEN

It was like a switch had been turned off. Mrs Foley stopped speaking. The sluice gates had been shut and the torrent of words ceased. She still brought in the trays — there had been no more sightings of Edward — but she did so in silence. No platitudes, no weather updates, no bland reassurances, she was just thin-lipped and expressionless. At first Patricia was unnerved and then as she grew stronger and wanted answers she realised she couldn't get them from a woman who refused to speak.

'I need to phone home.'

'Where are my clothes?'

'Why can't I leave?'

The truth was that Patricia was still very weak. Now that she had stopped drinking the tea she had become nervous of everything on the trays. She left soups or stews untouched. She nibbled at bread, imagining the butter had an odd taste. The less she ate, the smaller her appetite became. She did get out of bed occasionally, but her steps were slow and uncertain. Any sudden movements and she was overcome by dizziness. She found an old blanket in the wardrobe and, wrapped in it, she would sit very still by the window. Somehow the constant howl of the wind and the rattle of the window frame became more bearable if she could see the dark clouds moving across the sky and watch the mammoth rolling

139

sea swell and crash against the cliffs.

Pressing her forehead against the cold glass she dreamt of escape. Jumping from her window onto the porch below and then to the ground. Overpowering Mrs Foley and racing down the stairs to leave the house through the kitchen. Of course these plans would never come to pass. She knew she didn't have the strength and even if she did, how far would she get wrapped in a blanket with nothing on her feet? The pub was too far and she didn't know the way to the village. She remembered what Edward had said about the Foleys building the castle on this spot because it was so difficult to reach. Hard to get in, hard to get out. She daydreamed about Buncarragh and what was going on there. Where did people think she was? Did anyone care or were they so involved in their own lives that they hadn't really noticed? Oddly she only cried when she thought about Convent Hill. Wept, imagining the empty rooms, the pot plants going unwatered, the block of Cheddar growing dark and cracked in the door of the fridge. She longed to return to her lonely life. The loneliness that had driven her to this awful place now seemed like a state of bliss.

One afternoon she was lying in bed drifting in and out of sleep when a noise caught her ear. It wasn't coming from inside the house. She listened more closely. It was an engine and it didn't sound as if it was at the back in the farmyard. A car engine! She jumped out of bed, almost falling, her body unused to such exertion. At the window she pulled aside the net curtain and craned her neck to catch a glimpse of the drive at the side of the house. Jutting out in front of the wall she could see the bonnet of a car. It was a little blue Fiat. Rosemary had a car like that! Patricia pressed the side of her face flat against the window-pane to try and see more. A coat flapped. Mustard. Rosemary's coat, the one with the brown velvet collar. Rosemary had come to rescue her! She rapped her knuckles as hard as she dared against the glass. 'Rosemary, I'm up here! Rosemary!' she called out. The coat stayed where it was, being played with by the sea breeze. She banged on the window again. 'Rosemary. It's me, Patricia. Rosemary! Up here!' The coat moved and for a moment the face of her friend was visible but then she waved a hand and ducked down to get back in her car. She was leaving! 'No. Rosemary! I'm here. I'm up here.' She raced across the room and tried the door handle in vain. Still locked.

Frantic, Patricia picked up the chair from beside the bed and rushing at the window smashed a leg through a pane of glass. The noise and violence shocked her, and she stood still for a moment, before dropping the chair and rushing to the broken window. 'Rosemary!' she howled into the bitter breeze. It was too late. A horrified Patricia watched the blue bonnet inching backwards. 'No. I'm up here,' but her voice was little more than a whisper now. She pressed her palm against the window and sank to the floor. Her body was convulsed by weeping, her mouth stretched wide by gasping sobs. So close, but her tears weren't just for her missed opportunity to escape, they were the relieved tears of a woman who had discovered that somebody truly cared about her. Rosemary, silly, funny Rosemary had driven all the way from Buncarragh all by herself because she was so worried for her friend. Patricia threw herself onto the bed and let her tears soak into the pillow, until eventually she fell asleep.

She was woken with a start by a dishevelled Mrs Foley bursting into her room, a red and white tea towel flapping in one hand. She picked up the chair that was lying on the floor and put it back by the bed. Then she turned her full attention to Patricia. Mrs Foley's face was crimson with rage and spittle flew from her mouth as she spat out her words.

'You'd better learn to behave, Missy. Any more nonsense like that, I will tie you to that bed. Do you hear me? Hand and foot! Your precious Edward won't save you! Do you understand?'

This was a Mrs Foley that Patricia hadn't seen before. She seemed crazed and unpredictable. Dangerous. The tea towel was twisted tightly between her fists and Patricia was reminded of the night she had seen the old woman wring the chicken's neck in the outhouse. 'Do you understand me?' she asked again.

'Yes,' Patricia whispered and then a little louder, 'I understand.'

'Good. And maybe that will blow some sense into you.' The old lady waved a hand, trembling with anger, at the broken window, 'because I won't be fixing it.'

She slammed the door and turned the key.

Patricia didn't know how long she had been left alone for or what time it was, but it was dark outside when the door opened again and Edward inched his way into the room. He was carrying a sheet of cardboard. She knew her eyes must be red and swollen but she didn't care.

'I've come to fix the window.' He was speaking in a whisper. Patricia wondered if his mother knew that he was doing this.

He crossed the room and began to tear out a square of cardboard.

'It was my friend Rosemary. People are looking for me. You are going to have to let me go. I have to go home, Edward,' Patricia implored him. 'You can't just keep me here. It's wrong!' She had to make him understand.

He turned and walked to the bed. 'You're not to upset Mammy. Please. You don't understand, Patricia. Don't rile her. It will only make things worse for you.'

He sounded deadly serious. Patricia wasn't sure if it was the cold from the broken window or fear, but she was shivering. What was Mrs Foley capable of?

★ ★ ★

More days went by. How many? Patricia couldn't be certain. It became light, it got dark, the days crept past her window. Sometimes the wind whistled around the eaves, or she might wake to hear it roaring past the house, rattling the windows, but it never seemed to stop. Patricia struggled to remember what silence sounded

143

like. Once or twice she thought she heard a car or voices but it was just the crashing of a high tide or the wind in the branches. She found some old magazines in an otherwise empty wardrobe, and dutifully flicked through them. The *People's Friend. Woman's Weekly*. Not magazines she could ever imagine Mrs Foley buying. She read stories of romance. Nurses falling in love with doctors while they saved lives in Africa, Scottish chieftains grabbing red-haired farm girls roughly and throwing them down on banks of heather, but always with a happy ending. Patricia had no idea how her strange tale would conclude. They couldn't keep her here forever and why would they want to? It made no sense.

One morning Mrs Foley came into her room as usual and placed the tray along the side of the bed. Patricia ignored her. There was nothing to be gained from asking questions. How many times had she pleaded with the old woman to tell her about Rosemary, what she had said to her friend? But nothing. Just the plates of barely touched food collected at regular intervals.

Mrs Foley jabbed a finger at the tray. 'Some post for you there.' Patricia jolted with the shock of hearing a voice and rattled the cup and saucer. Before she could gather her thoughts and respond, the old woman had left, turning the key in the lock.

There were four envelopes. Two were white, one blue and the other a sort of pale yellow. They looked like Christmas or birthday cards. She opened the first one and pulled out its contents.

On the front of the card was a picture of two birds, doves perhaps, using their beaks to tie a knot in a long piece of red ribbon that spelled out in its curves and folds the word, 'Congratulations'. How odd. She opened it up. In black print it said, 'Congratulations on your wedding day', and below that was a handwritten note. 'We are all so happy for you. Many congratulations to yourself and Edward. Please come and visit. Love from Gillian, Jerry and the family.' Patricia didn't know what to think. She felt as if she was going crazy. Her stomach tightened and her breathing had become swift and shallow. The next card showed some wedding bells in a throng of roses and inside was a note from Carol Daunt. Carol Daunt? They hadn't even been friends in school. Why would she send a card? The third one was a cartoon of two rabbits sharing a carrot. Inside it said, 'May there be more than fences running around your garden!' The message was from Rosemary. 'Sorry to have missed you. Hope you are feeling much better. I'm so happy for you and Edward. I wish you a long and happy life together.' This was madness. Impatiently she ripped open the fourth envelope. It was from Rosemary's parents. They too shared her joy. Pushing the tray aside Patricia got out of bed and began to hammer on the bedroom door. 'Mrs Foley! What is going on? Mrs Foley!'

The sound of footsteps on the stairs followed by the familiar sound of the lock and then Edward's mother stood before her. She looked defiant. She smoothed her apron and in a perfectly calm voice enquired, 'What can I do for you, dear?' Patricia didn't know where to start. Her mouth opened and closed but no words came. Finally, she grabbed the cards and held them up to Mrs Foley's face.

'What are these? Why are people sending them?'

'Well, I suppose people are happy for you.'

'Happy? What for? I'm not married. You are keeping me a prisoner. What lies have you been telling people?'

'Edward loves you very much and the sooner you understand that then the sooner we can all carry on as normal.' She paused and the women stared at each other.

'This is madness. Madness! You are out of your mind!' Patricia screamed and then, breathless, crushed the cards into her fist. She stood barefoot, wearing nothing but a nightdress that wasn't even her own. Mrs Foley's face was steely as she met the young woman's eyes. Slowly she moved one foot away from the other, bracing herself, almost challenging her young charge to try and get past her. 'It's up to you, my dear.' And with that she turned on her heel, locking the door behind her.

The hours passed. Bouts of crying were interspersed with sleep. Darkness came but Patricia didn't bother with the light. Mrs Foley had turned it on when she had delivered the dinner tray but Patricia had quickly extinguished it, preferring to lie forgotten and unseen in the night. Her dinner sat on the floor, untouched. Patricia wondered how long it would take her to starve to death. Would Edward and his mother allow that to happen? Surely they would take her to the hospital before she died? Then she could raise the alarm and this torment would be over. Maybe they would just tell the doctors that she was crazy and the more she insisted she wasn't, the madder she would seem. That happened in films all the time.

★   ★   ★

At first Patricia paid no heed to the knocking. She assumed it must have been Edward with a hammer or Mrs Foley working on something, but then she heard voices. A man's voice! That wasn't Edward. It must have been the door knocker. There was a visitor in the house! She knelt on the floor and pressed herself against the door. Yes, that was Mrs Foley and the voice of a stranger. One of the doors at the front of the house was opened and closed. Patricia stood up. This was her chance to raise the alarm. Somebody from the outside world could tell people she was here. She looked around the room for something to make noise, but then decided to simply begin stamping on the floor. They might be sitting in the room below. After stamping loudly, she paused and listened, waiting for some reaction — feet on the stairs, a voice calling — but the house remained in silence. Had they left the house? Surely she would have heard them moving around the hallway? She stamped again, but still there was no response. Patricia moved to the door and began to hammer on it, but again there was no reaction.

'Help!' she called and knocked on the door as hard as she could. Silence. How could it be that she couldn't be heard? She banged again and yelled out for help. Nothing. Had she been mistaken? Had she imagined the voices? She went and lay on her bed.

A short while later she heard a door and the man's voice in the hall again. She hadn't dreamt it! Rushing to the door she began to drum hard against the wood with her fists. 'Help! Please help me!' She waited, but the only sound she heard was the front door being swung shut.

She crossed the room to the window and saw a priest cycling unsteadily down the thin gravel path towards the lane. She knocked on the window but she knew it was futile. Her rescuer had gone. She braced herself for the arrival of Mrs Foley. Doubtless, she would storm up the stairs to berate her for daring to make such a racket, but no visit came.

It was hours later when the door opened slowly and Mrs Foley placed a cup of tea delicately on her bedside locker.

'I thought you might have worked up a thirst.'

Patricia couldn't look at her.

'I had a nice visit there from Father Manning. He called out to meet Edward's new bride.'

Despite herself, Patricia looked at Mrs Foley aghast. This was so completely insane, she thought she might faint.

The old woman was leaning against the door frame, with a studied air of nonchalance.

'I explained to him that you suffer something terrible with your nerves. He was most sympathetic. Very understanding. We said a little prayer together for you. Do you feel any better, Patricia?' Mrs Foley's voice was cloying with mock concern.

Patricia wanted to get as far away from this woman as she could. She ran to the corner of the room and pushed her face against the wall, grinding her teeth with fury and frustration.

A small voice from across the room said, 'Ah, the power of prayer.' And the door closed with a click.

★   ★   ★

Downstairs a door was opened and then shut and she heard a little snatch of the theme to *The Late Late Show*. Saturday. It must be Saturday, she thought. How many nights had she lain in her own bedroom in Buncarragh while her mother watched the television in the living room beneath? In her mind she saw the faces of people she knew back home lit up by the flickering screen as they sat in front of their televisions. Not one of them thinking of her lying alone and helpless in the dark.

She must have fallen asleep again because the next thing she was aware of was someone gently tapping her shoulder. Opening her eyes with a start she could immediately make out Edward's large frame against the light spilling into her room from the landing.

'Edward?'

'Shush, she'll hear you,' he whispered urgently. Then getting his face so close to hers that she could feel his breath against her cheek, he spoke slowly and quietly. 'Tomorrow night. Be ready. And eat. The food is safe now.' He stood up straight and turned to the door. Just before he closed it he put his head back into the room and repeated in a whisper, 'Tomorrow night.'

Patricia stared into the darkness. What was going to happen tomorrow night? Was it something to look forward to or dread? Could she trust Edward? She felt more awake than she had in many days.

★ ★ ★

'Aren't you a good girl?' Mrs Foley cooed when she came to collect Patricia's tray. 'That's more like it. You'll be up and around in no time.'

Patricia smiled, before she remembered that she wasn't an invalid and Mrs Foley was her gaoler, not some selfless Florence Nightingale. She twisted her body to the wall and the old woman left her room.

The hours seemed to pass even more slowly when she was anticipating . . . what? What had Edward meant? The sunlight left the sky and still she waited. Would there be a sign? Might she miss it? She wouldn't go to sleep. Edward had told her to be ready.

Dinner came and went but nothing happened. Maybe Edward was wrong, or had something changed? She sat on her bed and listened for something out of the ordinary.

150

Despite her best intentions, she fell asleep. When she woke up someone had switched off her light. She turned it back on. The curtains were drawn. Sitting up, Patricia thought she could hear voices. They sounded excited or distressed and seemed to be some distance from the house. She leapt from her bed and hurried to peer out of the window. She just caught a glimpse of Mrs Foley, bent against the wind, with a coat pulled over her nightdress. She seemed to be shouting at someone. Feeling braver, Patricia pressed herself against the glass. She could hear Edward's voice coming from further away and there was something strange about the way the light played against the side of the house. An uneven orange glow. Mrs Foley appeared again, this time carrying a couple of heavy-looking buckets. A fire! There must be a fire somewhere. Was this what Edward had meant? Was this the moment, her opportunity to escape? She rushed to the door and tried the handle. It opened! On the floor in front of her was a brown tweed coat and an old pair of shoes in worn black leather. Edward! He must have left them for her. Patricia put her feet into the shoes — a little big but they'd do — and then slipped on the heavy coat. She paused at the top of the stairs and listened. The voices were still coming from outside. Holding on to the banister to steady herself, she made her way downstairs as quickly as she could. Mrs Foley had been at the front of the house so Patricia headed through the kitchen. Still unsure of her balance she leaned on the chairs by the table and slowly made her way

151

towards the back door. Reaching it she suddenly worried that it would be locked. Her heart felt tight and frantic. She lifted the latch and the old door fell towards her with the force of the wind.

Patricia stepped outside into the blast of chill night air. She found she was gulping it in like a drowning man who has just made his way to the surface. She felt giddy, elated even, to be outside.

Keeping close to the wall, she made her way across the yard back towards the lane. She felt the heat of the fire before she saw it. Turning the corner she could see the blaze was in the orchard. Banners of orange flames were furling against the night sky. Suddenly Edward and his mother appeared struggling with a hose. Patricia threw herself back into the shadows. She realised it would be too risky to head straight for the lane that led down to the road. She would have to cut through the fields behind the orchard and get back to the road that way. Keeping her head low, she darted towards the milking parlour and using it for cover made her way towards the field. It was much harder to see anything now but she knew that if she kept the glow of the flames to her right then she was heading in the correct direction. She seemed to be on some sort of narrow path and decided to follow it rather than risk cutting directly across the wet grass of the field. Putting one foot in front of the other, she kept trying to find the firmer ground. Already she felt a little breathless and tired, as the adrenaline wore off, and the reality of making her way through the rough unchartered territory began to take its toll on her. The path seemed to be taking her slightly downhill and all she could see of the fire were tiny sparks bobbing high above her.

The path became muddier. Cold water seeped into her shoes. She didn't care. The only option was to keep going. The sharp grass whipped painfully at her bare legs, but the road couldn't be that much further. She stopped to try and get her bearings. The glow from the orchard was still to her right but seemed further away than she thought it should be. If only a car would drive by so she could see some headlights and make her way towards them. When she started to walk again she was surprised by the way she had sunk into the mud. It took some effort to pull her feet out and she nearly lost one of her shoes. It didn't help that the cold air had found its way beneath her coat and her body had begun to shiver violently. Her feet were numb.

She smelled it first. The tang of salt mixed with something much darker, almost rotten. It reminded her of something and then it struck her; the marsh that they had driven over. She realised that she was no longer wading through a muddy field. The path must have led her down to the sea. She could hear the lapping of water. She turned to try and go back the way she had come but her left foot suddenly plunged her up to her thigh in the cold muddy sand. She gasped and fell backwards. When she righted herself she wasn't sure which direction she had been facing in. A fluttering panic took hold of her and she began to whimper. Reaching forward she found a clump of reeds to hold on to. Pulling herself with

153

whatever strength she still possessed, she managed to free her left foot which was now shoeless. She held on to the grass and tried to catch her breath. Looking around, she could just make out some shadowy shapes in the distance but nothing that looked familiar or could help her decide in what direction she should be heading. Summoning all her energy she stood up and took a couple of unsteady steps away from the sound of the sea, but then with a horrible jolt she found herself submerged up to her waist in the icy cold mud. She let out an involuntary scream. Immediately she worried that someone might have heard her but then realised that was what she needed to happen. She stretched her arms as far as she could but could feel no grass or reeds to get hold of. The cold circle of mud around her body seemed to be creeping higher. She twisted to her left and then the right, but there was nothing but a blanket of blackness surrounding her.

She called out: 'Help!' Even to her own ears it sounded feeble. 'Help me!' She tried to call louder but it was hopeless. Her violent shivering meant it was almost impossible for her to catch a breath. She could no longer feel her legs. Her flailing hands seemed to be finding more and more water. The tide must be coming in, she thought, and a crescendo of panic was followed by a deep sense of calm. This was to be her end. She let her body go limp and sink a little further. She remembered the story of the man coming home from the pub. They had found his bike. There would be no trace of her. A great tiredness settled upon her and she wondered if she might just fall asleep and never wake up. Warm, why did she feel so warm? She struggled with the buttons at the collar of her coat like a drunk trying to get undressed. The water was lapping around her armpits now. She couldn't tell if her eyes were open or closed. The darkness was everywhere.

At first she thought it was a noise in her head. A low growl. Maybe it was the wind. A car? A boat? But then long beams of light were thrust out across the water and Patricia stared at the hollow grey runway of illuminated waves. She half-expected to see something emerge from the surf. Then the beams of light shifted slightly towards her. They were wider and the engine sound was much louder. Finally, the beams hit her full in the face. She closed her eyes and did her best to wave her arms above her head. She tried to yell but couldn't.

The diesel and smoke of the tractor filled the air and then Edward's voice.

'Don't move. I'm going to get you out. Stay still.'

She saw the outline of him as he walked in front of the tractor's headlights but then he disappeared. The sound of splashing came from behind her and then she felt a tugging on her coat. Slowly, so slowly, her body shifted up through the mud. Her breasts were free and Edward had his arms around her now, heaving her towards him.

'I've got you. That's it. I've got you. You're safe now. Gently.'

Eventually her whole body had been freed and she found that she was lying on top of Edward. His chest was rising and falling with the effort of his exertions. He eased himself from beneath her and putting his arms under her, he cradled her like a bride before the threshold. Slowly, taking one careful step at a time, he headed towards the tractor, its engine still running. Patricia pressed her marble-cold face into the heat of his body. She could just make out his voice above the sound of the engine and the wind slapping the sea.

'Why? Why did you have to come this way? If only you had gone through the paddock. She'll never let you go now. Never.'

Patricia wasn't sure, but it sounded as if he was crying.

NOW

It was a long, low building with unpainted grey plaster walls and a short gravel driveway. It looked more like a large bungalow than whatever Elizabeth had imagined a nursing home might be. A chain made of white plastic protected the edges of the square of lawn that ran down to the road where a discreet sign announced that this was Abbey Court Care Home. It seemed so sad to Elizabeth that a man who had spent his life in the rugged splendour she had found at Muirinish should end his days in this bland suburban setting.

Brian pulled the car right up to the door and switched off the engine.

'So, I've got a few bits to do in town. I'll be back for you in, say, an hour and a half? That sound about right?'

'Perfect!'

After her initial shock at the news that her father was still alive, Brian had explained that he had just bought the land at Muirinish but that as far as he knew for the last four or five years Edward had been in full-time care. Before she'd had an opportunity to think about it, Brian had offered her a lift to the care home and rung his aunt, who normally only took in visitors during the summer months, but after a brief conversation had agreed to accommodate Elizabeth. It made a refreshing change to have someone else take charge.

The care home was about an hour's drive inland just outside Clonteer, the nearest town. Elizabeth had been nervous about spending that much time in a car with a total stranger but in fact the conversation flowed easily. At times she felt he was flirting and occasionally she was fairly certain that she was flirting back. Brian was one of those men who seemed very comfortable in their own skin and Elizabeth liked that. He had a confidence and seemed to take pleasure in making her laugh. It was fun to spend time with an unattached man with zero expectations.

After Elliot she had been on a few dates. She'd felt she should, not just to help her get over the humiliation of the divorce but also to reassert herself as a woman who could be attractive to men. It was the end of a relationship, not her life, she reasoned. The love of her life might still be waiting for her.

Well-meaning friends from Hunter had set her up on dates. A professor old enough to be her father, followed by a middle-aged man from Admissions who got so drunk he had been sick on her shoes. She had tried the various apps but after a few dates with men either still obsessed by an ex-wife, not divorced or an extremely noisy eater — other tables had turned to look! — she had decided to just be single for a while. It didn't help matters that none of her dud dates had bothered to get in touch hoping for a second chance. She appeared to be off the market whether she wanted to be or not. She had her work and her friends and then as Zach got older she found that she had begun to rely on him for company. Now she worried that doing so might have had something to do with the whole Michelle Giardino situation.

'Are you travelling by yourself?' Brian had asked.

'Yes. I have family up the country. My mother died. I'm back to sort things out.'

'I'm sorry to hear that. It's hard. I lost my mother three years ago.'

'She'd been ill.'

Elizabeth felt Brian stealing glances at her as they drove along.

'And have you family waiting for you back in New York?'

'No. Well, a son but he's visiting his father. I'm divorced.'

'Snap!' Brian said with a laugh. 'Two years. How about you?'

'Nearly eight for me,' she replied cheerfully.

'Turns out living on a farm isn't that much fun. She . . . sorry, do you mind me talking about this?'

'No, not at all. I love hearing about other people's unhappy relationships.' They both laughed. 'Where did you meet?' Elizabeth asked quickly, to confirm that her interest was genuine.

'A wedding. Where love stories begin. She was down from Dublin. My friend Kevin was marrying a friend of hers. We hit it off and then we dated long distance for nearly a year before I popped the question.'

'Had she . . . what's her name?'

'Sara without an 'H'.'

'Had Sara never been to the farm?'

'She had. I'm not really being fair. It was the winters more than the farm itself. She enjoyed it when she could get out and do things, we had a little boat, but the winters are long.'

'Any kids?'

'No kids. We tried but no joy. Now of course I'm so glad. Able to make a clean break of it. What about yourself?'

'A son.'

'Yes, you said. I suppose I meant, what went wrong?'

'It's complicated.'

'Jesus. That bad.'

They turned to each other and grinned.

★　★　★

As Brian drove away, Elizabeth found herself standing in silence outside the glass and pine front door of Abbey Court. She wondered why there were no other cars. Perhaps there was a car park she hadn't noticed. She crunched across the gravel and tentatively opened the door. Inside was a generous hallway covered in a shiny cream lino. A series of closed doors each had black plastic signs on them. 'Office', 'Staff', 'Day Room'. A corridor led in either direction across the back of the space. Elizabeth was just about to knock on the door marked 'Office' when a tall, thin man with a shock of ginger hair came around the corner of the corridor. He was carrying a dark blue rucksack, and his tight skinny jeans were punctuated by the sort of heavily padded trainers some of her cooler students wore in New York, but certainly weren't what she had expected to find in Clonteer.

'Can I help you?'

'Hello. I was hoping to see a patient.'

'Resident.'

'Sorry?'

'That's what we call them here. Residents.' He smiled, seeming to acknowledge that what the old people were called wouldn't change their circumstances.

'A resident, then,' Elizabeth said with a wry grin. 'I was hoping to see a resident.'

'Well, I'm afraid these aren't visiting times. The evening staff have just started their shift. Can you come back in an hour or so?'

'Oh, that might be difficult. I'm just visiting the area, you see. Do you work here? Could you bend the rules?'

'I'm a nurse. Day shift. Just finishing.' He tapped his rucksack to indicate his imminent departure.

Elizabeth tried to conceal her surprise. This was not how she had pictured a nurse. It seemed Abbey Court was going to defy all her expectations.

'I tell you what, if you take a seat in the day room for ten minutes I'm sure I can get you in.'

'Thank you. Thank you so much.' The nurse opened the door and Elizabeth stepped inside. Groups of high-backed chairs stood in small semicircles scattered around the large room. The far wall was glass and looked out onto a well-tended garden with some mature trees. It wasn't what anyone would have described as cosy but nor did it have a cold institutional glare.

'Can I get you a tea or a coffee?'

'But you must be going?'

'Ah, I'm in no rush. I might have one meself.'

'Coffee then, please. If you're sure, now?'

'Certain. It'll only be instant, is that OK?'

'Great, thanks.'

The nurse disappeared into a small kitchenette off to the side of the room and Elizabeth sat in one of the chairs nearest to her. A copy of the *Irish Examiner* was folded neatly on the table and a pile of heavily-used-looking board games was stacked against the wall.

'I'm Gordon, by the way,' the nurse called from the small room.

'Elizabeth. This is very kind of you.'

'No bother. Who is it you wanted to see?'

'An old man. Edward Foley. Do you know him?'

'Old Teddy? Oh, I do. He's a sweet old thing. Is it long since you've seen him?'

Elizabeth paused, unsure of how to answer the question. She didn't want to lie, but to tell the truth seemed like such an unwieldy story. Before she could decide on her response, Gordon added, 'I mean, he's not really with us any more, a world of his own, like, but he's no bother. You can't say that about all of them.' Elizabeth's heart sank. A wasted journey. There would be no answers. No deathbed reunion weeping for all the wasted years. The past would go unmourned.

Gordon emerged with two steaming mugs and chose the seat next to Elizabeth. 'A relative, is he?'

162

'Well, he's actually my father.' It felt odd and almost a little forbidden to be saying such words out loud, especially to a stranger. She felt her mother's disapproval.

Gordon raised his pale eyebrows. 'Really?' It was a question that asked so much. Why has no one mentioned his daughter? Where have you been? What are you doing here now?

Elizabeth decided it was easiest to just say, 'Yes.'

Gordon understood that it was best not to pry any further so picked up his coffee. 'Oh, do you take sugar? Sorry.'

'No. This is great, thanks.'

They both took a sip.

Outside two pigeons kept sentry, marching up and down the concrete path beyond the patio doors.

'Have you worked here long, Gordon?'

'No. Just a few months. I was nursing up in Dublin but . . . well, a bad break-up, and like the classic Irish boy I am, I came running home to Mammy.'

Elizabeth looked at Gordon. His head was bowed, his clear grey eyes studying the floor. She noticed how gaunt his cheeks were, the way his long jaw curved sharply up to his ears. She wondered who had broken his tender young heart.

'Sorry to hear that. And do you enjoy it here?'

'Ah, it's not so bad. The residents are mostly lovely, and the job is easy enough — well, apart from all the dying.' He shrugged and wrapped his hands around the warm mug. 'To be honest, come the spring, I'll probably head back to Dublin or maybe over to London. You know, lots of work, and God knows I'm hardly going to find a new boyfriend in Clonteer.' Something in Elizabeth's expression must have betrayed her surprise because Gordon immediately continued. 'I'm sorry. I didn't mean to shock you. I just assumed . . . '

'No, no,' Elizabeth interrupted him, 'my husband is gay.'

Silence. Why on earth had she said that? It must have been the talk in the car with Brian. The words floated in the air between them.

'Was,' she said, trying to clarify things, but Gordon looked even more surprised. 'Was my husband. Is gay. Sorry, I have no idea why I said that.'

'No, thanks for telling me. Always good to know there are more out there!' Gordon laughed. 'It's easy to forget living here.'

'I can imagine,' Elizabeth agreed with a grin.

The door from the hall was thrown open and a short woman with scraped-back hair and thick legs strode into the day room. She stopped short when she saw Elizabeth and Gordon.

'Oh. I wasn't aware anyone was using the day room at present. Gordon, isn't your shift over?'

Gordon stood up. 'It is. Elizabeth, this is our Care Director. It is Care Director, isn't it?'

A stern glare was aimed in his direction. 'Yes, Gordon, it is Care Director. Pleased to meet you, Elizabeth. I'm Sarah Cahill, Care Director here at Abbey Court.' The two women shook hands. 'Has Gordon been assisting you?'

'Oh yes, thank you. Very helpful.' Elizabeth had an uneasy feeling that she was going to get Gordon into some sort of trouble. 'I was hoping to see a relative of mine.'

'I explained about the visiting hours,' Gordon interjected hastily.

'Yes. Yes he did,' Elizabeth confirmed. 'It's just that I'm only passing through and I'm not sure when I can get back.'

Sarah smiled warmly. 'Not a problem. Not a problem at all. Gordon should have just come to find me.'

Gordon stared at her. His expression suggested that the last time he allowed a visitor in out of hours she had threatened to sack him.

'What resident is it?'

'Edward Foley.'

'It's old Teddy,' Gordon said to clarify.

Another stern look. 'Thank you, Gordon. Mr Foley is in room three. I wonder if you could show Elizabeth to his room please, Gordon?'

More smiles and handshakes and then Sarah was gone, clicking across the polished linoleum floor.

'Two-faced cow,' Gordon muttered under his breath.

'I hope I didn't get you into trouble.'

'No problem. She has it in for me, that one. Come on, I'll show you to Teddy.'

The room reminded her of when her mother had been ill. The sour smell of badly washed bodies mixed with the lingering stench of human waste. The room itself was narrow and long with a large window at the opposite end. A single bed

165

was pushed against the side wall and in it lay an old man. Elizabeth stepped towards him. His rheumy eyes were open but unfocused. Wisps of grey hair sprouted from his head, while patches of stubble dotted his parchment-yellow face where he had been haphazardly shaved by a busy nurse. He looked unkempt and uncared for. His green and white pyjamas were buttoned right up to his throat. The only sound was the slow rasp of his breathing, his dry lips hung apart.

'Now, Teddy,' Gordon almost shouted at the old man. Elizabeth started. 'There's a visitor here for you. Isn't that great?'

The old man did not seem interested in the news. His gaze didn't shift, his breathing didn't alter.

'Say hello to him. Squeeze his hand. He likes that.'

Elizabeth felt uncertain. It seemed too forward, too intrusive somehow.

'Edward,' she said and then a little louder, 'I'm Elizabeth.' Reaching forward she touched his arm. It felt so warm and thin beneath the fabric of his pyjamas.

Gordon pushed a chair towards her. 'Have a seat. I'm going to shoot off. Nice to meet you.'

'You too, Gordon. Thanks for your help and good luck with everything.'

'And you.' As he left the room he turned and said, 'Be patient. Teddy has his moments.'

Left alone with the man who was her father, Elizabeth began to question why she was here. Even if he suddenly became completely lucid what good could come from this? He knew

166

nothing of her life and she was completely ignorant of his. All she could tell him was that her mother had told her he had died many years before and what person on their deathbed needed to hear that? With Gordon gone she felt more comfortable holding the old man's hand. Stroking it, she repeated her name and then added quietly, 'And I'm your daughter.'

The rasp of air entering and leaving his lungs continued like a slow, steady drum.

'I was out at Castle House. It's very beautiful. You must have hated leaving it.'

His gaze didn't shift.

Elizabeth found that her eyes had filled with tears. She brusquely brushed them away. This was maudlin nonsense. She didn't know this man or anything about him. Why should she weep for him?

'Sorry to interrupt.' It was Sarah Cahill at the door. 'I was just checking everything was all right.'

'Yes,' Elizabeth said as brightly as she could. 'Everything is fine.'

'Gordon tells me you are Mr Foley's daughter?' Her tone suggested she needed some clarification.

'Well, technically I am, but my parents were estranged. We never knew each other.'

'I see. I see. Well, lovely that you got to spend time with him before it was too late.' The Care Director seemed sincere.

'Thank you. Yes. I never thought I'd get to meet him.'

'If you are interested there are some old family photos that he brought in with him. It's nice to have some personal effects in the room, if not for

167

them, then for the staff. Makes the residents seem more like real people.'

She reached down and opened the drawer in the bedside table.

'They're in there. I'm sure he wouldn't mind you having a look.'

'Thank you.' Elizabeth spoke quietly as if the two women were sharing a secret. Sarah withdrew, closing the door gently.

A small stack of photographs was at the front of the drawer alongside a packet of Rennies and an old ballpoint pen. She picked the pictures up and placed them under the bedside lamp.

A woman sitting on a tartan rug on the beach with two little boys. That must be the dead brother, thought Elizabeth. There was something about the way his lips were slightly downturned that reminded her of Zach. She peered closer to get a better look at Mrs Foley. Her grandmother was probably younger than Elizabeth in this photograph but had the air of a pensioner with her headscarf and tightly permed hair. What was most striking however was the way she was holding her sons. They were both gripped tightly to her sides. In contrast to the wide, tooth-filled smile their mother wore, both boys looked sullen and uncomfortable. It seemed an odd picture to have kept all these years.

The next photograph showed a youngish Edward, twentyish, Elizabeth would have guessed, posing proudly beside a cow, brandishing a rosette and a small silver trophy. Elizabeth compared the man in the picture with the old man in the bed next to her. How had that beaming youngster so full of joy and pride become this faded husk? She felt her eyes fill with tears once more as she remembered her own mother and imagined that she too must have been bright-eyed and full of hope and laughter as a young woman. She struggled to imagine a version of her mother that had ever been carefree. Old age was such a cruel price to pay for youth. Elizabeth sighed and picked up the next photograph.

At first she wasn't sure why the little girl in the red dress looked so familiar but then she realised that it was herself! She had never seen the picture before, though she had a vague recollection of the bright red pinafore. How old must she have been in this photo? Four or five? She looked so happy, her little face bursting open with laughter. She peered at the background. Just some green shrubbery. She had no idea where it had been taken. Then she was struck by the realisation that her mother must have had some contact with Edward over the years. How else would he have had this photograph? Had she met Edward before, unaware that he was her father? There was no writing on the back. No clues.

She shuffled through the next couple of photographs. A view of Castle House and some people she didn't recognise standing by a gate. The next one was a large group shot at a wedding. They were seen through that mauve haze that old colour photographs always seemed to have.

She examined the line of people standing awkwardly on the top step outside a faceless chapel. There was Mrs Foley, still severe but now looking a little older, wearing a large brown hat. The frothy bride was more handsome than pretty but her happiness lit up the whole picture. The groom . . . Elizabeth froze. He looked very like Edward. Perhaps it was the dead brother but surely he had died before any wedding day? She turned the photograph over and on the back there in the handwriting she knew so well was inscribed, 'Teddy and Mary — 1972'. The year before she was born. She looked at the picture again. That was definitely her father beaming at the camera with his arm around the bride. It made no sense.

Her mind was racing. Who was this man lying in the bed before her? Was he her father or just a smokescreen and Rosemary had been right about her mother being pregnant before she left? Was her real father walking along The Green back in Buncarragh, unaware of her existence? But if she wasn't the daughter of Edward Foley, why had she been given Castle House? Questions began to tumble into each other in an impenetrable heap. Why was the newly married Edward replying to Lonely Heart ads? Who had written the letters? Did her mother know Mary? Who was Mary?

Elizabeth hastily shoved the wedding picture in her jacket pocket and returned the other photographs to the drawer in the locker. She stared at the old man. His eyelids fluttered and he licked his lips. Was Edward Foley still in there? All the answers she wanted trapped inside this frail creature. This was so much worse than not knowing.

THEN

Escape was the last thing on her mind now. After Edward had rescued her, she had gratefully returned to what now seemed like the refuge of her bedroom and accepted a mug of hot sweet tea. Patricia didn't care if it was drugged or not. She had to stop shivering, but long before the morning came, a fever had taken hold of her. The sheets were soaked through with her sweat and when Mrs Foley had changed them for her, she lay under the weight of the blankets shivering so violently she thought she might break a tooth.

Patricia would have sworn that she had been awake all night but when she opened her eyes she discovered that not only had she been asleep but at some point she had been moved into a different bedroom. She now found herself in a high double bed with an ornate headboard made from some dark glossy wood. A large matching wardrobe stood against the end wall, while the wide window was opposite the bed. The wallpaper and curtains were almost the same shade of burgundy, which brought to mind dried blood. The heavy material around the window made the wind sound further away. After the trauma of the marsh Patricia felt safe. She slipped back into sleep.

Her lucid moments came and went but old Mrs Foley seemed to be a constant. Washing her face with a cool flannel, holding cups of tea up to her mouth, straightening the bedclothes and tucking her in. Patricia's throat felt sharp and raw so that speaking was difficult but she took comfort from listening to the whispered monologue of the old lady. 'Now, that will make you feel better.' 'A big sleep. That's what you need.' The prison guard had become a nurse and somehow Patricia found it much easier to feel thankful for her help.

'The doctor has been, and he has left us a bottle of tonic and a prescription, but Teddy will probably have to head into Clonteer for that.'

'The doctor?' Patricia rasped, the words like knives against her throat. 'When?'

'This morning,' explained Mrs Foley. 'You were very groggy, but you were a good patient. You sat up and let him listen to your chest and your back.'

Patricia lay down on her pillow and shut her eyes. Was Edward's mother telling the truth? Should she take the medicine? She felt so tired . . .

'What do you want, Mrs Foley?'

'What's that, pet? What do I want?'

Patricia searched her face for some clue to her intentions.

'Do you want me to die?'

The old lady recoiled. She looked truly wounded by Patricia's question, as if such a suggestion was unthinkable.

'How could you ask such a . . . no, I . . . I only want . . . ' She bowed her head and rubbed her eyes before abruptly turning and leaving the room. Patricia didn't hear the sound of the key turning in the lock.

A flurry of thoughts filled her head. Why had that question thrown the old woman? Was she planning to kill her? If she was, why hadn't she already done it? Had she reacted in the way she had because she had killed before? No, she was being ridiculous. She was just an old crazy lady who had lost her mind. Edward had helped her escape once. She was sure he would again.

Later, there was a gentle knock on the door, and then before she could answer, Edward stuck his head into the room. Without thinking, Patricia smiled, and he stepped forward.

'How are you?' he whispered.

'All right. Sore throat. Headache.'

Edward nodded.

'Thanks for rescuing me,' she continued weakly.

'I'm sorry, I'm just so happy I found you in time.' His dark eyes held her gaze and for a moment neither of them spoke.

'Did a doctor really come?'

'Yes. Yes, he did. That's why she moved you in here.'

Patricia screwed her face up to indicate that she didn't follow his logic.

'The double bed,' Edward said, pointing at it. 'We're married.' He held out his hands helplessly.

Patricia stared at him, unsure what to say. Being reminded of her circumstances, and how out of control they had become, made her almost dizzy. Her sense of panic began to resurface. She took some deep breaths. She didn't feel able to scream or shout. What did she need to understand? She licked her dry cracked lips.

'Why won't your mother let me leave?'

Edward squirmed, pulling at the bottom of his jumper, and turned away.

'I don't know. I don't know. She's not a bad person.'

'What does she want?'

Edward turned back towards her. 'She wants us to be happy.'

'Happy? Oh, my God. Was this the plan all along? Those letters, Edward, those letters!' She threw herself back on the mattress; the effort of speaking was agony.

Edward knelt by the bed and took her hand. 'This should never have happened. My mother was just helping me.' He paused and looked up at the ceiling as if asking a higher power what he should say to this woman lying before him. 'We needed you, she said so, and she was right. My mother writing the letters seemed simple, it was only after we met that I realised how wrong the whole thing was. I liked you and those letters, they made you like me.'

Patricia turned away from him and groaned.

Edward squeezed her hand tighter. 'I can't. You know I don't have the words. I can't explain. I don't know how to tell you.'

'How did you manage to never learn to read or write? You weren't a child when you left school, were you?'

Edward pulled at his collar. 'I just . . . when they were teaching it back in infants and first class, I just didn't get the hang of it and then the teacher, old Mrs Cassidy, gave up on me. She knew I was only going to work on the farm, so what did it matter? When I got to secondary there was talk of getting me special help but then, well, then I had to leave.'

Patricia looked at him. His face crumpled by frustration at his own shortcomings. This man wished her no harm. She trusted him.

'Edward, you can put an end to all of this. You can make this stop.' She leaned forward so that their faces were almost touching. She hoped he could see the desperation in her eyes.

'I can't!' Edward spat the words at her as if it was her own stupidity that prevented her from understanding why he couldn't help her. He pulled himself to his feet, unnerved by his own outburst.

'I'll go. Get well.' The click of the door as it closed. Patricia squeezed her eyes shut. She had no idea what was going on in Castle House or what would happen to her, but in that moment, without him, she found she missed Edward. Her Edward.

NOW

A skeletal, needle-free Christmas tree leaned against the hedge, a few strands of forgotten tinsel fluttering in the breeze. Elizabeth sighed. Her accommodation for the night didn't seem promising.

Brian had picked her up from Abbey Court and taken her back to her car in Muirinish. She had asked him about Edward's marital history but Brian knew nothing. Perhaps his aunt would know more. She followed him in her own car the four or five miles along the coast road till they came to a small cluster of houses. There were two street lights but no sign giving the place an actual name. Brian told her that it was just known locally as Coakley's Cross but it lacked the pub or shop or chapel that might have elevated it to the status of an actual village.

He led her from the cars to a gate that two houses shared. One was brightly lit and looked freshly painted, while the other was a nondescript bungalow that had seen much better days. Above the abandoned Christmas tree, hanging baskets of dead plants were hung from either side of the shallow porch. Of course this house turned out to be the one belonging to his aunt.

'Brian!' The old lady at the door seemed surprised to see her nephew.

'Auntie Eileen, this is Elizabeth, the woman I told you about.'

Hands were wiped on an apron and then a thin bony paw was held out to be shaken.

'Nice to meet you, I'm sure.' Her pale eyes were magnified by her thick glasses so that every blink was like a camera shutter closing. Elizabeth was mesmerised by her.

'Thanks so much for taking me in.'

Eileen held her head back to get a better look at her visitor through her bifocals. Then she turned and gave her nephew a quizzical glance.

'I rang earlier.' Brian was speaking very slowly and clearly. 'I explained that Elizabeth needed a bed for the night. You said she could stay. Remember?'

The old woman bristled with indignation.

'Of course I remember! Come in out of the cold. You are very welcome . . . ' Her voice trailed away.

'Elizabeth.'

'Of course, of course. Come in.'

Elizabeth took a step forward but realised that Brian was staying where he was. She turned to him.

'Thanks, then.'

'You're very welcome. Nice to meet you. Sleep well and safe travels.'

'Thanks. Take care.'

They both hesitated. Was this the moment for a handshake, a hug, a peck on the cheek? It seemed that none of those felt exactly right, as Brian gave an apologetic shrug and started to walk back to his car.

Elizabeth's heart sank. She did not relish the thought of her night ahead with only Auntie

Eileen for company.

'Close the door. Keep the heat in!' a voice from within commanded. Elizabeth painted a smile on her face and strode forward. A hall the size of a phone box forced her through the only open door into a dimly lit sitting room. A single bar on an electric heater glowed orange while above it a coal-effect fire moved in slow waves. In the corner of the room the light from a silent television spilled over the small two-seater sofa and a low coffee table, with a half-finished crossword abandoned on it.

'In here!' Eileen's voice called from the door at the other end of the room. Elizabeth was momentarily blinded when she stepped into the bright glare of the kitchen. It was a narrow room but down one wall was a large aquarium. It hummed and the blue-green light spilling from it gave Auntie Eileen the pallor of a Halloween ghoul.

'Goodness!' Elizabeth expressed her surprise at finding this enormous tank in such a small room.

'Beautiful, isn't it? They all belong to Johnny.'

It crossed Elizabeth's mind to ask who Johnny was but almost at once she realised that she had no interest in finding out more about him.

The two women stood and watched the small bright fish swimming with purpose on the other side of the expanse of glass.

'I could watch them all day.' Auntie Eileen turned and smiled at her visitor. Her large exaggerated eyes reminded Elizabeth of the fish in the tank.

'I'm sure you could. Very soothing.' Though Elizabeth wondered how anyone could ever relax in this room lit up like a nuclear reactor.

The old lady scraped a chair back from the Formica-topped table.

'You'll have a seat.' Elizabeth sat down, while the old lady leaned against the draining board of the sink.

'Did Brian say he found you down in Muirinish?'

'That's right. I was down looking at Castle House. Do you know it? The Foleys lived there.'

'Castle House? Is that the one almost in the sea?'

'Yes, it's just set back.'

'The one with an old castle ruin?'

'Yes. That's the one.'

'That's Castle House. It was the Foleys I think lived there,' Auntie Eileen explained helpfully.

'That's right.' Elizabeth wondered if the old woman was deaf.

'I never knew them but that was a fierce sad house. One funeral after another. It's like the place is cursed. What's your interest in the place?'

Elizabeth cleared her throat. 'Well, I'm the new owner.'

'Oh.' The old lady's face suggested that she had heard Elizabeth loud and clear. 'It must have lovely views, I'd say.'

'Lovely,' agreed Elizabeth with a smirk. 'I'm very interested in the history of the place. What were you saying about funerals?'

'Oh, I was only a girl. I don't really remember,

179

but when we went into town that way, my mother, God rest her, always crossed herself. It might have been a bad death . . . or did someone drown? Sorry now. I'm no good to you at all. I'll tell you the person you should speak to. You need to talk to Cathy Crowley. She was a Lynch back then and she grew up down there beside them. She might remember all the gory details.'

Elizabeth raised an eyebrow. She wasn't sure she was fully prepared for 'gory details'.

'That's great, thanks. Where could I find her?'

'Her husband manages the Co-op down in Muirinish. They're in the white house with the big hedges just beside it. I'd say now she would be your best bet. She's a great one for local history and all that sort of thing. Very interesting . . . ' The old lady's eyes drifted back to the fish tank and began to follow the creatures as if she was watching a very slow game of tennis. Suddenly, as if remembering that she had a guest, she put a hand on Elizabeth's shoulder and enquired, 'Have you had your dinner?'

Without thinking, Elizabeth told her that she hadn't.

'Oh, right.' Auntie Eileen looked worried. 'I don't normally do evening meals.'

'Well, perhaps I could — '

'No, no,' the old lady interrupted, 'I'll put you together something here. Sure, nowhere would be open at this hour.' She indicated the clock on the wall telling them that it was twenty past seven as if it was midnight.

Elizabeth thanked her profusely and then asked if she could go to her room. The old lady showed her back through the sitting room and then into the hall. One door was for the pale pink bathroom, while the other led to her peach boudoir. Elizabeth's overall impression was of nylon. The whole room seemed to bristle.

Left alone, she brushed her teeth and then sat on the end of her bed, her weight bringing the mattress close to the floor. For the first time in hours she thought about Elliot and Zach. How had the pick-up gone? She wondered if Michelle had dared to show her face. Elizabeth had to admit that she was almost glad to be sitting in this nylon shrine rather than having to deal with the embarrassment of Zach's sex life. Let Elliot pick up the pieces for once. She would try to call them later, once they were back in San Francisco and the dust had had a chance to settle.

A gentle knock on the door.

'Yes?'

'Your tea's ready when you are.'

'Thank you!' Elizabeth replied, thinking to herself that the old lady had managed to cook up a meal surprisingly quickly.

When she saw what was waiting for her on the kitchen table, the speed became less of a mystery. A small grey, almost blue, mound sat in a pale yellow pool of liquid. She thought it might be egg but really couldn't be certain.

'It's just some scrambled egg. I hope that's enough for you.'

'More than enough,' Elizabeth reassured her hostess and she meant it.

'There's some toast for you,' the old lady said, putting down a side plate with two slices of bread so white it was hard to believe they had seen daylight never mind the inside of a toaster. 'I have the kettle on for tea.'

'Lovely!' Elizabeth hoped that might help her wash down some of her meal.

She had scarcely taken a bite of the eggs, so dry it was hard to understand where the liquid had come from, when the shrill doorbell took Auntie Eileen from the room. Elizabeth used the opportunity to mess up her plate with her fork and tear the 'toast' in two to give the impression that she had consumed more than she had.

'A visitor for you!' Auntie Eileen exclaimed and Brian's smiling face loomed behind her shoulder. Elizabeth sighed with relief.

'Hello,' she called happily.

'Sorry. I'm interrupting your meal,' he said apologetically.

'Not at all. I was just finished.' Elizabeth stood up to prove her point.

'Really?' Auntie Eileen was incredulous.

'It was lovely. Thank you,' Elizabeth said to her hostess with all the sincerity she could muster.

Brian coughed. 'Well, I was just wondering if you fancied a drink down the pub.'

'Yes,' she blurted out.

Brian laughed. 'It's like that, is it? I won't have her back too late,' he said to his aunt, adding, 'If you want to go to bed just leave the key out.'

'I will, I will.' But the old woman was distracted by the food left on the table. She looked stricken, but Elizabeth refused to feel guilty.

The atmosphere in the car seemed different between them. The windows steamed up and their coats seemed noisy and cumbersome. Conversation was stilted. They seemed to have lost their easy, relaxed connection from earlier in the day. It was decided that they would drive back towards Muirinish. Brian explained that there was a sweet little pub called Carey's that sometimes had live music.

Elizabeth drank a couple of glasses of red wine, which was surprisingly good, while Brian had pints of stout. It turned out there was no music that night but the pub was busy enough and the turf fire gave the place a welcoming glow. Conversation became easy once more. Brian made her laugh and he leaned in close when she spoke. She noticed his thighs where his jeans were stretched tight across them. Elizabeth wasn't exactly sure if this was a date, but whatever it might be, she was enjoying herself. It was good to spend time with a man who knew almost nothing about her. He couldn't judge her as a mother or a daughter, he didn't know what she was like at work, or whether or not she should have spotted that things weren't right with Elliot. She was just a tourist, tracking down her roots. She drained her second glass.

'Will you have another?' Brian asked.

Elizabeth did want another but experience told her that she would regret it in the morning and she was planning to drive back to Buncarragh.

'No, I won't, thanks.'

'Right.' Brian seemed a little crestfallen. 'Well, I'm driving so I'd better not either.' It seemed the party was over.

'Will we hit the road?' he asked.

'Might as well. Don't want to wake your auntie,' Elizabeth said with mock seriousness, reaching for her coat.

Back in the car, the doors shut and the interior light went out. Brian had the keys in his hand but didn't put them in the ignition. There was silence. Elizabeth looked at his strong, almost angular, profile against the lights of the pub. He seemed lost in thought.

'Can I ask you something?'

'Of course,' Elizabeth replied, her heart beating just a little faster. Was he going to kiss her? She could feel the two glasses of wine urging her to say yes.

'Would you like to sleep with me?'

This was not the question she had been expecting. Brian seemed to have skipped several steps in their nascent courtship.

'What?'

Brian squirmed in his seat.

'I just wondered if you wanted to sleep together, you know, have sex?'

He sounded so matter of fact. Elizabeth wasn't sure what to say.

'It just seems a little abrupt. Sudden. You know what I mean?' She didn't want to upset him, but at the same time she was surprised that he was being so crass.

'Well, I just thought you are here for tonight. An attractive woman. We probably won't see each other again. I haven't done it in a while and I thought you might like the chance of no-strings attached . . . ' His voice trailed off and Elizabeth assumed that he could see the expression on her face in the light from the pub windows. Her surprise had turned to anger.

'I see. And do you offer your services to every single female traveller you come across?'

'No, no.' He raised his hands to placate her. 'I'm sorry, I didn't mean to . . . I really like you.'

'Well, that's encouraging. Good to know there is some sort of selection process.'

'Look,' he sounded defensive, 'I never meant to insult you or piss you off. It was just a question.'

'Well, the answer is no.'

'Fine.' Brian stuck the key angrily into the ignition but before he could start the engine the sound of Elizabeth's phone rang through the tension-filled car.

She writhed in her seat, trying to extract it from her coat pocket. When she did the display said 'Elliot'.

'Sorry. I ought to get this.'

'Fire ahead,' Brian muttered, clearly beginning to sulk.

'Hello. Everything all right?'

Elliot's voice didn't answer but just informed her, 'Your son has something to tell you.'

Your son? That didn't sound promising.

'Mom?' It was Zach.

'Yes . . . ' Elizabeth said the word tentatively, anxious about what might be coming next.

'Don't be mad, Mom.'

'OK.' If she was being honest, she was finding it hard to feel like a parent right now, sat as she was with a man in a car outside a pub, having an adolescent conversation about sex.

'Just tell me, Zach.'

'OK. Well, the thing is, I have some news . . . '
He was obviously playing for time.

'Just tell me!' she snapped.

Zach gave a tiny cough and then said quietly,
'You are going to be a grandmother.'

It was as if she had stared into the centre of
the sun. A hot white light seared into her brain.
She had no words. There wasn't a single reaction
that she could articulate. She felt breathless.
Finally Zach's voice came from the speaker.
'Mom?'

Elizabeth hesitated for a moment and then,
trying to summon a calm voice, said, 'I can't
speak to you right now.' And hung up. She sat
staring in disbelief at the screen of her phone.

Brian touched her arm, unsure of what had
just happened.

'Are you all right?'

Elizabeth turned to him and then they were
kissing. A mad, hungry embrace that owed as
much to despair as desire.

THEN

Staring up at the ceiling, or slowly tracing patterns on the wallpaper with her finger, Patricia could no longer name the days. Each morning the curtains were opened and sometimes the sun crept into the bedroom throwing warm pools of light on the threadbare carpet. Leaning forward, Patricia could catch a glimpse of blue sky.

The night sweats had stopped and every day she felt a little better. Mrs Foley continued to deliver trays of food and a banal commentary on the weather and life on the farm. Apparently some calves had been born. As Patricia grew stronger the bubble of rage inside her increased. She had done nothing wrong and she wanted to go home! Why was Edward so afraid of his mother? What was stopping him from just driving her to Buncarragh?

'Mrs Foley, you know I have to go home? You understand that, don't you?'

'Oh child, of course I do, but you aren't well enough to travel. I don't think you realise how unwell you are.'

'I'm well enough to sit in a car,' Patricia replied angrily.

Mrs Foley's nostrils flared indignantly. 'Oh, and you think Teddy has time to drive you all the way up the country?' She snorted with laughter. 'That boy is busy, very busy, working all the hours that God sends. And what for? So that you can lie up here like some princess being waited upon, hand and foot! You have some nerve, young lady.' And with that the old lady swept from the room, slamming the door behind her.

For the first time in what seemed like weeks Patricia felt more like her old self. If no one was going to help her then she would sort this out for herself.

She remembered that in her Enid Blyton books they were forever making ropes out of sheets. There were only two on her bed. She doubted they would reach the ground and even if they did would she have the strength to climb down them? It was unlikely. What if she just jumped? It was only the first floor after all. Looking down, though, the drop seemed much bigger than it did from the outside. What if she broke a leg, or even sprained an ankle? There would be no leaving Castle House for months.

An escape in the dead of night was another option. Patricia considered her chances of success. Would the noise of the stairs wake the old woman? And if she did manage to make it downstairs she didn't know what she'd do if the doors were locked.

That night, after she had picked at her dinner of boiled ham and cabbage, the same as the first meal she had ever had in the house, she recalled, Edward came into her room with a single cup of tea.

Patricia sat up to take it and as he handed it to her Edward sat on the side of the bed.

'How are you feeling?'

'Edward, I can't. If you cared how I was feeling, you would let me go.'

'I can't do that. My mother wants you to stay.'

'Speak to her!' she implored, touching the sleeve of his jumper.

He sighed. 'I have. I've told her we should let you go home.'

'And?'

'She's scared you'll go to the guards.'

Patricia felt so stupid. She had been so fixated on trying to leave and get back to Buncarragh, it had never crossed her mind that what was going on here was a crime. She could just phone the police. Her heart was beating faster. Something in her face must have betrayed what she was thinking, because Edward grabbed her arm and stared into her eyes.

'You wouldn't, would you? You'd never go to the guards?' He tightened his grip.

'You're hurting me,' she said, trying to squirm free.

'It would finish her. She . . . please, I will sort this out. Please, if you can just be patient, I will get you out of here. She has been through so much and she just wanted this so badly. I'm sorry that it had to be like this.' He dropped her arm and picked at the candlewick bedspread nervously.

'Your mother is mental, Edward, she's the one that needs locking up. She should be in a home!'

'You don't understand. She has been through so much.'

'What? What has she been through?' Patricia spat the words out. Angry and impatient.

189

'She changed,' Edward said quietly. He looked down at his hands as if they belonged to someone else. 'After James. After he died.'

For a moment Patricia was silenced. She could imagine how losing a child could destroy a mother.

'How old was he?' she asked quietly.

'Seventeen,' Edward replied in barely more than a whisper.

'What happened?'

He didn't speak, just examined the folds in the covers.

'You don't have to tell me,' she added softly.

'No. I . . . I should tell you. You ought to know.'

⋆　⋆　⋆

Edward wondered how to begin his story. Should he start after the two boys had finished milking, when they had stood in the yard, James hosing off his wellington boots? He could tell her that it was a beautiful summer's evening, the air still for once, and the sound of contented cows wafting lazily to them over the warm dusty fields. It was James who had suggested they take the boat out. Someone had told him that the mackerel were running and they still had a couple of hours of daylight. Of course Edward was going to agree. He was barely fourteen at the time and, having spent so much time alone on the farm, struggled to find his place amongst the packs of boys that roamed his school. James was more than just his big brother. He was his best, and only, friend. His hero, the man he wanted to become but doubted he ever would. James could control the herd with a few shouts, he was able to talk to girls, and their mother didn't yell at him or tell him what to do. Edward would never have admitted it to a living soul, but he preferred life without their father.

Maybe his tale should begin a couple of hours later as night was creeping up on them and the wind suddenly returned, whipping up the grey ocean, slapping their little wooden rowing boat with growing force. Edward was the one who said they should head back and he hadn't been able to disguise the fear in his voice. That was why James had stood up and started rocking the small boat from side to side. He had been laughing and teasing his younger brother. Edward had begged him to sit down but that only provoked James to rock the boat more violently.

He remembered he had reached up and touched James's jumper. Had he pulled it? Had he tugged it? He could still feel the damp wool against his fingers. Edward had just wanted his brother to sit down. That was all. He had never wished him any harm.

What happened next was like a magic trick, or when the film skipped at the cinema in Clonteer. James just disappeared. Where his man-shaped outline had been visible against the darkening sky was suddenly clear. His brother was gone. Vanished. He remembered looking over the side but the choppy waves held on to their secrets. Had James jumped in to frighten him? Surely,

191

he'd bob up to the surface in a moment, laughing and spluttering. He must be down there holding his breath. The seconds passed and became minutes and a horrified Edward had to accept that his brother was not coming back to the surface. He peered into the dark waves on either side but could see nothing. He wanted to jump in and slip through the waves like an oily seal till he found his brother but Edward couldn't swim. That was partly why James had been trying to frighten him. He peered into the distance, trying to see if his brother's dark-haired head had surfaced somewhere, but there was nothing. Edward felt sick and dizzy with panic. Where was James? He couldn't be gone. James had to be alive, he had to be, but where? He called out his brother's name, screamed it, but he knew that his voice wouldn't carry to where his brother could hear his cries.

Later on he would try to piece it all together. James must have lost his balance, perhaps because Edward had pulled at him, but maybe he just slipped on some of the mackerel in the bottom of the boat, or the rocking of the waves had grown more violent. He would never know for certain. They had found some blood on the metal oar lock, so it was assumed that James had hit his head as he fell overboard and then his rubber wellingtons would have filled with sea water, dragging him down to the murky forest of seaweed that wafted placidly below.

Edward had begun to cry. This was awful beyond imagining. He couldn't stay out at sea but equally how could he leave? He shouldn't just give up on his brother. What would their mother say? The tears grew heavier and his sobs became howls that were swallowed by the wind and the darkness. He couldn't go back to shore alone. It crossed his mind that he too should just jump overboard. Better that no one returned to Castle House than Edward without James. He leaned forward and wrapped his arms around his knees, paralysed by fear and grief.

He wasn't sure how long he sat like that but when he finally managed to control his breathing and stop crying, it was fully night. In the distance he could see the light on the corner of the house and a glow behind the curtains in the front room. He would have to go back. He had no choice.

The oars felt much heavier than before and the sea had turned to treacle, but he slowly made his way closer to the shore. The steady slap and creak of the oars were his metronome. A groan on each pull, then stretch and down and pull again. James had taught him to row. He began to cry again.

As the boat neared the shore he could see a small light floating in the darkness. At first he couldn't understand what it was but then he realised it must be someone on the beach with a torch. It would be their mother, worried and waiting. Soon she would hear the steady rhythm of the oars and the bow of the boat hitting the waves. He imagined her then, relaxing, thinking to herself that her boys were safe. He began to pull with less vigour, trying to delay what was to come. The horror as she stepped forward and saw that only one son had made it back to shore, and that boy was Edward. He began to shiver violently, the cold and shock and dread overtaking his body.

Finally he heard the crunch as the bottom of the boat hit the sandy gravel and he stepped out into the cold water. Ahead of him he could see his mother's face, like a Halloween head, lit up by the torch. She was shouting across the noise of the surf.

'I thought you were lost. What happened to you?'

Edward couldn't speak. He just heaved the boat behind him, dragging it up onto the shore. His mother picked her way across the edge of the waves to help him, but then she froze. The torch jabbed at the darkness, poking into each corner and pocket of the boat. Her voice was thin and high as she called his name. 'James? Where's James? Edward, where is your brother?'

Edward dropped the rope and stood with his arms hanging by his sides. The waves swirled around his ankles. He opened his mouth to speak but was engulfed by grief and guilt. He let out a cry and it seemed to cut through the night, like an animal caught in a trap. He rushed to his mother, but stumbled so that he found his arms were wrapped around her knees.

'No! No, no!' Her voice decreed that this was not happening. Her son was not gone. She had not lost her baby.

Edward's weight against her legs and the shifting wet shingle meant she had lost her balance and she fell backwards with a scream, her arms splayed out on the beach like Christ on his cross.

The waves rolled in and out. The two heaving bodies lay entwined with hearts that would be forever broken.

That was when everything changed.

Back in the bedroom, Patricia was staring at Edward, still waiting. He cleared his throat.

'We were fishing out on a boat. It got choppy and James fell overboard. It was all fierce fast. I think Mammy has always blamed me.'

He raised a hand to wipe away a tear.

Patricia put her hands around his shoulders to comfort him and he fell against her. They lay on the bed, Patricia shushing him like a baby till they both fell asleep.

NOW

They didn't sleep together. After about ten minutes of passionate kissing and roaming hands, Elizabeth pushed Brian away.

'I can't.' She was panting slightly.

Brian reached up and cupped her face in his hands.

'Are you sure? You seem to be enjoying it and, well,' he moved a few strands of hair from her face, 'you're a fine-looking woman.'

She didn't make eye contact. She liked him but the kissing had really just been a way to silence the noise in her head. A distraction from dealing with Zach's news. 'Yes. It's too much. I should head back. I have to call my stupid fucking son.'

Brian made no move to start the engine but put his arm around her and pulled her back into an embrace.

'Yeah, what was all that about? What's happened?'

Elizabeth let out a long slow sigh.

'My seventeen-year-old son has got his thirty-something girlfriend pregnant.'

'Fuck,' was Brian's brief response.

'Fuck, indeed.'

He made a whistling sound and added, 'I'm so glad I'm not a parent. What are you going to do?'

'I don't know. Try to talk sense into them both?' Elizabeth sounded very unsure.

Back at Aunt Eileen's, Brian gave Elizabeth one last slow kiss and then watched her walk up the path before driving away. Retrieving the key from under a metal hedgehog that doubled as a boot scraper, she let herself in. The house was in darkness but she managed to find the light switch for the bathroom and then a bedside lamp. Sitting on the low, soft bed, she pulled out her phone and stared at the screen. This was not a call she wanted to make. Deciding that it was best to speak to Elliot first, she dialled his number.

'Yes?' Elliot's voice barked down the line. He sounded as if he was answering the door to Jehovah's Witnesses. This was the side of Elliot that Elizabeth liked the least, when he went into full teacher mode.

'It's me, Elizabeth,' she replied.

'Why are you whispering?' he snapped back.

'It's late here, and I'm staying in a bed and breakfast.'

'Why aren't you at your mother's?'

'It's a long story. I'll tell you when I see you. Nothing bad. How's Zach?' she asked, trying to get the conversation back on track.

'Upset.'

'Of course. It's a lot.'

'With you. He's upset with you!' Elliot was the teacher talking to his dimmest student.

'What?' Elizabeth asked in an indignant whisper.

'He rang you to share his news and you wouldn't talk to him. Of course he's upset.'

Elizabeth couldn't believe what she was hearing.

'Our seventeen-year-old son is going to be a father and this is what we're talking about? Seriously?'

'We have to support him through this, Elizabeth. He's so young.'

'I know he's young,' she hissed angrily down the line, 'that's why I'm upset. How pregnant is she? What's their plan?'

'Options are limited. She is very pregnant. I can't believe you failed to notice, I mean, when did you last see her?'

Elizabeth tried to remember.

'I don't know. Before Christmas, but it's winter in New York. She was covered in coats and scarves. So they're planning to have this baby?'

She felt so useless and detached. Tears of frustration began to form.

This was her own baby boy they were talking about. She barely trusted him to pick up groceries from D'Agostino's. How could he be responsible for another human life?

'Look, maybe it's not that bad.' Elliot was trying to sound calm and reasonable now, which made his ex-wife feel the exact opposite.

'What are you talking about? Not that bad? It's a fucking baby, Elliot!'

'I know. I know that, but it's not like she's a teenager. She doesn't want to get married to Zach.'

'He's seventeen!' Elizabeth couldn't help interrupting.

'But that's the point. She's in her mid-thirties. I'm pretty certain she didn't plan for this to happen, but now that it has, she must be thinking that she might as well keep it or she may end up never having a baby. I don't think Zach is part of her plan.'

Elizabeth had to admit this made sense, which in one way was a relief but in another broke her heart for her son. She imagined how he must be feeling. Along with the fear, she knew that he would be puffed up with mannish pride. But if Michelle Giardino just wanted to walk away with the baby, he'd get over it, and there would be other grandchildren with a better sense of timing. She wondered if she was a heartless bitch for thinking this but quickly told herself that she was simply concerned with what was best for her son.

'OK. Well, I'll talk to Zach and then we can all figure out what happens next. Is she staying in California?' she asked hopefully.

'No. Heading back to New York in a day or two before they stop her flying.'

Elizabeth's heart sank. It would be on her watch.

'Great. Talk soon. Goodnight.'

'Bye.'

Elizabeth dragged herself into the middle of the bed so that there was less chance of her sliding down the slope of the mattress onto the floor. She slipped under the light duvet and turned out the lamp. The glow from her phone lit up the room and she tapped on Zach's name to call him. It rang. She waited. No reply and finally it went to voicemail. She sighed and hung up. She imagined Zach with Michelle, looking at 'Mom' blinking on the screen and telling his girlfriend horror stories about her. Her mind began to calculate the number of months that Michelle Giardino, maths tutor, had been coming to their apartment. At once a week at seventy dollars an hour that she couldn't afford, this baby had already cost her thousands of dollars. Her mind whirled with all the things she wanted to say to Zach and Ms Giardino. How would she ever sleep?

She woke seven hours later still clutching her phone. Noises were coming from the kitchen and there was the distinctive smell of frying bacon. Elizabeth rubbed her face and yawned. Hopefully breakfast would be better than the meal her landlady had provided the night before. She was starving.

Auntie Eileen was standing in the middle of the kitchen floor with a tea towel draped over her arm when Elizabeth walked in. It looked as if she had been waiting. The artificial glare from the aquarium made the room seem more suitable for an autopsy than breakfast.

'Good morning! Tea or coffee for you?'

Elizabeth normally preferred coffee but thought that tea was a safer bet. The table was set for one and she took her place. A small glass of orange juice stood beside a rack of toast which Elizabeth assumed must be cold. It was. This was in stark contrast to the plate her hostess took out of the oven and placed in front of her. The only clue to how long the plate had been in the oven was provided by the wrinkled dried-out state of the two sausages and strips of bacon. They looked like something that might have been found in a Neolithic tomb rather than on a menu. She sighed and reached for her tea. Perfectly good. Oh well, a liquid breakfast was better than nothing.

'How was your night?' the old lady enquired.

'Good, thanks.'

Auntie Eileen stood by the side of the table, leaning forward. Clearly she expected more details.

'It's a very sweet pub.'

'Yes, yes.' A vigorous nodding in agreement. 'More tea?'

'Oh yes, please.' Elizabeth pressed her fork against an unyielding sausage. 'So I was going to try and see that lady you spoke about last night. The one by the Co-op. I'm sorry I don't remember her name.'

'Cathy Crowley,' Auntie Eileen reminded her as she poured the tea. 'But amn't I after having a much better idea. Her mother, old Mrs Lynch, lives in a little bungalow there beside them. She's some age but she still knows it all. Sharp as a tack. Anything you want to know about Castle House or the Foleys, she's your woman.'

Elizabeth felt encouraged. She might get more answers than she had expected. 'Thank you so much. I'll do that.'

Auntie Eileen sucked her finger and then absented-mindedly dabbed some crumbs off the table and ate them.

'I was thinking last night about that place.'

'Castle House?'

'Yes. I was just wondering if you'll be back?'

'Back?' Elizabeth was slightly bewildered. Why

would she ever come back to this place?

'Well, you know, maybe you'd use it as a holiday home.'

Elizabeth felt so foolish. For a moment she had completely forgotten that she was a property owner in Muirinish.

'I had just thought that I'd sell it.' But even as she said the words she wondered if that was what she really wanted.

THEN

When she woke he was gone. All that remained was the indentation on the pillow and the memory of his body's warmth when she had stirred during the night.

Patricia wasn't sure if Mrs Foley knew what had happened but she seemed suspiciously chirpy when she brought in the breakfast tray and pulled back the curtains on another grey day.

'Sleep well?' she asked. Was that a smirk on her face?

'Yes, thank you.'

Mrs Foley went to the other side of the room and sat in the high backed wooden chair beside the wardrobe.

'I've been thinking.' She paused, and Patricia looked up from buttering her toast. A small knot of dread tightened in her stomach.

'Now that you are feeling much stronger, thank God, I thought it was time you helped out around the house, earned your keep.' The old woman concluded her proposal with a tight smile.

Patricia didn't know how she should respond. Part of her longed for the opportunity to get out of this room. The possibility of using the phone, or simply making a run for it down the lane, was exciting, but she knew she mustn't betray her enthusiasm or Mrs Foley might retract her offer.

At the same time, she bristled with fury that her gaoler thought she should be doing chores to help with the running of her prison.

As blandly as she could, Patricia simply replied, 'I see.'

'After you use the bathroom I'll sort you out with an old housecoat of mine and some slippers.'

Since her recovery from her fever she had been given bathroom privileges. She had been provided with a small silver bell to ring when she needed to go. Mrs Foley would then unlock the door and wait for her while she used the bathroom. Patricia had checked and the window seemed even further off the ground than the one in her room. Some days Patricia had rung the bell more than she needed to, just to hear Mrs Foley making the effort of climbing the stairs, but soon the old lady had become suspicious, and now she didn't respond if the rings were too close together.

Dressed in her borrowed finery an hour or so later, Patricia found herself seated at the kitchen table. She had thought the room might look different but it was exactly as she remembered it from the night after the pub, weeks before. Mrs Foley placed a plastic basin of potatoes in front of her.

'You can start by peeling those.'

Not feeling the need to respond Patricia picked up the peeler and began her work. Looking around, her eyes came to rest on the back door. She could just make a run for it. Even in her second-hand slippers, she guessed that she could outrun Mrs Foley and Edward would let her escape. Of that she was certain.

Mrs Foley turned from the sink and evidently noticed where Patricia's gaze was fixed. Walking slowly, she went over to the door and turned the large key in the lock, before removing it and placing it in the front pocket of her apron. She gave Patricia a long, hard stare.

'If you're not going to peel them spuds, we can just put you back in your room.'

Patricia began scraping the potatoes.

About ten minutes later the handle of the back door turned and someone rattled the lock with no success. There was a knocking and Mrs Foley went and used the key to open the door. Edward burst into the kitchen.

'Why was the door . . . ' he began, but noticing Patricia, stopped speaking.

'Look who has come down to join us,' his mother said, pointing at the table with a tight smile.

A look of confusion crossed Edward's face.

'I see.' He sounded very uncertain about what he was looking at. 'That's great.' He smiled at Patricia. She did not return his enthusiasm, but instead, with an expressionless face, reached into the bowl and took out another potato.

'I mean, great that you are feeling better,' he elaborated. Patricia gave him nothing. He deserved to squirm.

'I'll put the kettle on for you,' his mother chimed in.

'Fine, so. I'll just wash my hands.' As he walked to the door Patricia noticed that he was still wearing the shirt from the night before. Had that really happened? It seemed so hard to imagine that this man had fallen asleep cradled in her arms, when now here she sat like some modern-day slave, being held captive by a mad woman.

Patricia watched the tea being made and saw no sign of it being drugged, so drank a cup with the others. Very little was said. One of the neighbour's sheep had been with the herd this morning, so Edward was going to have a word and block up the fences. Someone Patricia had never heard of had driven by in a new car. Pellets were needed for calves.

After Edward had returned to work in the yard, the back door was relocked. Once Patricia had finished her peeling, Mrs Foley gave her a brush and instructed her to sweep the floor. As resentful as she felt, it was preferable to lying in bed all day staring at the ceiling, drifting in and out of sleep. When she was finished with her broom, Mrs Foley gave her a dustpan and brush.

'Good work.' Edward's mother was positively beaming. 'Now, I think that's enough for today. Let's get you back upstairs.'

Patricia didn't want to go back to her room to spend a long, dull afternoon but could think of no excuse to stay downstairs. She glanced around the kitchen looking for some task she might help with but nothing leapt out at her. She shuffled to the door obediently and made her way upstairs to her room. Once inside, Mrs Foley pointed at the borrowed slippers.

'I'll have those, thank you.'

Patricia took them off and handed them over. She felt completely powerless. The key turned in the lock and she was left alone, sitting on the bed in the dusty half-light of a perpetual Sunday afternoon. She began to weep once more. Everything seemed hopeless. Even her half-baked plan to call the police seemed impossible. She hadn't seen any sign of a phone downstairs, even though she knew there had to be one. She'd heard it ringing. It struck her that it had been some time since the phone had rung in the house. Had Mrs Foley got rid of it just to thwart her?

For the first time since arriving at Castle House, she decided to pray. Down on her knees at the side of the bed, she put her hands together and squeezed her eyes shut. The familiar words tumbled from her lips.

'Hail Mary, full of grace. The Lord is with thee. Blessed art thou amongst women, and blessed is the fruit of thy womb, Jesus. Holy Mary, Mother of God, pray for us sinners, now and at the end of our death. Amen.'

She waited. Had anyone heard her? She doubted it. All her prayers had gone unanswered thus far in her life. It seemed unlikely that she would be listened to now. The Holy Mother didn't care about her. Patricia was like a forgotten umbrella left damp and leaning against the door of the shop. She shut her eyes.

'Please deliver me from this place and bring me back to my home and my family. I know that I'm a sinner but I cannot see what I have done to deserve this. Please help me in my hour of need. Amen.'

She considered if it was worth bargaining with the Almighty, but with what? She didn't smoke or really drink. Her first-born could become a nun or a priest, but at this point the chances of her ever having a child or any kind of recognisable life seemed very remote.

Patricia bent forward and rested her forehead on the bed. She was so alone, but why was this any worse than her life had been before? Hadn't she always been alone? The years she had spent sitting downstairs in the kitchen waiting for a shout or a knock on the floor to signal that her mother needed something. The months since the funeral, still spent sitting in the same room but now with nothing to wait for. If only she had simply accepted her fate. It was her desire to change things, her last-ditch effort not to be alone that had led to this. For a moment she was outside herself, up near the ceiling, looking down on this foolish woman kneeling by a bed, mouthing prayers that would go unheard. A strange calm took hold of her. Maybe she should just accept her fate this time, not struggle. She wasn't thinking properly. Everything made her feel tired and confused. Getting up, she reached for the little bell. She would use the bathroom and then escape from the rest of the day into sleep.

★　★　★

The next morning, she woke early. A weak glow pressed at the gap in the curtains and her tired eyes scanned the familiar room. She noticed that on the floor by the side of the bed was a basket that hadn't been there before. Patricia peered over to see it more clearly. It appeared to be full of blankets. Odd. She hadn't complained about being cold and Mrs Foley hadn't mentioned giving her extra bedding. Her mind drifted to thoughts of the day to come. What chores might be in store for her? Would she be allowed to stay downstairs for longer? What were the chances of her being able to raise the alarm?

What was that? She thought she heard something. Leaning over the side of the bed she looked at the basket. The blankets were moving. Patricia froze. What was it? Had the mad old bitch put some sort of animal in with her? She sat up and pressed herself back against the wall, bracing herself for what might jump out. She held her breath. Then from the edge of the basket emerged a perfectly formed tiny pink hand.

NOW

Elizabeth was still shaking her head in disbelief as she put her overnight bag into her car. She had been worried that Auntie Eileen might have embarrassed her by not charging anything or maybe asking for a paltry fee. She had wondered how much she should insist on giving her. In the event, she needn't have worried. The old lady very matter-of-factly announced that she was owed eighty euros. Elizabeth hoped that she didn't look as surprised as she felt. That wasn't much less than the hotel at the airport. She decided she would check out Coakley's Cross on TripAdvisor.

Before she could drive off, Brian's car pulled up and he stepped out, looking freshly washed and shaved, with his hair slicked back and a crisp white collar peeking out from his dark jumper. Unlike most dates, he actually looked better in the morning light.

Elizabeth opened her door and stood up, leaning on the roof of the car. She dreaded to think what she looked like with her oversized anorak zipped up to her chin and hair that she couldn't remember checking in the mirror.

'Morning!' he called with a smile.

'You've just caught me. I'm back on the road.'

He was standing in front of her, the open car door separating their bodies.

'I'm glad I did.' He looked at the ground, and

then, only half lifting his head, said, 'Listen, do I need to apologise for last night? If I was out of order, I'm very sorry.'

Elizabeth wasn't sure how she felt. He had annoyed her, it was true, but then they had made out for quite a long time, and she couldn't deny that she was pleased to see him.

'You're fine, Brian. Don't worry. It was nice.' She held out her hand with a wide grin on her face. He shook it and the two of them laughed for no apparent reason.

'Are you heading straight off? I wondered if I could shout you lunch in Clonteer somewhere?'

'Well, I'm hoping to talk to some woman down in Muirinish, but then I was going to head back to Buncarragh, so that could work.' She hadn't been looking forward to returning to Keane and Sons; the idea of lunch was a welcome distraction.

'Great. I'll find out where is open and let you know. Should we swap numbers?'

'Sure.'

They both fished out their phones and exchanged their information. There was another brief awkward pause, neither of them sure if a peck on the cheek or a handshake was called for. Not wanting to get it wrong, Elizabeth ducked back into her car with a cheery 'See you later' and drove off.

The road down to Muirinish seemed much shorter in daylight and far more scenic. After passing Carey's pub, the road curved around the shoulder of a hill, giving her an uninterrupted view of the sea. To her right she could just see the top of the castle ruins sticking out from a group of tall pines. Her house. So strange to think that she owned an ancient Irish castle, even stranger to think that it was her family seat. She would have loved to call Zach to tell him about it, to share jokes comparing it to their tiny apartment in New York, but she knew that she shouldn't. He needed time to cool down and she needed time to digest the news of his impending fatherhood. What to say for the best? Was there anything to say? Apparently this baby was going to arrive and apart from loading Zach and a bunch of condoms into a time machine, there didn't seem to be a solitary thing she could do about it.

She slowed down as she went past the gates to Castle House and then at the fork in the road she didn't head over the causeway but followed the signs for Muirinish. She was keeping an eye out for a garage. The car was low on fuel but she also wanted to find something to eat. The lack of both dinner and breakfast meant she was starving. The narrow road, boxed in by hedges, curved through fields and past a few large newly built houses, until at the bottom of a short hill it widened out. On the right was a series of large grey buildings with curved corrugated iron roofs. A clock was painted on the side wall, telling the world that it would forever more be a quarter to three or fifteen minutes past nine. It was hard to tell since the artist had made both hands the same length. In a window there was a large red and white sign that said 'Good luck Cork'. Elizabeth assumed it referred to some upcoming sporting event but it might just as easily have been cheering the county on in case of an impending apocalypse. Further down on the left was another series of buildings painted in a shade of dirty mustard. The large sign declared this to be 'Supermarket and Hardware'. Elizabeth pulled over and got out of the car.

Inside there was a smell that reminded her of Keane and Sons in Buncarragh, but this store was laid out in a series of aisles like any modern supermarket. She headed to the back where she could see some chiller cabinets. Bringing a cellophane-wrapped sausage roll and a can of diet Coke up to the counter, she noticed a sign saying 'Free Wi-Fi'.

'Is there a café here?' Elizabeth asked the young woman behind the counter who was hunched over the till, her long dark hair hanging over her shoulders, while both very pink ears stuck out on either side. She looked up and squinted as if Elizabeth hadn't been speaking English. She made a noise that could be best described as an inquisitive grunt.

'The free Wi-Fi? Is there somewhere to sit and use it?'

'Where are you parked?' the woman asked, pulling a loose strand of hair from her mouth. Elizabeth really wasn't following this conversation but told her the location of her car.

'You can get the Wi-Fi out there. It's the only one and there's no password. Do you need a bag?'

She didn't. Elizabeth paid, went out to the car and picked up her glasses from the passenger

213

seat. Sure enough, when she opened her laptop, everything came to pass just as the cashier had described.

Elizabeth scanned her emails. Mostly junk, or group emails from Hunter she was safe to ignore. Another missive from Linda Jetter detailing the moods and movements of Shelly the cat. Was it wrong that Elizabeth cared so little? The subject line of the newest email read 'Our news' and it wasn't a sender that she recognised: canofsardino@me.com. She opened it.

Dear Elizabeth,
I wanted to call, but this seemed safer. I wanted you to hear me without voices being raised or accusations flying.
The first thing to say is that I am very sorry. I never intended for any of this to happen. I betrayed your trust and I am not proud of myself. You brought me into your home as an educator and I did not behave in a way that was proper. I understand that you must be very angry. My own parents are not very happy with the news either. You should call them!

Elizabeth pushed her laptop away. Was this woman trying to make jokes? She had only avoided being accused of statutory rape by a few months! A slight tremor had taken hold of her right hand. She couldn't remember when she had ever been this angry. She wanted to commit violent acts, cause bodily harm, scream at somebody. Elizabeth read on.

You will not be surprised that my life has not turned out the way I had planned. I have a failed marriage —

Elizabeth let out an involuntary grunt of disapproval.

— and a failed business. Please don't think I am trying to make excuses but Zach was the first person to make me feel good about myself in a very long time.

A scarf. Elizabeth wanted to get a long scarf, wrap it around Michelle's neck and pull really hard.

When I found out about the baby, I was shocked (I promise you, we had been careful), but then I began to realise that all of this had happened for a reason. I hope you can understand and forgive me. You have a child —

Yes, I do, thought Elizabeth, and you have robbed him of what's left of his childhood. The nerve of this woman!

— so you know what it means. I want to reassure you that this is my journey. Zach can't be a father right now and I don't want to ask that of him. He must continue on his own path. I am so sorry to have brought pain to your family, but please know that you have given me a gift for which I will be forever grateful.

Was this woman mentally stable enough to look after a baby? And as much as Elizabeth longed for this creature to vanish, surely her son should have some sort of say in what happened next. There was also a tiny part of her heart that rebelled at the notion of her grandchild being spirited away. She glanced back at the final paragraph.

I hope to see you in New York with Zach. Please don't judge me too harshly. I have made terrible mistakes but I finally feel that I have got something right.
Yours in motherhood,
Michelle.

Hope. Understand. Forgive. All Elizabeth wanted to do was throw her laptop out of the car window into a ditch.

THEN

Patricia began to ring the bell and didn't stop till she heard the key in the lock. Mrs Foley stepped into the room. She didn't seem at all surprised to find Patricia standing on the bed, backed against the wall, pointing at the basket on the floor.

'A baby? Why have you . . . ? I don't understand. A baby. Why is a baby in that basket?' Her voice was little more than a breathy rasp.

Mrs Foley stood very still and replied calmly. 'That's little Elizabeth. She'll be needing fed soon. I'll bring up a bottle.' And before Patricia could say anything else the door had been closed and locked. She jumped from the bed and began to hammer at the door with her fists.

'Edward! Edward! Where are you?' He must know the answer to this mystery. Where had the mad old crone found a baby? Patricia imagined some poor mother out in the world somewhere frantic with fear, wondering where her child had disappeared to. Behind her a small cry came from the basket. She banged on the door some more but then the crying got louder. Patricia bent down to the basket and for the first time looked at the baby's face. It was crinkled up in mid-cry but stopped as Patricia's face loomed into view and cast a shadow. The large blue eyes stared up at her and the infant's arms began to conduct a tiny orchestra. Patricia felt the urge to pick up the small human and hold her close but she stopped herself. This baby had to go back to where it belonged, and that meant she mustn't fall into Mrs Foley's trap. If she came back to find Patricia nursing the child then it would be so much harder to make her return the baby to its rightful mother. She got up and went back to the door.

'Edward! I need help!' The door bounced against her fist as Mrs Foley opened it and entered. She held up a baby's bottle full of milk.

'There you go. And don't forget to get her wind up after.'

Patricia kept her hands by her sides, refusing to take the milk.

Mrs Foley stared at her for a moment and then placed the bottle on the bedside table. 'It's there when you're ready. Oh, and Edward is off working so you can forget your wailing.' The old woman turned as if to leave but instead retrieved a padded bag covered in small pink roses from the landing. 'There's more nappies in there and lotion and talc.' She placed it on the floor under the chair. Patricia glanced down and as she looked up the door closed, followed by the familiar click of the key.

She sat on the bed, unsure what to do next. Part of her wanted to feed the little bundle in the basket but she knew that she shouldn't. This was not her baby. Somebody else had been caring for this child, loving her. She wasn't a newborn. Patricia guessed the baby was at least three or four months old, maybe more. She hoped that Edward would come back for his lunch. Maybe he could talk sense into his mother. This was serious. The police might get involved. The thought of a Garda car pulling up outside the house suddenly filled her with hope. If they came to rescue the baby, they could save her too. Her thoughts were interrupted by the baby crying. A few tentative yelps followed by a full-throated bawling. Patricia sat still. If she let the infant cry for long enough eventually Mrs Foley would have to come and investigate.

Minutes passed. This waiting game was going to be harder than she had imagined. It was torture listening to the distress of the little mite. She put her hands over her ears but it was no use. Maybe the baby would just give up and stop crying, though, if she was being honest, that didn't sound like it was going to happen any time soon. The whole room seemed to be filled with the desperate cries of this tiny creature. The little hands were flailing above the edge of the basket. Where was Mrs Foley? How could she listen to this? Patricia realised that this was a test to see which of them cracked first. She resolved that it would not be her. She sat on her hands just in case they decided to act independently and grab the bottle of milk.

More minutes slipped away and still the baby cried. Patricia leaned forward and caught a glimpse of the small face. It broke her heart. A tiny mouth, the howling centre of a beetroot-red set of features. She couldn't bear it. Cursing Mrs Foley, Patricia grabbed the baby's bottle and leaned down beside the basket. She tried to put the rubber teat into the mouth but the child

219

seemed beyond consoling at this point. Crying seemed to take priority over eating. Patricia tried shaking the bottle to get a few drops of milk into the mouth to remind the infant what all this crying was actually about. The baby twisted her head left and right. She seemed to have no interest in the bottle whatsoever. Patricia began to worry that perhaps the real mother had been breastfeeding. What was she supposed to do then? Would Mrs Foley let the infant starve to death before she called a doctor out? A sense of panic began to simmer. She reached into the basket and lifted up the baby, resting her in the crook of her arm. The crying didn't stop but the level of distress seemed to reduce. Patricia tried the bottle once more. After a couple of false starts the tiny mouth decided that the time was right. She gripped onto the teat and began to suck hungrily. Patricia's sense of relief was palpable. She stared down at the little human in her arms. The colour of its face was almost back to normal and the sense of contentment that her noisy sucking exuded was infectious.

'Is that nice, Elizabeth? Is it? Are you enjoying that? You are, aren't you?'

Patricia was sitting on the bed now, holding the warm bundle. Two beings trapped in this room against their will. Hopefully more people were worried about little Elizabeth. A mother would never stop looking and surely that meant one day both of them might be rescued. She looked at the tiny face unaware of anything other than the bottle she was clamped to. Could this baby be the answer to her prayers?

The infant had nearly drunk all the milk before she took her mouth from the teat and lay back in Patricia's arms. She had heard mothers talking about getting wind up after a feed, so draped the baby over her shoulder and began to rub her knuckles gently on its back, the way that she had seen others doing it. Soon a few small burps bubbled to the surface. Was that enough? She wasn't sure but decided it was best to keep patting the baby. She felt the curve of its stomach shift against her shoulder, followed by a milky belch that splashed onto the floor. Patricia lifted the baby up and looked at her face. She seemed very pleased with herself. Patricia couldn't help but laugh and kissed the baby on the forehead. She remembered all the tea soaking into the carpet in her old room and stepped over the milky stain at her feet.

Soon Elizabeth was asleep in Patricia's arms. When she tried to put the baby back in her basket, a flicker of distress crossed the little face and she gave a warning yelp. Patricia cradled her to her breast and went to sit by the window. Clouds were scudding across the sky and pools of sunlight picked out patches of the sea in a silvery blue. A lone seagull seemed suspended in the sky as it battled against the wind, but then, as if changing its mind, turned and allowed itself to be blown inland. Patricia remembered how beautiful she had found this view when she first arrived. Now it was a constant reminder of how isolated and alone she was. She tightened her hold around the baby.

About twenty minutes later she saw Edward

walking along the top of the paddock in front of the house. She freed a hand to bang on the window. He didn't seem to hear her so she knocked again with much more force. This time he seemed to have noticed the sound. He looked around as if trying to determine where it had come from. Patricia waved her free hand in order to catch his eye. It worked. Edward looked straight up at her window. Patricia stood and held out the baby, pointing at her. She could only imagine how shocked he was going to be by what she was holding, but instead it was Patricia who was stunned. Edward gave her a thumbs-up, smiled, and then waved before walking on. She stepped back from the window and placed her hand protectively on the baby's head. He was as mad as his deranged mother.

NOW

This woman didn't seem much older than herself.

'Mrs Lynch?' Elizabeth asked doubtfully.

The other woman seemed dressed to go out, her broad shoulders and stocky frame draped in a navy anorak.

'No. I'm her daughter. Was my mother expecting you?' She wasn't exactly unfriendly, but she spoke with a degree of caution.

'Who is it?' a reedy voice from within called out.

The woman at the door shouted over her shoulder.

'I don't know. Some woman looking for you.'

'Who? Who is it?' came the distant response.

'Sure, I'm finding out. Hold your horses.' And then, turning back, 'Sorry about that. You were saying . . . '

Elizabeth took a deep breath. She was still wound tight by Michelle's email, but she knew she shouldn't take it out on this woman. She smiled.

'Oh, yes. My name is Elizabeth Keane but I'm a relation of the Foleys from Castle House.' She was about to explain that Brian's Auntie Eileen had told her to call, but then she realised that she didn't know Eileen's surname. 'Someone told me your mother might be able to tell me a bit of the family history.'

A warm, damp hand with several surprisingly expensive-looking rings was thrust forward.

'Cathy. Cathy Crowley. Nice to meet you.'

'Nice to meet you too.' The two women stood smiling at each other nodding until Elizabeth spoke. 'Do you think your mother would be able to help me?'

Cathy opened the door fully. 'Well, all you can do is ask. She's a big age now but she's still a great one for knowing everyone's business. Come in.'

At the back of the cottage there was a small, dark kitchen. Seated at the table covered in a bright floral oil cloth was an old woman. She was a greyer, thinner version of Cathy. Blue-rimmed glasses were lifted and perched on her nose as the two women came into the room. A large black and white cat jumped lazily from a chair and sauntered towards the door.

'Mammy. This is Elizabeth . . . sorry, what was your family name?'

'Keane.'

'Keane,' Cathy repeated but at a louder volume.

'Keane? I don't think I know any Keanes.' The old lady peered at her visitor through her glasses.

'This is my mother, Ann Lynch. Mammy, will you have more tea?'

'I will if it's there.'

'It is. I'm just after topping it up. Elizabeth? A cup for you?'

'Thank you, yes, please.'

'Sit down there,' Cathy said, simultaneously placing a cup and saucer on the table. 'There's milk in the jug. Now you'll have to excuse me. I have to go in to the optician in Clonteer and I'm already late. Mammy, I'll be back to get you your lunch, so don't be lighting the stove.'

Old Mrs Lynch dismissed her daughter with a wave of her hand.

'Nice to have met you,' Cathy said to Elizabeth from the doorway.

'You too. Thanks for the tea.'

'Not a bother.' And then the sound of the front door slamming.

'I'm a little deaf. You'll have to speak up.' Ann Lynch had the air of a woman for whom strangers calling to interview her were a regular occurrence.

'I understand. Is this all right?' Elizabeth asked, raising her voice.

'Clear as a bell. No need to shout. Now what can I do for you?'

'You knew the Foleys from Castle House, I'm told?'

The old woman sucked her teeth and raised her eyes to the ceiling.

'I did. I did. God rest them.'

Elizabeth paused, waiting for Mrs Lynch to begin a litany of tragedies, but instead she appeared to be waiting for another question. Elizabeth reached into her pocket and produced the wedding photograph she had found at Abbey Court. She pushed it across the table to the old lady.

'I wondered if you could tell me who these people are?'

Mrs Lynch picked up the picture and peered at it.

'God help us,' she said with quiet affection. 'Isn't that Teddy's wedding day? I was there myself. Such a happy day. Would you look at Mrs Foley beaming. And poor Mary, there in all her finery. Terrible sad.'

Elizabeth leaned forward.

'What was so sad?'

'Well . . . ' Suddenly she stopped and took off her glasses. 'Sorry. Who did you say you were? What are the Foleys to you?'

Elizabeth hesitated. 'I am . . . my father was, is, Edward, Teddy Foley.'

Mrs Lynch looked puzzled and then it was as if a fog had lifted. She quickly put her glasses back on. A wide smile spread across her face and her eyes brimmed with tears.

'Elizabeth? Oh, my God. After all these years, just look at you! Elizabeth Foley all grown up and back in Muirinish!'

'You knew me when I was a baby?' Elizabeth found the old woman's emotional state infectious. She too felt close to tears.

'Knew you? Sure, didn't I raise you! You bounced on my knee next door, I couldn't fill the bottles for you fast enough. You were a lovely little thing. Elizabeth Foley. I can hardly credit it.'

'You raised me?' Now it was Elizabeth's turn to look perplexed.

'Well, for the first few months of your life. You know, after your mother died.'

'I don't understand. My mother only died last year.'

'No.' Mrs Lynch picked up the faded

226

photograph, shaking her head. 'No, dear,' she repeated softly and pointed to the bride. 'Mary Foley was your mother, but she died in labour. It nearly sent old Mrs Foley over the edge. That's why I stepped in to help. There was no way she could have coped and poor old Edward wouldn't have known where to start. They really were blighted, that family. So, it must have been the other one raised you?'

'The other one?' Elizabeth's mouth was dry. So many questions darting around her mind. Was this old woman right? She might just be confused.

'Patricia. My mother was called Patricia.' She spoke as clearly as she could, hoping to jog Mrs Lynch's memory.

'Patricia!' she called out triumphantly. 'If you had put a gun to my head I wouldn't have been able to remember that woman's name! And where was it she took you after?'

'Buncarragh. It's just on the Laois-Kilkenny border.' Elizabeth spoke the words calmly but she felt frantic. The possibility that what this woman was saying might be true seemed stronger every moment.

'Oh yes, I remember hearing it was somewhere up the country.'

Elizabeth wasn't listening. Her breathing had become fast and shallow. She had remembered what Rosemary had said about the baby appearing to be older. It was as if a heavy curtain had been cast aside, allowing light to flood in. Her mother hadn't been pregnant when she went to Cork. She had never been pregnant.

Elizabeth realised with a sickening jolt that she was about to cry. She hoped she could control it but no, out it poured like a flash flood of sobs and snot. She tried to speak but couldn't. Her face was contorted into a twisted mask of tears. She could hear her own voice making a shuddering moan.

Mrs Lynch looked horrified. 'Oh. Oh, I'm sorry. It must be a shock for you. I'm sorry.' She hauled herself to her feet and turned in small futile circles. 'There must be a hanky here somewhere.' Spying a roll of kitchen towel by the sink she went to get it. Elizabeth was desperately trying to control her breathing, but the hot sobs kept rolling through her body. Why had this hit her so hard? It was a shock but it was also a sharp, stabbing sense of regret. Her mother had loved her in ways she had never understood. She had taken another woman's child and raised her as her own. Somehow that love seemed purer. She hadn't been lumbered with a daughter, she had chosen to care for her and love her and protect her from her past. Discovering the truth now, when her mother was gone, seemed so cruel, so unfair.

Mrs Lynch shoved a thick wad of kitchen roll into Elizabeth's hand and slowly the howling tears subsided.

THEN

The room was dark and silent. The low bulb in the bedside lamp seemed to throw more shadows than light and the only sound apart from the occasional whistle of the wind around the eaves was the breathing of three bodies. A baby, a woman and a very confused man.

All day she had waited for him to come but it was only after dinner when the whole house seemed to be asleep that there was a soft knock on her door and Edward slipped into the room. He didn't look at Patricia or the baby but sidled over to the other side of the room.

Patricia spoke in a whisper so as not to wake Elizabeth.

'You knew about this baby?' She was standing at the foot of the bed, while Edward sat slumped, eyes on the floor, in the chair by the wardrobe. He remained silent.

'Did you really think that if you gave me a baby, I wouldn't want to leave this prison? Are you serious? That's what you thought?'

Edward twisted his head from left to right.

'It was Mammy. She said — '

Patricia wanted to scream so badly that she clasped her hands over her mouth. Edward groaned and wrapped his arms around his head,

Patricia moved forward and knelt before him.

'Edward.' She tried to sound as reasonable and calm as she could. 'We have to get this baby back to where it belongs. I don't know where you got it, but she must go back. This is serious.' Silence. 'Are you listening? Do you understand, Edward?'

She placed a hand on his knee and he looked up, catching her eye for the first time. 'She's mine,' he said in the softest of whispers.

Patricia wasn't sure if she'd heard him correctly. 'What? Your baby?'

'I'm her father.' His voice sounded dry and matter of fact.

It felt as if all the air had been sucked from the room. How was this possible? It wasn't possible. Edward was lying. He must be. How could they have kept a baby, a crying baby, hidden all this time? Then it came to her, like putting a name to a face or turning a corner to find you weren't lost after all: she remembered the pink soother. The one she had found in the other bedroom. She had forgotten all about it. Maybe he was telling the truth.

'Where has she been, Edward? Why didn't I hear her?'

Edward seemed less distracted now. He knew the answers to these questions.

'A neighbour. Mrs Lynch had her.'

'But the mother, Edward. There must be a mother, who is she?'

He simply stared for a moment and Patricia wondered if he had decided to stop speaking but then he ran his tongue over his top lip and said, 'I was married before.'

Patricia immediately wanted to correct him. He sounded as if he genuinely believed that they

230

were married, but she resisted.

'All right. But where is she? Who is she?'

He leaned forward and took Patricia's hand.

'Mary.' There was something in his tone that suggested that Patricia was supposed to know this fact already.

'Mary?' she repeated.

'Every bush, every bower, every wild Irish flower, it reminds me of my Mary on the banks of the Lee.'

Patricia dropped his hands and sat back. The song they had shared on the bridge. That moment, which she had found romantic, he thought had been his way of telling her about his wife.

'Edward . . . ' She was at a loss for words. The workings of his mind were a mystery to her, she didn't know where to start, how to explain her feelings so that he might understand.

'I thought that was just the old song, Edward. I couldn't have known that Mary was your wife.' She paused and looked at his impassive face. 'Do you see?'

'She died,' was his simple response.

Patricia thought of the rest of the song. Of course she was dead. For a moment she felt sorry for the crumpled man in front of her but then she remembered the baby. Tiny Elizabeth in her basket. This wife hadn't passed away years ago.

'When did Mary die, Edward?'

'Last year. The end of last year.'

Patricia froze and deliberately tried to slow her breathing down. She could feel panic bubbling in her chest.

231

'But Edward . . . Edward, you wrote to me late last year, so . . . '

'It was Mammy's idea,' he said quietly.

Patricia turned away. She couldn't look at him. At last the madness was explained. Edward didn't want a wife, Elizabeth needed a mother. Edward was still speaking.

'Mammy thought nobody would want me if they knew from the start that I had a baby. That's why I didn't tell you. She said you'd fall in love with Elizabeth once you met her, once you held her.'

As if to prove Mrs Foley wrong, Elizabeth chose that moment to squirm under her blankets and then let out a night-shattering cry. Edward immediately sat up with a look of panic. He clearly hadn't spent much time around his baby daughter. Patricia didn't know what to do. She desperately wanted to ignore the baby, not allow Edward or his mother to think for one moment that their plan might be working, but at the same time, the one blameless party in this whole twisted scheme was the baby. Why should she be made to suffer? Patricia picked Elizabeth up and began to pace around the room.

She looked down at Edward and spoke sternly. 'I'm doing this because somebody has to. Go and get her a bottle. Your mother said she'd left some out downstairs.'

He got up to go, but paused by the door. 'Do I need to heat it up or anything?'

'I don't think so. She drank cold milk earlier so she mustn't mind it.'

Edward left her and the baby. Patricia rocked

her gently in her arms while she made shushing sounds. Elizabeth continued to make it very clear that she needed to be fed.

Patricia looked down at the little red face and was relieved to not be worrying about some distraught mother wailing over an empty pram. At least this was her home and Edward was her father. She realised that the person she still needed to be worried about was herself. She was the one who needed to be rescued, not this baby.

Edward burst back into the room brandishing the bottle as if returning to the front with orders from a general.

'Here you go.'

'Thanks.' Patricia sat in the chair that Edward had been occupying and Elizabeth vigorously latched herself to the rubber teat. Her father sat on the bed. The baby's hunger and now her happy rhythmic sucking seemed to act as a balm on the room. Neither Edward nor Patricia felt nearly as stressed and upset as they had just a few minutes earlier.

'She needed that,' Edward said with an admiring grin, as if eating was a talent.

'She did,' Patricia agreed and then they sat in silence for a few minutes. She watched Edward watching Elizabeth.

'How did she die?'

'Mary? She died giving birth to that one.'

Patricia absorbed this information looking down at the baby slurping happily, oblivious to all the sadness and pain she had been born into.

'She started to bleed and they couldn't stop it.

By the time the ambulance came it was too late. She was gone.'

Patricia couldn't help but have some sympathy for this man. He wasn't a bad person, just naive. Too innocent to live in this world, especially with his life being dictated by his mother. Patricia wondered if Mary had been held against her will.

'How did you meet Mary?' she asked, trying to disguise her suspicions.

'Just by chance, and we hit it off.'

Edward wasn't lying. It was true, they had met by chance but that wasn't the whole story or even their first encounter.

What he didn't say was that they had been connected many years before. When he saw her behind the counter in the chemist's Edward hadn't recognised her at first. She was just a woman dressed in black standing at the dispensary. He had asked for the regular prescription of the pills his mother had been on since James drowned. It had been Mary who had noticed him.

'Edward?' she had asked uncertainly, a smile brightening up her thin, pale face. Suddenly he saw the ghost of a young girl he had known.

'Mary?'

They spoke then. She told him about her new job, there in the chemist's. The grandmother who had raised her had passed away so she thought it was time to make her own way in the world. She asked about Mrs Foley and Edward found it wasn't painful to talk to her. The words came easily. He was enjoying himself.

A stranger might have seen a man and a

woman shyly flirting across a counter but what drew them together that day wasn't a physical attraction or romantic chemistry. What connected them was what they had shared. They had both lost James. Mary had been his girlfriend at the time of the accident and his death had affected her deeply. At the funeral, despite her youth, she'd taken on the role of de facto widow and people shared their sympathy with her in almost the same way they did with the family. She had taken to wearing black and vowed to never love another.

So many years had passed, but in each other's company they felt alive. They understood one another because they both knew what they had lost. Edward found that he had invited her out to the farm one Sunday; his mother would like to see her. This was true. Mrs Foley had always been fond of Mary. James had begun to get himself a bit of a reputation locally with the girls so it was a relief to his mother when he started to go steady with someone. She went out of her way to praise Mary. 'A grand capable girl,' was her seal of approval.

Edward hadn't really expected her to say yes, but one Sunday, not too long after the meeting in the chemist's, she was sitting at the kitchen table dunking the Marietta biscuits she had brought into her tea. Conversation had been general. The farm, her grandmother's passing, the new job, but soon the talk had turned to James.

Edward and his mother never spoke of the missing brother and son, but the presence of

Mary in the house gave them permission. They feasted on memories of the young man they had all adored, but there had been no tears. They laughed about the time he hadn't put the hand brake on and the car had ended up blocking the entrance to the Garda barracks in Clonteer, the way he had named all the cows after the neighbours, how Dora the collie had continued to sleep on one of his old jumpers till death had claimed her too.

They arranged to meet again. A film in Clonteer. A walk along the headland on a Sunday. These weren't referred to as dates, but they knew they didn't want to lose each other. When Edward had kissed her it was as if a spark of James had been reignited. In truth, their brief little romance wasn't with each other, it was a celebration of a love they shared. Asking her to marry him seemed like the right thing to do, for his mother, for Castle House, for James.

Sometimes it was hard to recall, but there had been happy times. Mary stepping her way carefully across the fields, her belly growing, a picnic lunch for them to be shared sheltering against a high hedge. The three of them sitting around after dinner talking about the future. Old Mrs Foley had picked the site for her bungalow and she had found a design she liked from the book of plans. The sound of Mary's breathing when he woke in the night. The smell of her hair fanned out on the pillow next to his. Castle House had been transformed. It had all seemed too good to be true.

Her death had been unbearable. Cruel beyond

endurance. It was like having to say goodbye to James all over again. Mary had been the keeper of the past. Losing her meant letting go of any hope of happiness. He still remembered shivering on the rocks on the far side of the paddock while the ambulance took her body away. He slipped back into a state of guilt and sadness like someone returning wearily to an unmade bed. The future, any future, had seemed impossible to imagine as he stared into the starless night.

His mother had changed overnight. This time, however, it wasn't like when they had lost James. Back then she had disappeared into a dark place barely able to get out of bed. Edward had dropped out of school to look after the farm but there was no one to look after him. He had lived on sandwiches for months, until Mrs Lynch from the Co-op had advised him to call out the doctor. The pills had helped. His mother had left her room, and cleaned and cooked. True, she seemed distracted, almost sleepwalking through her days, but for Edward it was an improvement. When Mary had come on the scene for that couple of years, it was as if he had got his mother back; the woman who made decisions, the woman who took on tasks and completed them, the woman who knew exactly what to do. When Mary had died the change that came over Mrs Foley was different; it was a far more subtle shift. She didn't retreat into the darkness of her room, but became strangely driven. She couldn't allow this fresh tragedy to destroy them. She had seen Edward happy and she refused to accept that it was over. Mary could be replaced. A new woman would be found. A wife and mother. Castle House would be a home again. She could make that happen. It was as if she was willing a future for Edward into being.

Her plan had not been presented as a suggestion. It was simply what they were going to do. Giving the new baby away had been the hardest thing, but Edward knew he was in no state to take care of his daughter by himself, and so if that was what his mother said they should do, he didn't really have a choice.

Mrs Foley had read out the ads from the *Journal* and between them they had chosen three to reply to. Patricia was the only one that wrote back. She couldn't have known it as she sat at the kitchen table in Buncarragh, chewing the top of her pen, but she had sealed her own fate. Mrs Foley seemed to relish reading the letters to Teddy, and would often write and rip up two or three replies before she was satisfied and read them aloud for her son's approval. His mother's confidence in the plan meant that there was no turning back. He didn't dare tell her just how excruciating the dates were, but his mother must have guessed. She knew her son and his many limitations, but she also believed that he was a good man and any woman would be lucky to call themselves his wife. The end justified the means.

Elizabeth had begun to cry and the pungent smell that filled the room suggested the reason why. Patricia rolled the changing mat out on the floor, and placed the squirming little girl in the centre of it. Edward knelt on the floor beside her

238

and handed her a clean nappy from the pile that his mother had provided earlier.

'Can you put some warm water in that?' Patricia asked, handing him a plastic basin. Edward got to his feet and left the room.

Elizabeth lay on her back impatiently cycling an imaginary bike. Her face was raspberry-red and her cries were becoming more insistent. Patricia could hear the tap running across the landing.

'I hope I'm doing this right,' she said, almost to herself.

'Looks good to me,' Edward commented, coming back in with the basin.

'There is some difference between how you fold them. I think for girls you put the pins on the side.'

When Patricia peeled the old nappy off, she and Edward both recoiled in horror from the smell. It was shocking that something so toxic had come out of such a sweet little creature. They laughed and for a moment Patricia was lost in her task, making sure her tiny charge was clean and comfortable. Edward was watching her and the baby, and a contented grin had spread across his face. Catching sight of his expression, Patricia scolded him.

'Don't think this is working. Your mother's loony plan is not going to work. I'm caring for this little one only because I have to. She needs somebody, but I must go, Edward. You know that, don't you?'

'Yes.'

'You need to speak to your mother. You have

to talk sense into her. Will you do that for me, Edward? Will you?'

He just nodded his head slowly.

Elizabeth, with her fresh nappy, was back in her knitted dress and booties and gurgling happily. Patricia picked her up and held her out to Edward, who took her gingerly and held her in the crook of his arm. There was something about seeing a father holding his daughter that seemed so perfect. The baby had grabbed hold of one of his fingers and Edward was swinging her arm from side to side.

'You're a lucky man.'

Edward didn't look up from his daughter. 'I don't feel it.'

'That little girl has lost her mother. She has been through so much. I need to leave soon, Edward. Soon.'

The baby turned her tiny head towards Patricia, then smiled and seemed to wave.

NOW

A bank of fog sat plump and solid out at sea, obscuring the horizon. Elizabeth was sitting on the low stone wall in front of Castle House worrying about haemorrhoids. She could hear her mother's voice. 'Don't sit on that cold stone, you'll give yourself piles.' Growing up it had seemed to Elizabeth that her mother believed the world was out to get her. 'Don't leave the house with that wet hair.' 'It's not an hour since your lunch, you can't swim yet.' 'Stop leaning against the storage heater, you'll curl your spine.' She had rolled her eyes and silently mocked her stupid mother for spending her life in a constant state of worry and fear. Now here she was outside this house with its blank windows and sagging gutters, wondering what had happened to her mother here. Why had she fled, leaving her husband behind? She knew so much more about her past than she had a few days before, but the mystery as to what had actually gone on in this house forty-four years ago seemed deeper than ever.

After leaving old Mrs Lynch's house she felt completely disorientated, almost sick. The seismic shift in everything she had always believed to be true had hit her with such unexpected force. She sat in her car and allowed it to almost drive itself back to her birthplace. At least that much was the truth.

The kettle had been reboiled and more tea made before Elizabeth had managed to get her shuddering sobs under control. Handfuls of paper towels turned to pulp by her tears and snot sat on the table in front of her. Mrs Lynch couldn't stop apologising, as if somehow it was her decision to rewrite history.

The two women had held hands and slowly more of her history had been revealed. Her mother, the woman who had given birth to her, had been called Mary. Everyone had been delighted when Edward had found her after living alone with his mother and the memory of his dead brother for so long. When news emerged of the pregnancy people were happier still. The dark past of Castle House was over, and the Foleys could look to a future filled with new life.

Mrs Lynch had recalled everything she could about the night Mary had died. The sound of an ambulance waking half the parish and the next morning people piecing together where it must have been going. Everyone was braced for bad news and, like dark clouds delivering rain, it came. She told Elizabeth about the funeral. Teddy holding the tiny baby, her, she was that baby, and his mother, Mrs Foley, leaning on his other arm, hardly able to walk, she was so broken by grief. People had offered help, delivered food, called up to the house, but everyone had been sent away.

A couple of nights later, Mrs Lynch had been watching the television, when there was a knock on the door. It was Teddy, soaked to the skin in the rain, holding his baby. He was a man of few words but from what she could gather, his mother wasn't coping very well and he wondered if their neighbour Mrs Lynch could take care of the baby for a while. Naturally she had been apprehensive, her own children were school age by then and she hadn't relished the idea of nappies and sleepless nights, but Elizabeth had been a model baby. The calmest, happiest child that she had ever seen. A couple of months went by and there was no sign of the Foleys taking back their little one. Edward would call down with milk, or a bucket of spuds, and check in on his daughter, but always headed home empty-handed. Mrs Lynch had begun to feel as if this child would be hers forever. Then she heard a couple of rumours that Edward was courting. She couldn't quite believe it. Mary wasn't more than a few months dead. But then with no fanfare it was announced he had remarried.

While people couldn't begrudge Teddy Foley a little happiness, this did seem odd. Not just because it was so fast, but because this was a man who had never had a girlfriend, barely spoken to a woman, and now in the blink of an eye he had managed to bury one wife and then find another one. Of course Mrs Lynch imagined that baby Elizabeth would be going home. She assumed that this rushed wedding had been brought about by a desire to give the baby a new mother, but that wasn't what happened. Edward explained that his wife was ill and wasn't up to looking after the child. A week passed and then another but still she was ill. At

243

the time there were two schools of thought. Those with wilder imaginations began to suggest that no wife existed at all. Only one woman had been seen with him and they had had a blazing row outside Carey's. The whole marriage was just Edward Foley finally parting ways with his sanity. The more sympathetic amongst the community believed that he had managed to find a new bride but worried that this one was even more sickly than Mary. They braced themselves for further tragedy to visit Castle House.

As it transpired everyone was proved wrong. Patricia Foley recovered after a few weeks and one evening a nervous Edward came to Mrs Lynch and returned home with his precious parcel.

By this point in the tale Elizabeth had begun to weep again in earnest and Mrs Lynch decided that her audience could bear no more. She glossed over the subsequent events, bringing her story quickly to an end by saying, 'And then we heard Teddy's new wife had left and taken you with her.'

'Why? Why did she leave?' Elizabeth pleaded, her mouth as red and wet as her eyes.

Mrs Lynch got up from the table, busying herself at the sink.

'No one knew. It was all very sad. But now if you'll excuse me I must get ready. Cathy will be back to take me down to the hairdresser's.' It was a lie but she had spent enough time with this woman who had unwittingly trailed such sadness through the house. It seemed incredible that this was what had become of the happiest of babies.

The interview was over and Elizabeth had stumbled out to her car.

The fog seemed to be edging closer. Elizabeth pulled her scarf tight around her neck and got up from the wall. So many lies. Her father wasn't dead and the mother she had buried wasn't really hers. Had her mother, the woman who had raised her, stolen her? But Edward knew where they lived, he could have come to find her whenever he wanted. Why hadn't he come?

Around the side of the house, the wind picked up and Elizabeth zipped up her coat to stop it flapping open. She was below the ruins of the castle now. It seemed much bigger from this angle than when she had seen it from the farmyard. She felt dwarfed by it. This was the ancient home of the Foleys and as far as she knew she was the end of the line. Or was she? Who knew what other secrets these walls held and now there was also the promise of her unborn grandchild. She pulled up her hood. There was too much going on in her life. When were things going to become easy? How many more dramas would she have to endure before things became simple? That was all she wanted. To go to work, come home, make grilled cheese sandwiches and read a book until bedtime. She turned around, stretching her arms out, and let out a wild yell, which was whipped out to sea by the breeze.

THEN

Edward had slept in the room with Patricia and Elizabeth. The baby had been the first to drift off and then Patricia, sitting on the bed, had allowed her head to lean back on the pillows for a moment before sleep had claimed her too. Edward had stood up and looked at the two sleeping figures before him. He thought of Mary then. The simple, happy life that might have been, rather than this unholy mess. He leaned down and turned out the lamp. He waited for a moment and then, like a ghost in the darkness, he lay down on the floor beside the bed. The rough thread of the old carpet felt good against his cheek, and the sweet scent of baby talc and lotion soothed him towards sleep. He listened to the soft breathing and told himself that he could fix things. There had to be a happy ending for someone in this sorry tale.

At some point in the night Patricia had woken. She lay there listening for Elizabeth but then realised she could hear heavier breathing. 'Edward?' she whispered, but he didn't respond. He must be asleep, she thought to herself, not bothering to wonder why he was still in the room. As she waited to fall back to sleep she had an unexpected feeling of contentment. Was this all so terrible? Edward was a kind man and she adored the baby. Maybe she should stop struggling and embrace this as her life. She had

246

read somewhere that if you were drowning the best thing to do was not to fight it. Just breathe in the water and fill your lungs. Should she do that? Just inhale and surrender herself to this new life? Was pretending to choose something that very different from actually wanting it? Later when Elizabeth's crying had woken her, she turned on the bedside lamp and found that she and the baby were alone once more.

The next day after breakfast, Patricia had been armed with some tired-looking yellow dusters and a tin of polish to dust and clean a room she had never even stepped foot in before. It was one of the front rooms by the entrance hall and Patricia doubted it had been used in a year or more. Dead flies were scattered on the windowsills and woodlice lay in dusty graves in the corners of the room. The door had been left ajar so that she could hear Elizabeth if she started to cry.

Patricia didn't like to admit it but cleaning did give her a strange sense of satisfaction. She was methodical and thorough. She tackled the window frames and pictures first, then the floor and finally the furniture. It irritated her that she hadn't been given access to the Hoover. She knew there was one, she'd heard it, but for some reason she wasn't considered responsible enough to use it. Did Mrs Foley think she was going to ride it to freedom?

Kneeling on the windowsill trying to get cobwebs out of the folds in the curtains, she looked outside. A dense rain was being driven almost sideways across the front of the house. Today was not ideal for an escape attempt. She

247

got down and looked around. How long had this furniture been here? The small brown sofa with a gold trim along its cushions looked so old she doubted that even Mrs Foley as a blushing bride had ever seen it looking new. The carpet on the floor was threadbare enough to have been rescued from the ruins of the castle.

An engine! Patricia threw down her duster and pressed herself against the window to see if she could catch a glimpse of the vehicle. A flash of dark green disappeared behind the side of the house. It was just Teddy. She returned to her work, wondering if she would share the fate of the flies, to be found one day, a crisp husk waiting uselessly at the window.

A few moments later, Edward stuck his head around the door.

'A letter for you there.' He held out an envelope and smiled.

Patricia crossed the room and took it without uttering a word. She had to keep reminding him that this situation wasn't normal and would never become anything close to that. Her feelings from the night before had unsettled her. Was she beginning to crack? Had Mrs Foley's plan begun to work? She must not consider surrender. Edward left her alone.

Turning the envelope over she saw that it was addressed to Mrs Edward Foley. Her first instinct was to crumple the paper in her fists and throw it away, but she was fairly sure that the handwriting belonged to Rosemary. She checked the postmark. It was Buncarragh. Her heart beating faster, she sat down and ripped it open.

Dear Patricia,
*Sorry not to have written sooner but then
you haven't exactly kept the postman very
busy yourself! I want to hear all your news.
How's married life treating you? Are you
sick of milking cows yet? I hope it is all
going very well and that the two of you are
very happy.*

*My big news is at the top of the page.
I've bought a house! I'm thrilled with
myself. It's only small but it is all mine.
It's a few doors down from Busteed's and
looks out on the trees by the river. I sold
my site on the home place so I thought I'd
better do something with the money and
not just spend it all on cakes and frothy
coffee. I'm officially a grown up! It's not a
hundred per cent yet but I think I might
be going into business for myself too. Mrs
Beamish is being a right cow. If I have to
attempt one more shag hairdo, I might end
up in prison. I'm not safe with the scissors.
Fat bot's mother came in the other day
with a picture of your one, Jane Fonda! I
felt like suggesting Kojak might be more
her style . . . ha ha!*

★　★　★

Patricia's reading was interrupted by voices
coming from the kitchen. They were getting

249

louder and sounded angry. She pushed the letter into the pocket of her nylon housecoat and went to the door to hear better. It was Edward's voice but she could make out only some words.

' . . . got to go . . . ' and then something she couldn't quite catch followed by ' . . . never be happy.'

Mrs Foley sounded furious. 'Be a man! You've always been . . . ' then it sounded as if she had turned away because her voice seemed more distant, but then full volume again,' . . . with that baby.'

Edward's voice was even further away. It sounded as if he must be heading for the back door. 'Mammy! There is only one thing that . . . ' His voice became muffled, so Patricia crept into the hall and edged along the wall towards the kitchen. Mrs Foley's voice thundered through the closed door. 'Edward Foley! You listen to me and you listen carefully. You lost your brother, you lost your wife and now you want to lose your daughter! You're a fool and I will not let you do it!' The back door slammed violently and Patricia scampered back to her dusting before she was discovered.

Her back against the door, she found herself breathing hard. She had never heard Edward speak like that before. She felt that something in him was about to crack. If she kept up the pressure on him, maybe it would snap, and he would finally defy his mother.

Upstairs Elizabeth began to cry. Patricia put down her duster and hurried off to see what the baby needed.

The afternoon was long and dark. The wind was at its worst and drove the rain in angry squalls against the window. It was the sort of day that would have sent Patricia into a downward spiral, thinking about Buncarragh and the lives that were marching on without her, but today she barely had a thought for the damp darkness that shrouded the house. Having fed and changed Elizabeth, she had watched her sleep for nearly an hour and then when the baby had woken with a small flurry of cries she had picked her up at once and held her to her breast as she paced the room. Patricia bent down and kissed the tiny ear which in turn made the little mouth wrinkle into a smile. She put the baby on the bed and gently tickled her belly. The smiles became a gurgle of laughter and that small happy face became Patricia's world. She slipped off Elizabeth's knitted lemon booties and examined her perfect little feet. So beautiful. She blew kisses into the sole of the right foot, then the left, and Elizabeth began to cackle, a laugh like no adult would ever make. It was an expression of pure happiness, not designed to please anyone, or demonstrate anything, but simply because the sensation on her feet filled her to bursting point with joy. It thrilled Patricia. For the first time, she had a glimpse of what lengths a mother might go to to keep her child happy.

The key turned in the lock, and Mrs Foley came into the room. The bubble of baby joy was immediately burst. Patricia stayed on the floor by the side of the bed. The old woman's eyes looked red, as if she had been crying, and in the fading light from the window she looked tired and drawn.

'Patricia,' she said by way of a greeting. Patricia said nothing.

Mrs Foley sat on the high-backed chair. The two women looked at the baby on the bed and Elizabeth, as if sensing the attention, wiggled her legs in the air.

'Sweet child,' observed Mrs Foley.

'Yes,' agreed Patricia.

A silence descended on the room and the old woman put her hands on her thighs as if she was about to launch into a low keening ballad. Patricia could sense her eyes boring into her. She felt the familiar ripples of anxiety starting in her stomach. What had the old crone got in store for her now?

'Has Teddy been talking to you?'

Patricia turned to look at her visitor. 'Talking?'

'Telling you things? His story?'

'What do you mean?'

Mrs Foley gave an exasperated sigh. 'You know things haven't been plain sailing for him?'

'I do,' Patricia replied cautiously.

'Well then, you know he hasn't had it easy.' She leaned forward, her dark eyes fixing Patricia with a hard stare. Mrs Foley spoke slowly and softly, picking her words with care. 'You are not going to upset that boy any more.'

Patricia's mouth was dry and she found herself leaning away from the old woman. What was she planning to do? The thought that

Edward's mother was about to try and kill her suddenly seemed very real. She got to her feet and moved to the foot of the bed.

'Do you understand me, girl?'

'Yes. Yes, I do,' Patricia said quickly, not wanting to upset Mrs Foley any further.

'So, if you don't want to take care of this baby, I'm not going to make you.' Mrs Foley stood up and before Patricia could react she had reached down and picked up baby Elizabeth. She carried the squirming bundle towards the door. 'Happy now?' she spat at Patricia.

The two women locked eyes. Only the baby moved a muscle and even she seemed to sense that now was not the time to cry. Patricia's mind was swirling, unsure of what her next move should be. Clearly this was some sort of game, but what was winning and who decided which woman lost? Through her confusion, one thing was sure: if winning meant losing the baby then she had no interest in victory.

'Wait!' Patricia called across the room. Even the way Mrs Foley was holding the child, not cradled in her arms, but gripped against her hip with one elbow like laundry, made her anxious. She dreaded to think what fate would befall Elizabeth if she was taken from this room.

'Yes?' Mrs Foley sounded calm, uninterested even. Patricia held out her arms to take the baby. One horrible moment of not knowing, and then Mrs Foley broke the spell, walking over to Patricia and handing her Elizabeth.

'If you're sure,' she said with a triumphant smirk.

NOW

Elizabeth wasn't certain why she had come back here. To pay her last respects, or did part of her still hope that the old man might suddenly be jolted back to consciousness by her presence and reveal her past? She parked her car on the apron of gravel outside Abbey Court. Quite a few of the spaces were taken, so she hoped it might be a better time for visiting.

Inside, the doors to the day room were open and several older people sat slumped in chairs, staring into the middle distance. A few of them had visitors with them, some chatting, others just sharing the silence. No one greeted her, so Elizabeth headed straight for Edward's room.

He looked as though he hadn't moved since the day before: still propped up on pillows, arms crossed over his chest, eyes lightly closed. It wasn't clear if he was asleep or simply resting. His parchment skin had a recently washed sheen to it even though there was an orange stain around his thin lips from whatever he had been fed. Patricia stood at the door for a moment just looking at him lying in his bed. This man, who her mother had erased from her childhood, was now the only real link she had to her past. Her father. She stepped forward.

'Hello, Daddy.' Elizabeth knew she was being foolish, but couldn't help herself. She wanted to hear her voice say those words. There was no

254

reaction from the bed, just the slow, even rasp of the old man's breathing. She went and sat beside him. The picture of the wedding was still in her pocket and she had intended to return it, but now she had second thoughts. Surely it meant more to her than anyone else? She couldn't imagine the collection of bones in front of her held together by faded pyjamas was ever going to want to see the face of his bride once more. They sat in silence. Somewhere nearby an electrical hum shuddered to a halt. Footsteps squeaked by on the polished lino of the corridor.

As if to give her visit a purpose, Elizabeth reached out and took her father's hand. It was warmer than she had expected and the skin was rough and cracked. Their fingers were inter-linked and she studied his nails and knuckles and imagined the last time they had touched her. How tiny she must have been.

Without warning Edward suddenly turned his head to look at her. She gave a little start of surprise. It was as if the dead had come to life. His dark eyes were open and staring at her and the tip of his tongue was moving gently against his dry lips.

Trying not to sound alarmed, Elizabeth leaned forward.

'Hello.'

Her father gave a small cough and swivelled his eyes towards the bedside locker. Elizabeth picked up the plastic sipping cup he was looking at and held it to his mouth. He sucked at the raised hole in the lid three times and then moved away. She put the cup back.

'Is that better?' she asked.

Another cough.

'I'm Elizabeth.' She was going to add that she was his daughter, but then thought better of it. She didn't want to give him a shock. Her return to his life shouldn't end it.

A look of pain took hold of her father's face and then he spoke. But what had he said? It sounded like 'gorilla'.

'I'm sorry. I don't understand.'

He spoke again. This time a different word. Hill? Heel, maybe?

'Are you in pain? Will I get a nurse?'

With a great effort he stuck his tongue out and licked his lips before swallowing. His hand tightened its grip on hers.

'What is it? What do you need?' Elizabeth hoped that someone might come into the room. She was feeling out of her depth. The look of pain came over his face again. He said something else that Elizabeth couldn't understand, but then his eyes widened and he moved his other hand to hold hers.

'Mary!' The name rang out.

Elizabeth squeezed his hands. This old man had seen her mother in her face!

'No. I'm not Mary. I'm Elizabeth,' she tried to explain but Edward wasn't listening. He just kept repeating 'Mary!' over and over again. He seemed distressed.

'What is it, Edward? Mary isn't here.'

He threw his head back on the pillow and began to shake violently. Elizabeth didn't know what to do. He seemed to have gone into a spasm or a fit of some kind. She raced to the door and called out into the corridor.

'Nurse! Can I get a nurse, please! Please, I need a nurse.'

Around the corner came a plump, dark-haired lady in a nurse's uniform and behind her the nice ginger-haired boy she had met the day before. They rushed into the room.

'I don't know what's happening. He was fine and then . . . '

The nurses were gathered around the bed. Gordon, the young one, turned to her. 'Better go wait in the day room.' He sounded solemn and firm, so she did as she was told.

It was only when she sat down on one of the high-backed chairs that she realised she was shaking. A girl, surely too young to be a nurse, noticed her and offered her a cup of tea which she gratefully accepted. This couldn't be how they said goodbye. He had to survive this, whatever 'this' was. Had she upset him, or had the convulsions always been going to happen? Trying to steady her hands, she sipped her tea.

After a few minutes, tall, red-haired Gordon appeared. She obviously looked worried, because he smiled to let her know at once that things weren't as bad as she feared.

'He's OK. We gave him a sedative, and the doctor will be out to him soon.'

'Thank you.'

Gordon sat down beside her. 'These things look much worse than they are. We see them all the time. I think it's more upsetting to watch than it is for them.'

Elizabeth nodded doubtfully.

'I was talking about you last night.'

'Were you?'

'It turns out my Aunt Patty went to school with Teddy.'

'Your aunt went to school with my father?' It seemed unlikely.

'Ah, there's a fierce clatter of them. Twelve kids. My father is the baby, like.'

'Right.'

'Anyway, she had the whole story. I couldn't believe it. The drama. It's amazing. I mean, we just see these old people sitting in here,' he indicated the other occupants of the day room, 'half of them gaga, but you forget they've all lived lives. Like, did you know about his brother?'

'The one that drowned?'

'Yeah. Wasn't that fierce sad?'

'It was, yes.'

'And then the wife. Was that your mother?'

'She was, yes.' Elizabeth was beginning to feel uncomfortable. She wasn't sure she should be talking about Edward's life as if it was just idle gossip.

'Aunt Patty said she probably was. And then the mother to top it all off. Awful.'

Elizabeth was tempted to pretend she knew what Gordon was talking about but her curiosity got the better of her.

'The mother? What do you mean?'

'Well, you know. The bad death.'

'Bad death?'

'The suicide, like.'

'Edward's mother killed herself?'

'Sorry now, I thought you'd know. According to Aunt Patty, she went out and hung herself from a tree in the orchard. It was poor Teddy found her.'

Elizabeth just stared at him. She didn't know what to say. This couldn't be true, could it? Surely someone, old Mrs Lynch, would have told her?

'I'm not sure that can be . . . ' she began, but just then Sarah Cahill, carrying a thick pile of files, appeared at the door.

'Nurse. Are you still on shift?'

Gordon jumped to his feet.

'Sorry, I was just — '

'May I borrow you?' Sarah interrupted him with a tight smile.

'Of course.' And the two of them were gone.

Elizabeth thanked the young woman for her tea and stood in the reception area, not sure what she should do. Edward would be sleeping and although she was fairly certain that Aunt Patty had got her wires crossed, she felt she should find out for sure. Mrs Lynch was the obvious person to check with, but if she drove out to Muirinish again she definitely wouldn't get back to Buncarragh tonight. As she made her way back out towards the car her phone rang. Brian.

'Hello?'

'Hello. Where are you?'

'I'm just leaving Abbey Court.'

'Great. Are you still on for lunch?'

Elizabeth's heart sank. She was in no mood

259

for a silly flirty lunch. Her decision was made.

'I'm really sorry, but I've got to head out to Muirinish again to check on something.'

'Oh.' He sounded deflated. 'Well, never mind. I've got stuff I should be getting on with anyway.'

'Thanks.' She hardly knew this man, why did she feel like a bitch? 'Nice to meet you.'

'You too. Thanks for everything. Bye.'

'Bye.' She hung up feeling as if she had just dumped someone.

★ ★ ★

Back in Muirinish, Elizabeth had almost given up waiting for the door to open, when the diminutive grey-haired figure of Mrs Lynch appeared behind the frosted glass. When she saw who her visitor was she did not look thrilled.

'I promise not to burst into tears!'

Mrs Lynch gave a half-hearted chuckle.

'Sorry. I think I must have dozed off in the chair. Did you forget something?'

'No. It was just, well, I wanted to check something with you. It's probably nothing.'

'Well, you'd better come in, so. My legs aren't great for standing. They're not great for anything to be honest,' the old woman said as she made her way slowly back into the gloom of the house towards the kitchen.

'Tea?' she offered but her tone suggested the answer she was hoping to hear.

'No, thank you. I'm grand.'

Mrs Lynch retook her seat from that morning. The large black and white cat didn't look as if it was going anywhere on this visit so Elizabeth sat down beside it.

'So, what can I do for you?' Mrs Lynch put her hands on the table with the air of a professional. Elizabeth was reminded of a bank manager or head teacher.

'It's probably a misunderstanding, but I just wanted to check: somebody told me, Edward's mother, she, well, she didn't take her own life, did she?'

The expression on the old lady's face was the only answer Elizabeth needed. Before Mrs Lynch could speak, she demanded, 'Why didn't you tell me?'

One of the old woman's hands was now twisting the small gold chain around her neck. 'You were so upset. I was going to tell you but then I just thought it would be too much for you.'

Still slightly indignant, Elizabeth could nevertheless see her point.

'It wasn't as if it mattered really. Not to you. It was just more tragedy to be heaped upon the Foleys.'

Elizabeth thought about poor Edward left all alone at Castle House.

'When did it happen?'

'Oh, God. That was a long time ago. I remember it was around the time the second wife went off with you.'

Elizabeth wondered how this news played a part in her story. 'Did it happen before my mother left? Was it the reason she went away?'

Mrs Lynch shook her head sadly. 'I'm sorry. I

261

really don't know. What you have to remember is that I never set eyes on that woman. There were no announcements. I didn't know she was here. I didn't know she was gone. Word got around, that's how things worked. With poor old Mrs Foley, God rest her, it was very different. The guards were here, asking questions around the place, sure everyone knew.'

'And . . . ' Elizabeth hesitated, 'she was found in the orchard?'

Mrs Lynch sucked her teeth. Clearly the details were too much for her. 'As far as I know, yes. And,' she continued as if reading Elizabeth's mind, 'it was Teddy that found her.'

'I see.'

'Have you been in to see him?'

'I have.'

'And how is he?'

Elizabeth wasn't sure what to say. 'Fine. I mean, he doesn't seem very . . . ' Her voice trailed away.

'I know. Sure, if those were your memories wouldn't you want to lose them too?'

The cat beside Elizabeth gave an extravagant stretch and began to lick its back paw.

THEN

Two whole days had passed since Patricia had seen Edward. Was he avoiding her? Had the argument she had overheard been the end of his fight to release her? Was his mother making him believe she had decided to stay? Certainly, since she had asked to keep the baby Mrs Foley was treating her differently. She was no longer watching Patricia's every move; even her bedroom door was sometimes left unlocked. She had come and watched Patricia while she tried to feed Elizabeth a jar of baby food, and helped her wipe up the orange carrot goo as it was unceremoniously spat out. Patricia wanted to escape, she had to, but she also understood that it was now more complicated than that. She couldn't just wander away barefoot into the night, she had no idea how far her weakened body could manage, and why should she when she was still hoping that Edward was going to help? Then there was the baby. Could she really leave this place, abandoning Elizabeth? She wasn't her baby, she kept reminding herself of that, but she didn't belong to anyone else. Who else could care for her and, yes, love her? Patricia could hardly articulate the feelings, but it was good to be needed. She loved the weight of the hot little bundle in her arms as she paced the bedroom. The little girl was even more vulnerable than she was and that gave her a patience and a strength she hadn't had before. She couldn't act rashly, not now she had to think about someone else.

Mrs Foley called from downstairs. She needed help. Patricia rolled her eyes and imagined that soon she'd be on her hands and knees cleaning out the grate of a fire she had never seen burning. She checked Elizabeth in her crib. Fed and changed, she was sleeping, her fists balled up over the blankets, tiny spit bubbles in the corners of her mouth. Patricia smiled and went to get her housecoat. It wasn't on the hook by the door, Mrs Foley must have put it in the wash. She remembered there was another one in the wardrobe. She was putting it on when she felt something in the pocket. Rosemary's letter! She had forgotten all about it after hearing the fight. She sat on the bed and took it out, smoothing the crumpled paper on her lap. She found where she had stopped reading.

. . . Kojak might be more her style . . . ha, ha!

The big scandal is that Fiona Dunn is after leaving Tony! His mother was in the salon and told us the whole story. Apparently they went to Lanzarote for their holidays and they met this couple from Dublin. Anyway she is after running away with your man and he has left the wife. Tony's mother was calling her every name under the sun. I suppose everyone has forgotten how Fiona got with Tony. She just dumped poor John Hickey from a great

height and apparently he was after buying
a ring and everything. At least there are no
kids. The scandal!

I don't know if you have been in touch
with your brother at all, but in case he
didn't tell you, Mrs Cronin died a couple
of weeks ago. I know she was a friend of
your mother's. She had a stroke and then I
think it was her heart. Probably for the
best.

I was sad to see the For Sale sign out-
side your house . . .

Patricia stopped. She read the sentence again.
'For Sale sign outside your house.' What was she
talking about?

I know you have made your life down in
Cork now but it made it seem so final.

No. This must be some sort of mistake.

I hope you don't mind me saying, but I
really miss you. I'd love to see you. Maybe
in the summer I could take a couple of
days off and come down to visit you and
meet the famous Edward!

The words on the page were dancing in front
of her eyes. This couldn't be true! That house
was hers. It was her reward, for nursing their
mother, for the sacrifices she had made. It must
be Jerry, and that Gillian dripping poison in his
ear. She knew she shouldn't have trusted that

slimeball Murphy the solicitor. He'd do anything Jerry said because he had the business. This wasn't right. She had to stop him.

Clutching the letter in her hand, she went to the door. It was open. She rushed down the stairs.

'Edward! Where are you, Edward?' she called.

Mrs Foley came out of the kitchen, wiping her hands on a cloth.

'What is it? Is the baby all right?'

'Yes, yes,' Patricia said impatiently, pushing her way past into the kitchen. 'Where's Edward? I have to speak to him!' Her voice was louder now. Her feeling of hysteria was building. Something awful was happening and she had to stop it.

'He's out working. He'll be in for lunch.' Mrs Foley was not going to indulge this behaviour. 'You need to calm down, my girl,' she said sternly, but Patricia had caught a glimpse of Edward through the window. He was on the far side of the yard, walking towards the milking parlour. She lunged at the back door. It was unlocked. She stepped outside and called his name. 'Edward!'

He turned, astonished to see her outside. She began to run barefoot across the uneven farmyard.

Mrs Foley was at the door, barking at her. 'Patricia! Come back here.' She began to make her way unsteadily after her in pursuit.

Edward ran towards Patricia and they were now standing in the centre of the yard. Her light housecoat was being lifted by the breeze and was

266

flapping around her.

'What is it?' He put his hands on her shoulders, to steady her. Patricia's face was now stained with tears and it was hard to understand what she was saying.

'Jerry. My brother, Jerry, is trying to sell my house!' She brandished Rosemary's letter as evidence, but the wind caught it and carried it up into the grey sky, sailing around the side of the castle towards oblivion. Patricia sank to her knees, while Edward tried to hold her up.

His mother had joined them. She was holding her hair back from her face with one hand. 'What is it? What is wrong with her?'

'I'm not sure. Bad news.'

Patricia leaned against him and pleaded. 'Please. I've got to go home. I've got to!' She twisted her head towards Mrs Foley. 'Let me use the phone. I must call someone! I must!' She was hysterical with frustration and panic. 'Please, Edward! Please!' His face showed no emotion. He grabbed her under one arm and lifted her up. His mother held her other arm tightly.

'We need to get her back to bed.' It was Mrs Foley speaking but Edward didn't disagree. Patricia was frantic. He couldn't be doing this.

'Edward, you said I could go. You said you'd help me. Please. Please let me go. I have to go!'

She felt a sudden sharp pain on the left side of her face where Mrs Foley had slapped her.

'You need to calm down.' They began to half-carry, half-drag her back towards the house. Patricia struggled but it was useless. She felt the skin of her feet being torn and scratched as they

267

pulled her across the yard and then into the kitchen. She was wailing now, screaming at the top of her voice. Words failed her.

Up the stairs they pulled her and then she was pushed onto the bed.

'Hold her,' Mrs Foley commanded and Edward, her Edward, eyes almost shut, as if he was in pain, pinned her down while his mother went across the room and picked up Elizabeth, who had begun to wail in unison with Patricia.

'Leave her now,' the old woman barked without a backwards glance as Edward trailed after her. The door was slammed and locked.

Patricia leapt from the bed and began to hammer on the door.

'Edward! Please! Don't do this!' She pummelled her fists against the wood until they hurt. 'Just one phone call! Please! Please!' She slumped to the floor and buried her head between her knees, her body overcome by sobs and fatigue. Her house. The only thing she possessed in the world. She felt as if she was being slowly erased. Soon there wouldn't be a trace left.

Hours crept by. Occasionally she could hear Elizabeth crying in another part of the house. She longed to be the one picking her up, cradling her, and kissing the sweet soft top of her head. Patricia tried to sleep but the cuts on her feet had begun to pulse with pain. She wondered if they would get infected and then she would die alone in this room. She began to cry again.

Much later (had she been sleeping?), she heard the scrape of the key in the lock. Patricia turned her face towards the wall.

'Patricia?' It was Edward's voice. He spoke in a whisper.

She turned and saw him silhouetted against the landing light. He was holding the baby. She reached out her arms and he placed Elizabeth into them. Patricia held the baby tightly and pressed her cheek against the child's face, breathing in deeply.

Light was still flooding into the room and Edward hadn't moved.

'I'm sorry.'

Patricia glared at him and hissed over the baby's head, 'Sorry? You say you're my friend, you claim you want to help me, but you are just as bad as her!'

'No. I . . . please, Patricia. I do want to help. I will. I promise.'

'I don't believe you, why should I believe you?' She shut her eyes, willing him to leave the room.

'I brought up some hot water.'

'What?' She didn't understand.

'For your feet. They'll need cleaning.'

She wanted to scream. If she hadn't been holding Elizabeth, she would have struck him. How could this man, who was holding her against her will, allowing her old life to be taken away from her, also be this man, who wanted to care for her?

'Edward, please tell me you understand.'

'Understand what?' He was carrying a steaming basin in from the landing.

'That you understand I must leave. You can't keep me here. Let me use the phone. Please,

Edward.' She was sitting up now, trying to read the expression on his face.

'There is no phone.'

'There is. I've heard it ringing.'

'Mammy ripped it out. She did it weeks ago.'

Patricia was dumbfounded.

'You just let her?'

'She didn't tell me she was going to.' He sounded reasonable, as if they were talking about his mother throwing out an unread newspaper.

'Didn't you think to get someone out to fix it?'

He looked at her blankly for a moment, just blinking.

'She wouldn't like that.'

Patricia gave a long sigh. This was useless.

Edward was on his knees now, soaping up a flannel in the basin of hot water. Gently he took hold of Patricia's right ankle and began to carefully soak the torn skin.

'Is that too hot?'

She felt defeated, by him, by his mother, by his kindness. 'No. That's fine.'

She closed her eyes and the warm flannel slowly made its way around one foot and then the other. Under the arch, through the toes, across the ball, up the heel. Patricia thought of Edward on his knees helping a sick calf, or drying off a new lamb. There was such tenderness in this man, but he couldn't seem to grasp the pain he was causing her.

When he had finished washing her feet, he wrapped them in an old towel and very gently pressed them dry.

'There. That's better.'

He gave a wide smile and before she could stop herself she had given a smile of thanks in return.

Edward folded the towel and stood up. He looked sad. Sadder than she had ever seen him. Had he washed Mary's feet, she wondered. He put the basin outside the door and then looked back at Patricia.

'Good night, so.'

'Good night.'

'Patricia?'

'Yes?'

The light was behind him so she couldn't see his face, but his voice sounded strained, almost cracking with emotion.

'I am going to help you.'

NOW

Of course, the place was familiar, but it was more than that. Elizabeth found she had a silly grin on her face as she drove past the Renault dealership on her way back into Buncarragh. It was a relief to return to a world that held no mysteries for her. It felt like a refuge after the Pandora's box of Muirinish.

The Christmas lights were still up, but the town didn't look as melancholic as when she had arrived the week before. Shops were open and people trotted with purpose along the streets, greeting neighbours, pausing for gossip. Elizabeth decided not to stop in town but instead drove straight up to Convent Hill. She had to go a little way past number sixty-two in order to park and walking back to the house she had a clear view down over the whole of the town. The chapel, the church, the trees marking the path of the river. Buncarragh. Growing up here she had always felt like an outsider. It was the reason she had been in such a hurry to leave, but now it made sense. She had been from somewhere else all along. She stopped outside the house where she had been raised and thought about her mother. The woman she had always thought of as so conservative, worried about what other people might think, had turned out to be somebody else entirely. Risking everything, she had left her life behind to find a husband, and then returned alone, but with another woman's child. Elizabeth wished she could see her mother just once more, to thank her for her life, to tell her how much she appreciated all the sacrifices, but also to ask her why she had kept it all a secret right to the very end? Why she had never returned to Muirinish and left Edward all alone on the farm? Maybe she had told the lie for so many years, she had forgotten the truth. Elizabeth looked at the tarnished door knocker and remembered the hours her mother spent with her tin of Brasso and an old cloth, making sure it shone like gold.

Tomorrow, she would leave here and, if she was being honest, she doubted that she would ever return. New York. She was looking forward to getting home and starting work again, but she dreaded her reunion with Zach and meeting the heavily pregnant Michelle. The night before, sitting in her bedroom in the Cork Airport Hotel, she had finally spoken to her son. It hadn't been easy. She didn't know how to be with him any more. How could she best be his mother? Part of her wanted to scream at him for being so stupid and irresponsible, but hearing the fear in his voice as he tried to sound capable and mature, she also wanted to hold him tight and protect him from this huge event that was going to derail his life. No matter what assurances Michelle might be giving, if Zach knew what the mother of his child had said to Elliot and Elizabeth about not involving him, he seemed to be ignoring it. He spoke at length about how he saw his role as a father. She didn't mention the email. His naïve desire to be more of a friend than a parent to the new baby broke Elizabeth's heart. He was so clueless, still such a child himself. Of one thing she was certain: this situation was going to get much worse before it got better. She had also spoken to Elliot. It seemed the last few days of playing Daddy had been enough for him. Will had got him a Weimaraner puppy for Christmas so he wouldn't be making it over to the east coast for the birth. For that at least, Elizabeth was grateful.

On the long drive back to Buncarragh, decisions had been made. The first and most important was that Convent Hill didn't matter. Elizabeth wasn't going to open another drawer or pack a single box to ship home. She was going to let her Aunt Gillian and Noelle loose on the place and then put it up for sale. Having made the decision, she felt released, as if a burden had been lifted. She had also decided that Castle House would be sold. She had to admit that there had been a small sentimental urge to keep it, maybe renovate it one day and retire there or use it as a holiday home, but unless she won the lottery that was never going to happen. Besides that, the house might be a part of her personal story, but it was such a dark, sad part that it made more sense to let it go.

Inside number sixty-two, Elizabeth picked her way slowly through the rooms. Piles of blue and white rat poison were scattered around the house, but happily she encountered no actual rodent residents. She had thought she might change her mind about not keeping anything, but room after room was filled with ornaments, pictures and pieces of furniture that she knew she could live without. Unless she was planning to open a Patricia Keane museum, what would she do with it all? Yes, her mother had loved all these things, but holding on to them wouldn't bring her back or make her more present. If anything, looking at her sewing basket or the old toffee tin filled with random buttons made her absence more vivid.

The last room she went into was her mother's bedroom. The curtains were still drawn from the night Elizabeth had spent there. She pulled them open. The view she could have described with her eyes closed. The telegraph pole. The dormer window in the roof of the house opposite that always reminded her of a ski chalet. That long crack running down the side of the house next to it, which had been there for as long as she could remember. Elizabeth reminded herself that she would never see these signs of her past again, but found she felt nothing. These things were just familiar, that was all, not special. She was surprised she was being so unsentimental. She wondered if she would have felt differently if she had a brother or sister to walk through the house with. Another person to share the memories. What did it matter? Then she suddenly remembered why she had come into this room. She opened the wardrobe door and retrieved the wooden box. Opening it to take out the package of letters, she found the knitted baby bootie. She had forgotten all about it. This must have been hers. She smelled the wool and smiled.

Noelle was in the window of the shop changing the display when Elizabeth arrived. She waved enthusiastically through the glass and began to reverse carefully through a selection of Hoovers and grass strimmers. Once inside Elizabeth was led upstairs to say goodbye to Uncle Jerry and Aunt Gillian. She quickly deflected any questions about her trip to West Cork by telling them that they could help themselves to the contents of Convent Hill, and when they were done she was just going to send in a firm that did house clearances. Gillian beamed at the news, whereas Noelle gave the impression of someone who had already had a good look around and hadn't found anything to her taste. As Elizabeth had expected, Paul immediately offered to take the house off her hands. 'Avoid all the estate agent's fees,' he explained. She was firm. It was very kind of him, but she wanted to keep everything businesslike and not mix things up with family. Paul hid his disappointment and immediately suggested that she hand the house over to Donal Fogarty to sell it for her.

'Is that the Donal who was your best man?'

'Yes.'

Elizabeth smiled. 'Well, I'll certainly think about it.'

She was offered a bed for the night but she had already decided that she would drive straight on to Dublin so that she could return the car and not get caught up in traffic the next day. She was done with Buncarragh.

The Keanes gathered on the pavement to wave

her off. They promised to stay in touch. 'See you soon!' they called and almost sounded as if they meant it. Elizabeth waved and drove away. She hadn't gone far when she indicated and turned down a side street on the left. It brought her past Busteed's bar and on to Connolly's Quay. She wasn't sure if she'd stop but there was a space right outside Rosemary's house, which she took as a sign.

The bell was followed by excited yapping before Rosemary appeared at the door, dressed in a long black velvet coat and a purple crotched hat that brought to mind an Abba album cover. She didn't seem particularly surprised to find Elizabeth Keane on her doorstep.

'You're back.'

'I am. But I'm actually just on my way to the airport.'

'I see. How was Cork?'

The question seemed loaded, so Elizabeth took a hunch and answered it with one of her own.

'Did you know?'

Rosemary pursed her lips.

'Well, you'll have to walk with me.' She held up a red and blue string bag with books in it. 'If I don't get these back today, I'll have a fine.'

'Perfect.' The library wasn't too far.

Rosemary set off at surprising speed and it took Elizabeth a couple of strides to catch up with her.

'So?'

Rosemary stared straight ahead and took a few more steps before answering.

'I didn't feel it was my secret to share. If your mother didn't see fit to tell you, then I told myself it wasn't my place to do it for her.'

'Did she tell you what happened?'

'Yes. Well, a lot of it anyway. She had a very bad time of it down there. As far as I could make out, she was practically a prisoner.'

'A prisoner?' Elizabeth was alarmed. She thought she knew all the secrets. 'My father locked her up?'

'No. I don't think so. In fairness, she only ever spoke well of him. No, it was mostly the mother. What they call mental health issues these days, but back then she was just a lunatic. She sounded like a right nut job. You'd never have guessed it from meeting her though. She had me fooled. Your mother never went into detail, but she told me about you, and who your mother was.'

They had reached the corner now and were waiting to cross the road.

'And my father?'

Rosemary looked puzzled. 'Your father?'

Elizabeth paused, momentarily unsure of how much to reveal, but decided that full disclosure was best.

'He's alive. I mean, he's still alive.'

Rosemary made no attempt to hide her surprise.

'Well, wasn't she a dark horse, your mother? I would have sworn she had told me everything. Did you meet him?' She strode across the road; not even this news was going to distract her from her mission.

278

Elizabeth nodded. 'Yes, but he's in a home now. He's more or less gone. I couldn't get any sense out of him.' She recalled his dark eyes looking into hers and calling out the name of her mother.

'I wonder why Patricia would have kept that a secret from me?'

'So, you were friends when she came back?'

Rosemary hesitated. 'Yes.' She sounded doubtful. 'For a while anyway.'

'What happened?'

The old woman stopped walking and looked Elizabeth in the eyes.

'Sorry,' Elizabeth said. 'You don't have to tell me.'

'No. No, it was you, actually.'

'Me?'

'I'm not proud of how I behaved back then. I was young. That's my excuse.' Rosemary gave a sad smile and continued down the footpath. 'When your mother came back, things weren't easy for her. She was changed. Much weaker and very shaken by what happened to her, it was tough. Your Uncle Jerry had tried to sell Convent Hill, and then of course everyone wanted to know about the new baby and what had happened. People were shameless, they'd just knock on the door and ask to have a look at you. Well, it didn't take long. Soon the story was everywhere.'

'Story?'

'The one I told you. That she must have been pregnant when she left Buncarragh. Fair dues to your mother, she never changed her version of

279

events. Your father had died and she had returned home with you. Even the priest tried to get involved. I remember he was up sniffing around asking questions. He offered to say a mass for your dead father. He was very put out when she refused. You probably don't remember but you never went to mass when you were little.'

'Didn't I?' Elizabeth had assumed she had always been dragged up to the chapel.

'No. Not till Father Lawlor died. It took a long time, but slowly the whiff of scandal moved on. Other, more shocking things went on, and your mother made sure she was never a repeat offender.' She turned the corner by the post office and started up the small hill that led to the library. 'It can't have been easy, but she managed to get her reputation back.'

'But why did you fall out?'

'I'm ashamed to admit it, but I think I was jealous. You were her everything. I was too young to understand that you were all she needed. She fussed over you, she talked about nothing else, it was all about the baby Elizabeth. Anyway, one day I snapped. Please don't judge me too harshly, but I'd had enough and I just reminded her in no uncertain terms that you weren't hers. You were someone else's baby. Looking back, I suppose I was trying to hurt her and I must have, because we never spoke again. Not a word.'

Elizabeth wasn't sure how to respond.

'I'm sorry,' she said quietly.

'I have very few regrets in my life, but that is one of them.'

They had reached the front of the library.

Elizabeth reached out and took Rosemary's hand.

'Thank you.'

'No need. No need. Safe travels.' She raised her bag of books in farewell and strode into the library as if she was keeping the whole town waiting.

THEN

She had been ringing the bell for what seemed like hours. Why did nobody come? She knew that Edward would have finished the milking by this time, so he and his mother should both be downstairs. She was desperate for the toilet and Elizabeth had begun to whinge and cry. Patricia was about to ring again when she heard the sound of heavy footsteps on the stairs. Her door opened. It was Edward.

Patricia was shocked. He looked awful. His face was covered in sweat and he was out of breath. His clothes were soaked from the rain and there were splatters of mud covering his trousers. A redness around his eyes made it look as if he had been crying. He was holding a coat over one arm and was a carrying a large heavy bag in the other.

'You'll need this,' Edward said gravely, holding out the grey wool coat.

'I have to go the toilet.'

'Well, hurry!'

'Take her for a second.'

Patricia lifted up Elizabeth and Edward dumped the bag and coat on the bed before taking her. 'Hurry!' he repeated.

When she came out of the bathroom Edward was waiting on the landing at the top of the stairs. 'Put this on.' She took the coat from him and while she put it on he went back into her room and grabbed the bag. 'I've packed a few nappies and a couple of bottles. It should be enough.' He thrust Elizabeth back into her arms, and almost ran down the stairs.

'Where are we going?' Patricia called after him.

'Buncarragh,' he said without looking back. 'You are going home.'

Patricia couldn't believe what she was hearing and stood rooted to the spot. 'What?'

Edward stopped just before the kitchen door and barked at her. 'Hurry up!'

Holding the banister with one hand and Elizabeth with the other she came down the stairs as quickly as she dared. In the kitchen the lights were on but there was no sign of dinner.

'Where's your mother?'

'Never mind. Put these on.' Edward kicked a pair of zip-up boots lined with sheepskin towards her. She recognised them. Mrs Foley often wore them.

'What about your mother?'

'Don't worry about her. We must hurry. Come on!' He was holding the back door open and the chill of the evening air was cutting through Patricia's nightdress. She buttoned her coat, slipped her feet into the boots and followed Edward out into the yard. He was heading for the car. Throwing open the passenger door for her, he ran around and got into the driver's seat. Patricia climbed in, hugging Elizabeth close to her chest, and shut the door, relieved to be sheltered from the cold wind. The engine started, the headlights cut a path down the lane and they moved off. Patricia's breathing was fast and shallow. Was she really going home? Had her nightmare finally ended? Edward suddenly lunged across the car and pushed her head.

'Keep down!' He sounded almost hysterical, so she did as she was told. They drove in silence, bouncing across the potholed lane towards the road. They turned out of the gate and Edward sped up.

'You're OK now,' he said and she sat up, kissing the baby's head to reassure her.

'Have you got a blanket for Elizabeth?'

He looked completely stricken. 'No. I forgot. I wasn't thinking. Sorry. I'm so sorry.'

Patricia was worried he might crash the car, he seemed so stressed. Trying to calm him down, she said, 'Don't worry, I'll just wrap her in the coat.' And she did.

The tunnel of light in front of them led them across the causeway and then under some trees. They were leaving Castle House behind them. Patricia half-expected Mrs Foley to jump out of a ditch in front of them and drag them all back to the house. She glanced at Edward. He was gripping the steering wheel hard and leaning forward, concentrating on every inch of the road. His breathing still seemed laboured and even in the glow of the dashboard she could see the gleam of perspiration on his brow. Elizabeth began to cry.

'I think she might need changing.'

'We can't stop yet. We'll get petrol in Bandon. You can do it there. I'm sorry.'

She wanted to ask questions but she didn't

284

want to distract him. He was taking her away from Muirinish and back to Buncarragh and if that meant Elizabeth had to cry all the way to Bandon, then so be it.

She had no idea what was going through Edward's mind as they sped through the dark roads. Patricia looked at the warm lights glowing in the windows of the houses that they passed. Some were right on the road, some set back, new bungalows, cottages, large country houses. Lives being lived in each one. Dinners being put on tables, televisions being gathered around. Were they happy? Was someone sobbing behind the curtains that were leaking light out into the darkness? What would they make of this strange trio speeding through the night?

After Bandon, Elizabeth slept. At first the villages they went through had people standing outside pubs, and lights in the windows, but as the miles slipped by and the hour got later, the bars were in darkness, and the fish and chip shops had kicked out the last of their customers. The whole country seemed deserted. The telegraph poles and hedges flashed by and Elizabeth's warm, even breathing was the only sound in the car.

Patricia thought back to when he had driven her down from Cork in silence. The agony of that journey. She remembered how worried she had been about her hair and getting her skirt wrinkled. Sitting in the car now, with no clue what she looked like or even when she had last had a bath, that other journey seemed like a lifetime ago. She stole a glance at Edward. They weren't even halfway yet and part of her still feared that he might change his mind. His mother's will would seize him across the dark empty miles and reel them back to the Foley castle. Eventually Edward seemed a little calmer and Patricia risked asking him a question.

'What's your plan?'

Edward didn't react and she wondered if he had heard her.

'Plan?' he said without looking at her.

'Are you going back?'

'Of course.'

'What about your mother? Won't she come looking for me? Is . . . ' she dreaded hearing his answer, 'is Elizabeth staying with me?'

'Don't worry about my mother. Don't worry.'

He didn't mention the baby. Patricia began to feel afraid.

'Elizabeth, Edward. What is going to happen to Elizabeth?'

He gave a strange tight cough and then replied, 'I, we, can't look after her. I'll send you money.'

Money. She was heading back into the real world where she had to worry about such things. She wondered if she had a house to return to. She squeezed the baby a little tighter.

'Thank you.'

Somewhere north of Clonmel, Patricia's head was nodding towards sleep in a blur of cat's eyes and briefly glimpsed tree trunks when Edward said her name.

She looked over at him.

He was still hunched over the wheel, staring ahead intently.

'I did care for you. I hope you know that.' His words were hoarse.

Patricia shut her eyes. She still had so much rage inside her. If he cared for her why had he allowed this to happen, to continue for so long? How could he be so cruel to someone if he had feelings for them? Then she thought of him, having to return alone to Castle House. Living with his mother and her fury for . . . well, forever. He could never escape. Edward was as much a victim in this as she was. She let the wisps of hair on the baby's head rub against her face.

'I know, Edward. You're not a bad man.' She considered saying more, telling him how he must escape his mother, or at least get her help, but she decided against it. There was no point upsetting him further.

Only a fox standing at the bottom of the lane that led up to the town dump witnessed Patricia's return to Buncarragh. As the car glided beneath the street lights she found she was holding her breath. Everything was just as it had been when she left, but deserted and still. How could it be the same when she could barely remember the naive young woman who had left this place so long ago? The artificial light made the town seem almost two-dimensional. Words slipped from her mouth, like an incantation she had repeated many times before. 'My friend works there. That's the family shop. These are the new traffic lights. Straight on. Left at the fork. Up the hill.'

They had arrived. The car pulled to a halt outside number sixty-two. The first thing she noticed was the For Sale sign outside.

'Look at that!' She pointed at the board, seething.

'It's not sold,' Edward replied simply.

'True.'

The engine switched off, they sat in silence in the car. Still Patricia feared that there would be some last-minute hurdle, or disaster. He would reach for the baby, or suddenly start the car again and drive into a wall.

'Have you keys?' he asked.

'Under the plant pot.'

'Right.'

Edward took a deep breath and heaved open his door. Patricia edged hers open too and then he came around the car to help her. She stood on the pavement while Edward got the bag from the back seat.

He carried it over and placed it at her feet. 'Thank you.' She had begun to shiver in the night air.

'You'd better get in.'

'Right.' But she didn't move.

The steam from their breaths floated between them as a single cloud,

Edward placed a hand under the baby's chin and lifted her face towards his. He bent down, and Patricia heard him whisper to his daughter.

'You be a good girl now. This is for the best. It's all for the best.'

When he raised his head he couldn't look at Patricia and his mouth was contorted into a twisted ribbon of pink.

'Goodbye, so.' His voice was high and strained

and he ducked into the car as quickly as he could.

Patricia suddenly felt awful. She had only thought about herself and Elizabeth and what was best for them. She had never really considered at what cost. Now she watched aghast as this man with tears streaming down his face struggled to start the engine of the car. Without thinking she stepped forward and rapped her knuckles against the window. Edward stepped back out of the car, and stood up with only the baby separating them. Patricia raised her face to him and he kissed her on her lips. Standing on tiptoe, she pressed back against him. It was a gentle embrace, with no hint of lust or passion. His lips were so much softer than she had imagined, but the stubble on his chin scraped her face. She stepped away, and then raised her hand to wipe away his tears.

'Thank you, Edward. Take care of yourself.'

He said nothing, just bent and kissed the baby's head and got in the car.

The power of forgiveness.

She pulled another woman's coat over the head of another woman's baby and watched the man she had never married drive away.

When the red lights had reached the bottom of the hill and disappeared, Patricia lifted Elizabeth up and kissed her on both cheeks.

'We are home, my baby!'

The key was where she had expected to find it, and opening the door she allowed the familiar smells to wash over her. Had she ever thought that stepping into this hallway could feel this wonderful?

Pushing open the door to the sitting room, she carried Elizabeth over to the sofa and wedged her between two cushions. From the hearth she picked up the largest poker and marched outside. Nobody watched as she flailed the heavy fire iron in the air and smashed the For Sale sign in two.

NOW

1

She felt a bit cheated. So much had happened to her while she had been away, but still New York refused to acknowledge it. The same movie posters were on billboards as when she left. The ugly red dress was still in the window of Inspirations, that weird store on the corner of 33rd. Armando behind the meat counter at D'Agostino greeted her as if she had been in the day before. Even Shelly the cat refused to respond when Linda Jetter brought him back to the apartment. By the time Elizabeth woke up the next morning, she had begun to doubt herself. Ireland seemed so far away. As the daily soundtrack of car horns and sirens started up outside her window, she wondered if she had ever sat on the wall looking out to sea at Castle House. Had her father squeezed her hand? Were Gillian and Noelle trawling through Convent Hill, as she lay in bed tracing the cracks in her bedroom ceiling? Peeling herself out of bed, she resolved not to dwell on her Irish trip. Today was not about the past. She had to focus on the life she was living in the here and now. Zach would be home soon and she was finding it hard to imagine what it was going to be like. A week ago, their conversations were about college applications and his homework, now he was going to become a father. For God's sake, she was going to be somebody's grandmother! It was insane. She let out a manic yelp to express her bewilderment as she stepped into the shower.

Zach's homecoming was not what she had expected or hoped for. He walked through the door with a backpack that dwarfed him and a very pregnant Michelle. The apartment seemed far too small for three people. Elizabeth was incredulous that she had failed to notice the pregnancy in December; how could she have missed it? They squeezed into the living room and sat down. Zach stared sullenly at the floor and gave monosyllabic answers to his mother's enquiries about his trip. Michelle over-compensated, smiling brightly and going into great detail about some vegetarian restaurant Elliot had taken them to in San Francisco. Elizabeth wondered when they would address what was very nearly the elephant in the room.

'I'm putting my stuff away.' Zach got up and hauled his luggage with him. When he was gone Michelle leaned forward, affecting a look of remorse, and in a conspiratorial whisper said, 'I'm afraid Zach isn't very happy with me.'

That makes two of us, thought Elizabeth. 'Oh?' She couldn't bring herself to ask more.

'I explained about the baby.'

'Explained?'

'That I would be the primary caregiver. That I don't want this event to overwhelm his life.' She smiled at Elizabeth in a way that suggested they were kindred spirits in this plan.

'It might be best if you left us. I think we have

a lot to talk about and that might be easier if . . . '

'Of course,' Michelle said, getting out of the sofa with remarkable speed for someone so encumbered. 'I'll go.'

And then she left. Just went. There was no goodbye to Elizabeth or Zach.

The moment the front door closed, he thrust his head around his bedroom door. 'Did Michelle leave?'

'Yes. Yes, she did.'

Zach's face darkened. 'Did you tell her to go?'

'No. I didn't. I promise you, Zach, I didn't. I think she just felt that you and I needed to talk.'

He leaned against the door frame, not looking at his mother.

'Come on,' she said kindly. 'Come and sit down. I've missed you. Ireland was fairly crazy.'

He stepped forward and they hugged. It felt good to hold her boy.

'Are you hungry?'

He nodded his head against her shoulder. 'Starving.'

Zach sat on the single high stool in the kitchen while his mother made him a sandwich.

'Pickle?'

'No, thanks.'

'Mayo?'

'Yes, please.'

Elizabeth rested her hips against the sink and watched her son eat. He devoured the sandwich in great gannet-like bites and then went to the fridge to help himself to a glass of milk.

'Thanks.' He wiped his mouth with his sleeve.

They exchanged a smile. She didn't want to be angry with him.

'Michelle told me what she said.'

Zach stared into his milk. 'It doesn't seem fair. How come she gets to decide?'

Elizabeth felt she had to tread carefully. She knew this wasn't just about him becoming a father, but also his way of saying something about her and Elliot. How their break-up had affected him. It hurt her to think that he felt he had missed out. In her mind things had been so much better when it had been just the two of them.

'Of course the baby will want a father, but, well, you have to make decisions now that will make you the best possible dad.'

Zach put his glass down on the counter. 'What do you mean?' he asked defensively.

Elizabeth took time to gather her thoughts and chose her words carefully.

'It's just that if you go to college — '

'But, Mom!'

'If you go to college,' she repeated, speaking over his interruption, 'you'll be better placed to provide for your child. Be someone they can aspire to be.'

'Aspire to be?'

'Yes.' She was trying to sound reasonable.

Zach's eyes flashed with anger. 'And I suppose you think I want to end up like you!' He gestured at his mother with a look that was a mixture of pity and disgust before leaving the kitchen and slamming his bedroom door.

Elizabeth sighed, and then, turning back to the

sink, washed and dried his glass.

Later that night, she was sitting in the living room, marking up poems for her return to work, when Zach pushed open the door.

'I'm sorry, Mom.'

She took off her glasses and rested the book over the arm of the chair.

'That's OK. But, Zach, and please don't be mad when I tell you this, OK?' She looked at him to check and he nodded.

'Kids get to slam doors, not parents. Please listen to Michelle.'

Zach crossed the room in a couple of steps and slumped to the floor at her feet. He put his head in her lap and wrapped his arms around her legs the way he had when he was just a small boy. She stroked his hair and bent forward to give him a hug. Her son holding on to the last few moments of his childhood.

Over the coming weeks normality seeped back into their lives like an anaesthetic. Zach went to class and Elizabeth returned to tutorials, lectures and faculty meetings. Of course, she filled in friends like Laura and Jocelyn on everything that had happened, but it was as if she was describing somebody else's life, another woman's crazy, out-of-control family. Groceries got picked up, papers were marked, report cards were signed, laundry got dropped off. Sometimes two or three days would go by without Michelle's name being mentioned. Elizabeth exchanged emails with estate agents in Ireland but that all seemed so far away and unconnected with her real life of hauling her heavy tote bag of books up the stairs from the subway, or calling her landlord to get the bulbs in the hallway replaced.

It was early February and the snow storm that had been forecast was just starting. Heavy flakes were falling outside the windows of the apartment and Elizabeth could tell it must be sticking because the sound of the traffic on Third had become eerily muffled. She had just crawled into bed when there was a knock on her door.

'Yes?'

It opened and Zach stepped into her room. His face looked drained of blood and he was holding his phone out like a gift.

'Michelle called. Her waters broke. She's gone into labour.'

Elizabeth leapt out of bed. This was really happening.

'OK. You're OK, Zach. You're fine. Where is she right now?'

'The hospital.'

'Yes, Zach, that's good, but which one? The snow is pretty heavy out there.'

'She's in the Murray Hill medical centre.'

'Well, that's good. That's great. You can walk over there.'

She looked at him, expecting him to go and grab his coat and boots, but he didn't move.

'Are you going to be there?'

'I guess.' Zach was passing his phone from one hand to the other as if it was too hot to hold. 'Mom?'

'Yes.'

'Will you come with me?'

Elizabeth could see that his bottom lip had

begun to quiver, but she was firm.

'No, Zach, I think you should do this by yourself. Don't you?'

'I guess,' her son replied, but still he didn't move.

'Well, go, then!' she said with a laugh and pushed him into the tiny hallway. He grabbed his coat and slipped into his tall unlaced snow boots. At the door he looked back at his mother and she reached in to give him a hug. 'Call me when you are a daddy!'

It was just after seven a.m. when her phone woke her. Zach. She scrambled to answer it.

'Hello, hello! Is everything OK?'

'Yes. All good here. Your son is a father.'

Elizabeth felt the tears fill her eyes and spill down her cheeks. Despite the circumstances, there was such joy. A new little life.

'What did you have?'

'A boy!' He sounded triumphant. 'You have a grandson, Mom. Come see him!'

Elizabeth laughed. 'I will, I will. Let me just jump in the shower and I'll be right over. Give me thirty minutes.'

Navigating the snow drifts on street corners and picking her way along the parts of the side-walks that hadn't been salted meant it was closer to forty-five minutes later when she was reunited with Zach. He was in a small, nondescript waiting area. A thin bald man in his thirties was asleep in a chair. Zach beckoned his mother out into the corridor. They hugged.

'Do you want to see him?'

'Of course! How's Michelle?'

'Good, I think. I wasn't there for all of it.'

Elizabeth knew better than to ask questions. She assumed it had all been a bit much for him. Was a seventeen-year-old supposed to experience childbirth? Would it affect all his relationships with women from now on? Banishing such thoughts, she followed her son down the hallway.

'He's just along here in the newborn nursery.'

'I thought they kept the babies with the mother these days.'

Zach had stopped in front of a large window, and was pointing impatiently. 'That's him. The one on the right.'

Elizabeth peered through the glass and saw nothing but a blotchy purple and red face, its mouth wide open in a silent scream.

'Oh, Zach. He's gorgeous.' She hugged her son.

She was just about to ask him about names when the slap of swinging double doors distracted them both. An older man, a doctor Elizabeth assumed, was walking towards them. As he reached the unlikely couple standing outside the nursery he took off his tortoiseshell glasses and rubbed his other hand through his grey hair. He looked serious.

'Mr Kleinfeld?'

'Yes,' Zach replied.

'I'm Dr Rice. Alan. We met last night.'

'Yes. I'm Zach.'

The two men shook hands.

'I'm his mother,' Elizabeth explained.

The three of them stood together in silence. Something didn't feel right. People only wait for bad news. Zach reached for his mother's hand.

'Perhaps you'd prefer to step into one of our family rooms.' The doctor indicated a door a little further down the hall.

'Yes, no,' Zach corrected himself. 'Just tell us here.' His voice was thin and high. Elizabeth squeezed his hand harder.

'I really feel you might be more comfortable — '

'Please!' To Elizabeth, Zach sounded the way he had as a small boy pleading for a treat or for the answer to a riddle.

Dr Rice rubbed his tongue along the inside of his bottom lip and then spoke.

'We aren't sure, but we think Ms Giardino may have had an adverse reaction to the epidural. Tests will tell us more later.' A small cough, and then he continued. 'Shortly after your son was born, the mother went into respiratory failure. Efforts were made to resuscitate her, but I regret to say, those efforts failed.'

Zach looked at his mother, more frightened than she had ever seen him.

'I'm so very sorry, but Michelle is dead.'

Zach gasped and violently jerked backwards as if he'd been struck. Elizabeth had to put her other arm around him to steady his body. He collapsed against her. She could feel his hot tears on her neck, his howls soaking into her padded jacket.

Dr Rice stood awkwardly beside them.

'It's a great deal to take in. Again, the family room is at your disposal if you'd prefer.'

Elizabeth just wished he would leave them.

'If you've any questions, anything at all, here's my card. Please feel free to call me.' He paused before repeating, 'I'm so sorry', and then moved away.

'Thank you, Doctor,' Elizabeth mumbled, taking the business card with one hand while rubbing the other up and down her son's back, trying to comfort him. As if anything could bring him comfort. This wasn't right. This boy wasn't built for this sort of pain. Elizabeth was suddenly filled with a terrible rage. What was wrong with the world? Why? Why would the gods conspire to test her child in this way?

Over Zach's shoulder, Elizabeth could see her grandson struggling inside his tightly wrapped blanket. His face was even redder than before. It was as if that tiny human shared her anger. The two of them bonded by a fury at the world. She knew what she had to do.

2

Memories don't just vanish, they hide. Like a tiny boat trapped in heavy seas trying to catch sight of the shore, sometimes glimpses of the past appear. But some days the wind drops, the clouds part and there is a clear uninterrupted view of land.

In Abbey Court Care home, Edward lay in his bed just before the dawn and everything was revealed to him. The barren vista of his life. He tried to sort through his memories, searching for the happier ones; a summer's evening bringing in the cows, frying up a pan of mackerel for breakfast, Mary on their wedding day, but it was useless. He had no choice. Only one dark day kept looming into view.

He was at the kitchen counter doing it the way he had seen his mother doing it for Patricia. Grinding the tablets with the back of a spoon, and putting them in the teapot. They were the pills the doctor had prescribed for his mother after James had died, but she had stopped taking them years before. Patricia had only ever had one or two, but he needed to be sure, so he crushed six of them.

'You're making tea?' It was his mother coming into the kitchen.

'I fancied a cup. Is that all right?'

'Don't let me stop you. This is a rare treat, getting waited on.'

The kettle was boiling so Edward filled the pot, and put a mug for himself and a cup and saucer for his mother on the table.

'What about madam upstairs?'

'I'll ask her in a bit.'

He let it brew for a few minutes and then poured.

He picked up his mug and blew on it but didn't drink. He tried to watch his mother surreptitiously. She was slurping loudly.

He remembered they had spoken then, but couldn't recall the words. What had they talked about? Strange that of all their conversations, that one wasn't etched on his memory.

He did know that his mother had yawned and said, 'I don't know what's wrong with me. I can't keep my eyes open.'

Had there been a moment? Had his mother guessed what he had done? Was there a look? He hoped there hadn't been. He prayed that she had never known.

Her head had fallen forward against her chest and her body had slipped down in the chair. Edward had waited then for a few more minutes, before tapping her on the arm. Nothing. 'Mammy?' His mother remained slumped and unresponsive.

He went to the back door and pulled on his jacket and scarf. Outside the light was fading. He hurried across the yard and got the wheelbarrow from outside one of the outhouses. He wheeled it as quickly as he could to the back door. He didn't know how much time he had.

Back inside he gathered his mother up in his arms and carried her outside and placed her as gently as he could into the wheelbarrow. It had started to rain. He pushed his load along the side of the house into the lane. The rough terrain coupled with speed disturbed Mrs Foley and one arm flopped over the side of the wheelbarrow and scraped along the stone wall. Edward saw blood. He froze, waiting for his mother to react. Her face remained still, her eyes closed, her mouth hanging open. Struggling with the heavy weight of his load, Edward took a sharp left into the orchard. Here it was much slower going, trying to ease the front wheel across the soft ground through the long wet grass. They passed the blackened trunks of the trees he had set alight to provide cover for Patricia's failed escape. Up ahead a rope lay coiled at the foot of one of the tallest apple trees. Just seeing it lying there like a serpent ready to strike made Edward stop. His breath, heavy from his efforts, floated in clouds before him. Was he doing the right thing? Was this really the only solution? He looked down and observed his mother's head hanging to one side, the pink of her tongue edging over her bottom lip. Edward began to cry. No. He had to keep going. This was his plan and it was the best way out that he could think of. Not just for Elizabeth and Patricia, but for his mother too.

Her plan was never going to work. He'd told her. The letters. He'd said to his mother, 'What will happen when they find out?'

Mrs Foley had waved away his concerns. 'We'll cross that bridge when we get to it.' Except they hadn't. They had all fallen off that bridge and were now drowning in the mess she had made.

He threw the rope over the highest strong branch and then tied it off lower down on the trunk.

His mother couldn't have coped with her failure. Edward could have borne her disappointment in him, he had lived for most of his life with that, but she couldn't have faced a future where she wasn't able to make things better. Somehow, even after everything that had happened, she believed she had the power to change things, to rescue him. Edward didn't know how she could have survived such disappointment. This was the kind thing to do. It had been his mother, all those years before, who had taken the gun out and shown him how to shoot that heifer after it broke its leg. He remembered them standing together in the field, trying to hide his tears as the bark of the gunshot echoed up into the darkness. She had turned to him and told him that it was for the best. He bent down and scooped up her body. This was for the best. It was.

He laid his mother down on the wet grass, the rain splashing against her face. Wiping his tears away to see better, he went to the wall and picked up the small wooden stepladder they had always used when they were picking the apples. He opened it and tried his best to steady the feet on the uneven ground. He lifted his mother's body and leaned her against the steps. He raised a hand to reach the noose but it was too high. He shifted his weight and fell against his mother's wet body. He felt her warm shallow breath on his face. Keeping her upright, he climbed a couple of steps until he had managed to grasp the rope. Then, using all his strength, he hauled his mother up in the air. He groaned with the strain. She slipped, he caught her. The ladder began to rock, but with one final effort he managed to slip the noose around his mother's head. For a moment they were face to face. He wondered if he should kiss her goodbye. No.

He looked away and let go. Her body dropped, knocking the ladder and sending Edward sprawling to the ground. He left the ladder where it was and stood up. In horror, he watched as his mother twitched and kicked. What was happening? It should be over. Her body twisted around towards him, and he saw, thankfully, that her eyes were still shut. He scrambled towards the wheelbarrow. He had so much to do. Still his mother's feet kicked. One of her shoes had come loose and landed on the grass like a windfall apple. Edward didn't know what to do. It was not meant to be happening like this.

He pushed the wheelbarrow towards the house, making a low whimpering sound. As he reached the gate he looked back. His mother's right leg was shuddering. He couldn't bear it. He would cut her down! Just as he set off towards the hanging body, everything suddenly became still. The rope was still swaying slightly and the rain was dripping from the trees, but his mother was gone. Edward sank to his knees. He bowed his head in front of his mother's corpse hanging from a rope and felt relief. Huge, life-changing relief. It was over, finally over. Her pain, her disappointment, her longing, all of it: she was at peace.

Night had fallen. Edward got up and pushed the empty wheelbarrow through the darkness back to the yard. Even before he went back into the house he could hear Patricia's bell ringing in the night air.

Now, more than forty years later, an old man in Clonteer lay in the early morning light and thought he could hear that sound once more. Maybe he could, or perhaps it was just the breakfast trolley clattering in the hallway. He wondered if Patricia had received his letter. The one he had written himself. It had taken him two attempts, sitting at the kitchen table, holding the

305

biro like a spoon, copying the word from the piece of paper where Mrs Lynch had written it out for him. Miss Buggy in the post office had written the address. For days, he had fretted about what he would do if Patricia replied. Who would he get to read it for him? He needn't have worried, because no response came. Then, three, maybe four years later, an envelope had been waiting for him when he got back to the empty house after work. Nothing but a photograph of a little girl. She was wearing a red pinafore and laughing at something he would never see. Elizabeth. He had put down the bright photograph and looked at what surrounded him. The cream walls with dark clouds of damp gathering in the corners. Old lino on the floor, worn away to the flagstones by the door. The ticking of a clock to remind him that time was passing. He had smiled then. What he had done had been for the best.

In the day room, two nurses were sharing a joke in the kitchen area. The sound of their laughter reached the room of Edward Foley. His eyelids flickered and his breathing became uneven. Inside his chest his heart fluttered and then, just as he thought to himself, this is it, it's over, it was.

AFTER

The tide was full and the sky was perfectly blue. Elizabeth could hardly believe how different it all seemed. As they drove across the causeway, the water sparkled in the sunshine, and she knew this had been the right thing to do. 'Nearly there now,' she called to the boys in the back. Her boys. That's what she called them. Zach was sitting with his son who was strapped into a car seat that neither he nor Elizabeth were convinced had been installed properly.

It hadn't been easy but in the little more than two years since her last visit to Muirinish, life had changed a great deal. After Michelle's death, Elizabeth had such a strong, unshakable belief in what she should do. She talked to Zach and he was enthusiastic about the plan. Michelle's parents took a little more convincing but, conceding that they were too old to start caring for a baby, they agreed that it made sense for their grandson to at least be close to his father, while being cared for by a responsible adult. Elliot thought she was crazy, but then, he hadn't even managed to care for a puppy. Will and the Weimaraner had moved out.

At first, things had been difficult. Convincing Zach to stay in school and arranging a leave of absence for herself from Hunter had been a struggle, but she had muddled through. She had graded papers from home and, although still unsold, she had managed to rent out Convent Hill. Then there was an unexpected but extremely welcome change in her circumstances. The Giardino family had reached a sizeable out-of-court settlement with the medical centre following the badly performed epidural, and they had decided to put half in trust for their grandson and give the rest to Elizabeth, to help her raise the child. The money was a godsend. She was able to return to teaching part-time at Hunter and her little family decamped to a modest duplex apartment on the top two floors of one of the few un-gentrified brownstones in Williamsburg.

Elizabeth loved being a mother again. It was so much easier the second time around, and, she reminded herself, that wasn't just because there was no Elliot this time. Of course, there were nights when she couldn't sleep, or her grandson refused to sleep, when she sat in the dark holding the baby and thought about Michelle. Poor woman. Elizabeth didn't rewrite history, she never pretended that she had been fond of the woman, but it did break her heart that Michelle had been robbed of time with her son. He was a magical little boy. Elizabeth thought of her own mother too. She had wondered if looking after another woman's baby might give her some insight into the mind of Patricia Keane, but, if anything, she felt she understood her less. Elizabeth was impatient to tell her grandson about his mother, show him pictures, allow him to ask questions. Had her mother never felt compelled to tell her the truth? Times were different then, she supposed, but it still bothered her. Surely the truth had always had a value? Or maybe back then other things were more important? They must have been or why else would secrets have been a way of life?

Castle House had found a buyer and the new owner was waiting for them as their car bumped and bounced its way down the lane. Hair slicked back, and wearing a freshly ironed shirt, Brian gave them a wave. The purchase had been purely practical. He wanted a yard adjacent to the land and it was a reasonable price. He still hadn't decided what to do with the house, probably just wait till it had joined the castle as a ruin. Elizabeth hadn't known he was the buyer until he had texted her to inform her about her father's death. There had been nothing left to bequeath in the will, the land had been sold to Brian years earlier, and Elizabeth already had the house, but there was the question of Edward's remains. The solicitor who had power of attorney had contacted Brian to see if he had a number for the previous owner of Castle House, and indeed he did. Elizabeth hadn't been sure what to do. Being so far away, she didn't know if she could arrange a funeral, or where Mary was buried, so she had just asked for a small private service at the crematorium in Cork. Today was to be about the ashes.

Elizabeth got out of the car and gave Brian a peck on the cheek.

'Great to see you.'

'You too. You've picked a great day for it.'

'Yes.'

They both looked around at the ruins, the blue sky peeping through the narrow misshapen windows. A banging sound brought them back to the car.

Zach was knocking on the car window.

'Mom, let us out!'

Elizabeth laughed. 'Sorry, sorry.'

She opened the back door, and then she and Zach both struggled with the car seat.

A large white Range Rover was coming down the drive. It seemed to fill the whole lane. Elizabeth looked and waved. 'Oh, good. She made it.'

The car pulled up beside the other two and Cathy Crowley stepped out, before going around the car to help her mother Ann Lynch from the passenger's side.

'Are you all right there?'

'I'd need a ladder. I hate this car.' Eventually the old lady's feet made contact with the ground and they walked over to the small waiting group. Elizabeth noticed how nicely dressed they were. She hoped they weren't expecting a formal ceremony or some catered event afterwards.

'Nice to see you both again. I'm so glad you could come.' Elizabeth smiled and reached forward to shake hands.

'And this is my son Zach. Cathy Crowley, Mrs Lynch.' She hoped she was doing this correctly. Zach stepped forward awkwardly and offered his handshake.

'And who is this little man?' Mrs Lynch asked, taking hold of the little foot that was being wiggled in front of her face by the child that Zach was holding.

'That is my grandson. His name is Foley.'

Mrs Lynch smiled. 'Foley. Isn't that lovely?'

'Well, we're all here so I should get his great-grandfather out of the car.'

Elizabeth went to retrieve a large plastic container, with a screw-top lid.

'I've never been to one of these before,' Mrs Lynch declared proudly.

'I must admit, nor have I,' her daughter added. 'What happens?'

Elizabeth looked at Brian and Zach, hoping that one of them might have something to say, but they just stared back waiting for her to explain.

'I'm not entirely sure either. There are no hard and fast rules. I just thought we'd spread his ashes out into the sea. If anyone wants to say something they can. I think that's it.' She gave a shrug.

'The first thing I'd say would be we shouldn't do it here.' Brian pointed at the paddock in front of the house. 'The wind is coming straight in off the sea, and we'll end up wearing him.' Mrs Lynch made a sound that suggested she would not enjoy that. 'We'd be better off going around the side, below the ruin, where there's a bit of shelter.'

Elizabeth looked at Mrs Lynch. 'Will you be all right getting around there?'

'She has her stick. She'll be fine,' Cathy answered for her mother.

Under the castle walls, Elizabeth unscrewed the lid of the plastic urn and then hesitated.

'Would everyone like to take a handful?' She

311

held out the container.

The ladies looked a little uncertain, but did as they were told.

Five handfuls of dust were released into the air and the wind picked some of it up, lifting it high and out towards the sea, while some of it just landed on the grass at their feet.

Mrs Lynch sighed and crossed herself. 'Poor Edward. He is released.' The adults nodded sombrely in agreement.

As if to lighten the mood, Foley began to flail his small plump arms and laugh as the dark cloud of ash floated away. Smiling, Elizabeth turned and looked at her grandson. Tiny fragments of dust had begun to settle on his skin.

Acknowledgements

The aspect of writing that I enjoy the most is its solitary nature and yet to reach the point where you are holding this book in your hands has taken the talent, effort and patience of so many.

First and foremost I am hugely indebted to my editor Hannah Black. She has just the right mix of discipline and indulgence to get me past the finishing line. Her notes are unerringly useful and earning her praise makes all the days of doubt and despair worthwhile.

The whole team at Hodder provide wonderful support and make me feel like a fully fledged novelist. Heartfelt thanks to Carolyn Mays, Lucy Hale, Alice Morley, Louise Swannell, Emma Herdman and Ian Wong. Claudette Morris made this book. Alasdair Oliver and Kate Brunt made it beautiful. Dominic Gribben held my hand while I read it aloud and if you discovered this book outside of the UK, then we both need to thank Joanna Kaliszewska.

I must thank my early readers, Gill, Jonothan, Niall, Paula and Rhoda. Their eagle eyes and rational brains were invaluable.

As always I am so grateful to Melanie, Dylan and Hannah at Troika for keeping me busy but not so busy that I don't have time to write a novel.

Becky and Kelly for managing my life so seamlessly.

And finally I must thank my mother, well, for so many things, but in this instance for giving me the seeds of the story that grew into this book.

I've loved spending time in Muirinish and Buncarragh and I really hope you have as well.

We do hope that you have enjoyed reading this large print book.

Did you know that all of our titles are available for purchase?

We publish a wide range of high quality large print books including:
Romances, Mysteries, Classics
General Fiction
Non Fiction and Westerns

Special interest titles available in large print are:
The Little Oxford Dictionary
Music Book
Song Book
Hymn Book
Service Book

Also available from us courtesy of Oxford University Press:
Young Readers' Dictionary
(large print edition)
Young Readers' Thesaurus
(large print edition)

For further information or a free brochure, please contact us at:
Ulverscroft Large Print Books Ltd.,
The Green, Bradgate Road, Anstey,
Leicester, LE7 7FU, England.
Tel: (00 44) 0116 236 4325
Fax: (00 44) 0116 234 0205

Other titles published by Ulverscroft:

HOLDING

Graham Norton

The remote Irish village of Duneen has known little drama, and yet its inhabitants are troubled. Sergeant PJ Collins hasn't always been this overweight; mother of two Brid Riordan hasn't always been an alcoholic; and elegant Evelyn Ross hasn't always felt that her life was a total waste. So when human remains are discovered on an old farm, suspected to be those of Tommy Burke — a former love of both Brid and Evelyn — the village's dark past begins to unravel. As the frustrated PJ struggles to solve a genuine case for the first time in his life, he unearths a community's worth of anger and resentment, secrets and regret.